THE FRIGID NI~~G~~
ENOUGH F~~OR~~ SNOWY . . .

The cab of the truck was a roaring furnace, and Snowy tried to persuade the kid to feather back the heater, to no avail. So he cranked down his window halfway, letting in a soothing, icy blast.

"Whaddayou, a goddamn Eskimo?" the kid screamed.

Snowy said mildly, "Buddy, where I come from, it's not so wise to mouth off to a guy as big as me, especially for a little twerp as skinny—" Snowy blinked. "What's wrong?"

"Jesus Christ." The kid was staring fearfully at Snowy, mouth hanging open.

"What—?" Snowy halted a motion to scratch his head, and realized what the kid was seeing. His hand had turned furry, the fingers tipped with milk-white claws. It was his normal hand. He felt his face. Sheila's spell was fading. . . .

CASTLE KIDNAPPED

CASTLE
Kidmapped

John DeChancie

ACE BOOKS, NEW YORK

CASTLE KIDNAPPED

An Ace Book/published by arrangement with
the author

PRINTING HISTORY
Ace edition/November 1989

ISBN: 0-441-09408-2

Ace Books are published by The Berkley Publishing Group,
200 Madison Avenue, New York, New York 10016.
The name ''ACE'' and the ''A'' logo are trademarks
belonging to Charter Communications, Inc.

PRINTED IN THE UNITED STATES OF AMERICA

10 9 8 7 6 5 4 3 2 1

To the Memory of
Robert P. Mills

The voice I hear this passing night was heard
  In ancient days . . .
    The same that oft-times hath
  Charmed magic casements, opening on the foam
    Of perilous seas, in faery lands forlorn.
                                            —KEATS

On the Approach Path to
Greater Pittsburgh
International Airport

GENE FERRARO HEARD the groan of servomechanisms, looked out the window of the Lockheed 1011, and saw the plane's flaps slide down and lock into place. The sound of whooshing air got louder and the engines revved up and whined, providing more thrust to compensate for increased drag.

Below, the ground was still shrouded in haze, but occasional features began to appear: here a sprawling shopping complex, there the winding ribbon of a freeway. Gene turned from the window, sat back, and sighed. The stewardess came by, whisked away his empty coffee cup, and hurried off on her rounds. Gene pushed up on the serving tray in front of him and locked it back into place. Presently the "No Smoking" and "Fasten Seat Belts" lights came on. The first directive didn't apply, but Gene obeyed the second.

He looked out the window again. Everything suddenly whited out as the plane plunged through low cloud, but shortly things cleared again and the ground reappeared, now a little closer.

Everything seemed fine. He was glad to be back home, even though he had enjoyed his stay in southern California. Los Angeles was . . . well, a different world, all sun and surf and blond leggy women. Glitzy as hell, daubed in Technicolor shades. Everywhere palm trees and tangled freeways and pastel stucco houses with orange Spanish tile roofs. Also smog, and lots of crazy people. And automobiles, lots and lots of those. Who had said that California had the most of everything and the best of nothing? It was true, Gene thought, but there is something to be said for sheer quantity. He had liked the place, but had had enough after two weeks. He'd bade goodbye to Linda Barclay and took the first nonstop flight out. Linda wanted to spend more time with her mother before going back to Perilous.

And after dutifully visiting with his own folks, that's exactly where he was going: Castle Perilous.

It no longer seemed like a dream to him—the castle, that is. He had long come to accept Castle Perilous as reality. It was either that or the most elaborate and convincing shared hallucination in medical history. But Gene could no longer regard the latter case as anything but the remotest improbability. The castle was real; it was an actual, physical place, made of cold hard stone. He had bumped his head against it on occasion. It had hurt.

A dream castle carved of adamantine rock . . . and energized by the stuff of magic, also undeniably real. Magic oozed from every crack and crevice in the place, lay pulsing in every stone. Castle Perilous was a magical construct, its existence maintained from second to second by a spell laid long ago, as legend had it, on a great demon called Ramthonodox. . . .

He had a sudden urge to urinate and suppressed it. Damn, he thought. One drink too many. But it was only two vodka and tonics, wasn't it? Surely, that wasn't enough to—

The urge soon turned into an immediate and crying need. Cursing his kidneys for picking such an inconvenient time to fail him, Gene unlatched his seat belt, got up, and made his way to the back of the plane.

A stewardess blocked his way.

"Sir, where are you going?"

"The obvious place."

"We're going to be landing in just a few minutes, sir. You'll have to wait."

His bladder felt like a water balloon being squeezed. "Can't."

"Sir, you'll have to! Passengers have to be strapped in for landing."

"But look—"

"Please, sir, it's regulations!"

Gene exhaled. Then very quickly he said, "Voodoo. Who do? You do!" It came out as *Vudoo-hudoo-yudoo!*

The phrase was an incantation for a general facilitation spell that Sheila had taught him, one of the very few spells he had mastered, and the only one in his repertoire that was efficacious in this world, on Earth. It was an all-purpose enchantment, one that simply increased the ease of performing any task or solving any problem. Set up optimum conditions. Success depended heavily on the skill of the enchanter. Unfortunately Gene was strictly an amateur in matters magical; but he tried hard.

"What did you say?" the stewardess asked, wincing as if from a sudden headache. She shook her head once. "Did you—?"

"You were about to tell me that I could go if I get it done real quick and be back in my seat in a jiffy."

She blinked. "Huh? Oh." Vaguely puzzled, she nodded. "Uh, yeah. Go ahead. *But hurry!*"

Feeling like the dam above Johnstown, Gene hurried.

Reaching the door, he found it had been locked—automatically, most likely, during takeoffs and landings. He shoved a shoulder against it and pushed, to no avail.

Well, hell, it wasn't a complete humiliation to let go in your breeches. Must have been something he ate, or drank, or whatever.

Use the facilitation spell again? Nothing to lose.

He repeated the incantation and tried the door again. There seemed to be some give. He cast the spell once more, trying to get some feeling into the recitation, even though doing so made him feel slightly foolish. Gene knew he alone was to blame; he had come up with the silly phrase, a simple mnemonic. Sheila had told him that the words actually didn't matter, as all magic was mental. The words simply focused the energy.

"Voodoo!—Who do?—*You do!*"

The door opened with a click and he stepped in. The urge vanished as soon as he closed the door, but that didn't surprise him as much as seeing that the rear bulkhead of the

cubicle was missing, the curving outline of the plane's fuse-
lage forming an oddly shaped doorway. Stranger still, the
doorway led into a large stone-walled crypt. A young man
dressed in medieval costume stood well away from the aperture, facing it. He regarded Gene, then bowed deeply.

"Your Excellency," the boy intoned.

Judging by the costume, Gene took him for a castle servant, specifically a page. Gene didn't recognize him.

"What the hell is going on?" Gene demanded.

The page bowed again. "Pardon the intrusion, Excellency.
His Majesty wishes to speak with you immediately on a matter of the greatest urgency."

"He's back? No kidding. How in the world did you wran-
gle the portal here?"

"I believe His Excellency the Royal Librarian effected the
technical details, sir."

"Is Osmirik around?"

"He waits without, sir. He also is most anxious to see
you."

"Sounds like a real emergency. Well, okay. But that stewardess out there is going to be mighty confused when I don't
come out of here. She'll think I pulled a D.W. Cooper."

The page gave him a puzzled look. "Your pardon, sir. I
do not quite take your meaning."

"Forget it." Gene made a motion to step over the toilet
seat, which hadn't disappeared. But he halted. "Wait a minute. My father is supposed to meet me when I land."

"I believe, sir, that a temporal adjustment will be made
for you when your business is concluded."

"Time travel again, huh? Last time we tried that little trick
it took four hours of mumbo jumbo. Oh, well, when duty
calls . . ."

He straddled the commode and stepped into the room. The
servant did not move closer.

Gene said, "Clever, that bit about making me think I was
going to wet my pants. Was that Osmirik, or did Sheila come
up with it? Sounds like her style."

"All will be explained shortly, sir."

Gene looked around. The only door to the place was in the
far wall. He heard a pop, and turned in the direction he had
come from. The aperture had disappeared, and with it the

privy of the L-1011. He was now inside Castle Perilous. Or so he thought.

He turned to the servant and motioned toward the door. "Through there?"

The page gave no answer as he took two steps backward, his expression one of guarded expectation.

"What's the problem?" Gene wanted to know. He started forward.

A rumbling sound issued from above. Gene looked up to see a wall sliding down from a slot that ran the width of the ceiling.

"Damn!" Gene dashed forward but didn't make it. The wall slammed down and cut him off, stranding him in darkness and echoing silence.

QUEENS

THROUGH THE OPEN window, Jeremy Hochstader heard the telltale sound of a police radio and knew he was about to get busted.

It wasn't much of a sound, just the momentary blurt, the pop, of a transmitter being keyed, the kind of static that might come from, say, a CB radio. But it had come from directly below the window, in the narrow alley to the side of the apartment building where a vehicle could not squeeze. Therefore, the noise had probably come from a walkie-talkie; which meant, probably, plainclothes cops; which meant one was waiting at the bottom of the fire escape, blocking off Jeremy's only avenue of retreat. Which meant that in a few short moments, there would come the pounding of heavy fists against his apartment door.

He was not normally paranoid. The sight of a squad car in front of the building would ordinarily be of no concern. But Jeremy knew that Mark DiFilippo had been arrested. DiFilippo was Jeremy's drug connection, among other things. The charge had been simple possession, but Jeremy had heard that the arrest had been carried out by Federal agents, and he was suspicious. Obviously they had DiFilippo on bigger stuff. Obviously what had happened was this: DiFilippo had plea-bargained his way out of the drug-dealing counts and had been arraigned on charges of computer crime: illegal use of interstate telephone lines, diversion of monies from various bank accounts, illegal use of credit card numbers, and other state-of-the-art, high-tech offenses, all perpetrated on the clutter of computers and peripheral equipment that lay about Jeremy's fourth-floor walkup apartment. They were willing to go relatively easy on DiFilippo to get the hacker. Him, Jeremy.

The evidence was everywhere. Floppy disks made precarious piles on desks, shelves, floors, even on the refrigerator. Recorded on the disks was program after illegal program, some of which Jeremy had written, some of which he had "downloaded"—stolen—and some of which he had copied with blithe disregard for U.S. copyright law. But copyright infringement—even "willful infringement," which technically was a felony—was the least of his problems.

DiFilippo must have talked.

In fact, the pizza-faced little wop must have sung like Caruso. Told them everything. Handed over all the account numbers, spilled everything about all the scams, the Trojan horse programs, the money-market accounts—everything, all the dope.

Dope!

All this took a second to race through Jeremy's mind when he heard the squawk from the plainclothesman's walkie-talkie. Leaping out of the chair, he rummaged through the debris on the coffee table and came up with a small plastic bag half filled with white powder. He dashed to the bathroom, emptied the bag's contents into the bowl, flushed the commode. Then he rinsed out the bag and threw it out the window.

At least there wouldn't be any drug charges to load on top of the hacking rap. . . .

Except for the marijuana. Which was . . . *where?*

Heart pounding, Jeremy rifled through the place but came up empty. It didn't matter much; there was no end of contraband strewn all over the joint, pills hiding in the mildewed depths of the sofa, uppers on display in jars in the kitchen cabinets, downers clutched in the paws of dust bunnies under the bed. Anything they would find would go straight to the lab and come back inevitably tagged: *Illegal.* Even Jeremy didn't know what all was lying about. He'd lived in this dump for two years and was the world's worst housekeeper. With a sickening feeling, he sat back down in front of the Macintosh and stared into the blank, gray screen of the CRT. It looked as empty and as featureless as his life.

He did not pause to marvel at how he had arrived at the certain knowledge that cops would soon be beating down his door. He had no need to look out the window and see the cop covering the fire escape. Jeremy knew the cop was there.

A few floors below, heavy feet thumped up the stairs. There came the sound of gruff voices, and again the fartlike sputter of walkie-talkies.

So it all comes down to this, he thought. No matter how bright he was—and he was very, very bright, always had been—it's come down to a major felony rap, probably a conviction . . . and jail.

Jeremy did not want to go to jail. That fate he feared more than any other. He was young—only twenty-three—slight of build, and possessed not one ounce of physical courage. In jail he would be dead meat. They'd use him and abuse him and throw him away like a candy wrapper. At the very least he'd get AIDS.

Jeremy didn't think much of himself, for all that he knew he was one of the best hackers in the city. He had been on the verge of becoming a successful free-lance microcomputer systems consultant. He had already done a few jobs for some small brokerage houses on Wall Street, mainly on the recommendation of his uncle George, an independent stock analyst. But his age was a handicap, and so were his looks. Jeremy looked about fifteen. He couldn't go to work for a company. No sheepskin. He'd flunked out of Columbia two years ago.

So when money got tight—and when Jeremy was into heavy speedballing, money got *really* tight—he would fire up the Compaq (his favorite rig for modem work) and dump cash into his account with stolen credit card numbers. DiFilippo had finally wondered where all the green stuff was coming from, and threatened to shut Jeremy off if the information was not forthcoming.

"It's gonna stop snowin', Jeremy. Christmas ain't gonna come this year. Unnerstand? Come on, tell Santa where you're getting the cash to pay for this stuff."

Jeremy had told him, and DiFilippo wanted in. The rest was history.

I'm just another goddamn drug-abuse statistic, Jeremy thought ruefully. Just like in the TV public-service spots. How dumb. How unoriginal.

I did drugs, and I lost my job, my wife, my kids. . . .

Jeremy liked coke. The subject here is not soda pop. He had a pronounced affinity for the crystalline alkaloid commonly processed from the dried leaves of the coca plant: cocaine. Coke, snow, nose candy . . . (plug in the current sobriquet). He'd started out packing his beak with the stuff, snorting it, then had graduated to freebasing and shooting the gunk into his veins along with some heroin to lubricate the pipes. Speedballing made you feel loose and smooth and good—damn good. Speedballing was fun, as long as you took it easy, watched your chemistry, and didn't pull a John Belushi.

Well, he hadn't, but he hadn't been able to avoid one of the . . . like, real *obvious* pitfalls. The money thing. Feeding the habit. No, he'd blundered into that one like a baby.

He *was* a baby, he guessed. Never grew up.

Tell it to the judge.

Pushing its way past the numbness, panic finally welled up inside him. Deep voices and ponderous footfalls came from the landing one floor down.

Jeremy jumped up and ran to the door. On the way, almost as a reflex action, he snagged the Toshiba laptop. Throwing the door open, he dashed out and ran up the stairs, carrying the small computer like his grade school lunch bucket.

Behind him he heard a confusion of voices, footsteps, pounding, and then shouts.

"He's flown!"

"He didn't go out the window!"

"Maybe up on the roof?"

"What's he think he's gonna do, fly?"

It was four flights to the roof. Jeremy didn't think at all on the way up. There was nothing in him but blind fear. But when he banged through the door and ran out onto the black tar expanse of the roof, he finally wondered where he was running to.

But of course there was nowhere to run to. He knew that, and he knew that he could never face arrest and jail.

He went to the edge of the roof and looked over the low tile-capped wall. Someone was climbing the sooty cage of the fire escape. All Jeremy could see was the top of an incipiently bald head and the flash of a yellow T-shirt, but he knew who it was: the cop. The guy was shouting into his walkie-talkie. The alley below was empty. Jeremy saw no squad cars in the alley behind the building, nor any in the part of the street that he could see. But how many cops does it take to bust one skinny nerd of a twenty-three-year-old in the thrall of arrested adolescence?

Three. Two to hold the nerd and the other to beat the living shit out of him. Just for the sheer joy of it.

It was clear what he had to do. He didn't think he could get out of it. They had him dead to rights. All the money in his many accounts would be impounded, so it would be a public shyster for him, no fancy hired-gun lawyer who might be able to get him off or at least get him probation or maybe even into a halfway house or something. No, he was going to do hard time. The best he could hope for was minimum security. But even that would be hard to face.

Jeremy was scared. So deeply scared that he would do anything . . . *anything* to get out of this. Out. He wanted out.

He realized that he was already standing on the slippery terra-cotta tile of the wall, staring down into the alley, the hard, unforgiving bricks of which lay eight full stories below. He teetered forward. Could he do it?

He could, if he closed his eyes. Doing so, he stepped off the roof into thinnest air, still holding the computer.

He hit immediately, and he didn't understand. He hit hard, but not as hard as he should have. He should have been a sack of shit and bones lying in the alley. But here he was . . . somewhere else.

Where the hell was he? He sat up and looked around. He was in a hallway, in a building, somewhere. Not his apartment building. He was sitting on a gray flagstone floor, the tan case of the little Toshiba lying upside down about two feet from his right hand. The corridor walls were of dark stone. He craned his head around. Behind him, the corridor ran in semidarkness to its vanishing point. What was in front of him was the problem: the top of the apartment building, only he couldn't figure out how it could be there. Beyond his outstretched legs the corridor extended a few more feet to a stone arch. But through the arch . . . well, there was the roof of the apartment building. Only it was canted kind of crazily, tilting to the right and sort of away. The angle was goofy. So, where the hell was this place?

The yellow-shirted cop appeared, peering over the wall. He seemed to be searching the alley below. Jeremy stared at him, but the cop didn't see him at first. Then the cop did. He looked, then squinted. He blinked a few times, then looked again, right at Jeremy.

"What in the name of—?"

Then the roof and the building and the cop were gone, replaced by a view of a long, dim corridor.

Silence.

Jeremy rubbed his eyes and looked again. Nothing changed. Here he was in a place that looked like a church, or maybe a castle. And he had no idea of how he had got here. None.

His mind a total blank, he sat for a long spell before reaching for the computer and slowly getting to his feet. His rear end hurt, but it wasn't bad. He hadn't hit his head, he was pretty sure. Wherever he was, it was very quiet. He listened. Nothing. No voices, no heavy policemen's footsteps. Nothing.

He turned away from the stone arch and began walking very slowly down the long, dark hallway.

QUEEN'S BALLROOM

SHEILA JANKOWSKI WASN'T worried yet, but she was getting there. Gene was now two days overdue. The guards posted at Halfway House, on the other side of the Earth portal, were reporting no sign of him. And no phone calls. But that didn't mean much; you never knew when Gene would get the yen to ramble. Usually he satisfied his wanderlust in the castle. Inside Perilous there was no end of worlds to explore (well, actually there were exactly 144,000 of them, but let's not quibble). Earth was a world, too, though, and was in fact one of the castle's worlds. So, if he was off exploring, he was still doing it inside the castle. To be technical about it.

But that made Sheila feel no better. Gene still should have reported in.

She let her gaze wander to the huge chandeliers all aglow with hundreds of candles. She sighed. Best to take her mind off Gene for a while. Worrying would do no good. Just listen to the music, watch the people dance.

It was the annual Servants' Ball, a Castle Perilous tradition, and this year the organizing committee had invited some of the castle's Guests. Traditionally the lord of the castle and his family were invited, but Lord Incarnadine had been away for over a year. (No one was worried. The servants were used

to their liege's prolonged absences; one of the elderly chambermaids could remember a ten-year disappearance; but that
was who knew how long ago.) So in Incarnadine's stead,
some of the more prominent Guests were invited, including
Gene, whose official title was now Honorary Guardsman and
Knight Errant Extraordinary.

"Good evening, milady."

Sheila turned to find the castle chamberlain—Jamin by
name—bowing in front of her.

"Good evening," Sheila said.

Jamin straightened up, smiling broadly. He was a middle-
aged man with wispy red hair and twinkling eyes. "I pray
her ladyship is enjoying herself this night?"

"Oh, yes. Wonderful. You people have done such a good
job. And thanks ever so much for inviting us. We're very
honored to be included."

Jamin again bowed deeply. "It is you who do us the honor,
milady."

"Oh, no," Sheila protested as the musicians struck up
another number. It was nice music, Sheila thought. Sort of
medieval-sounding, but then again not quite like anything she
had ever heard before. Not that she was an expert in musi-
cology.

Jamin said, "Beg to inquire, milady—might I have the
honor of this dance?"

"Huh? Oh, sure!"

She was not at all sure she could do any of these dances.
The steps looked fearfully complex. It was all orchestrated,
somehow, like a square dance.

Laying a hand on Jamin's proffered arm she said, "If you
don't mind clumsy old me. I just might step all over your
toes."

"It's simple, milady. Allow me to show you."

Jamin executed what looked like a simple box step, with
one or two side steps thrown in.

Sheila tried it. "Well, I don't know," she said. "But if
you're willing, I'm willing."

" 'Twill be my delight, milady."

Maybe a little magic would help, she thought. Wriggling
her right finger she cast a facilitation spell that always worked
well inside the castle.

Jamin took her in his arms and they began to dance.

Sheila did the best she could, and apparently she wasn't doing badly. They whirled across the dance floor amidst the crowd and the music and the candleglow.

"Marvelous, milady!" the chamberlain beamed.

Sometimes it was all too much for Sheila. Being treated like an aristocrat, being called "your ladyship," living in a fairy castle, a dream world, to say nothing of all the magic, the mystery—it was just too much. When would she wake up to find that she had never left her empty, overmortgaged house in Wilmerding, Pennsylvania? When would she come crashing back to reality? For clearly this was not reality as she knew it. It couldn't exist, this world that she had stumbled into a year or so ago.

Could it be a year already? Of course that was reckoning by castle time. Who knew what relationship castle time had with Earth time? Or maybe there was no relationship at all. Castle Perilous, it was said, was timeless.

The tempo changed, slower now. She could see the musicians' strange instruments. Some looked like recorders, some like lutes, but others were multisegmented affairs, made of wood, set about with stops and valves. A few looked like nothing she could describe.

"Pardon the intrusion, old boy, but may I cut in?"

She turned her head to see Cleve Dalton tapping Jamin on the shoulder.

Jamin bowed graciously. "By all means, sir."

"Thank you, Jamin," Sheila said.

"Milady." Jamin backstepped, still bowing.

She began dancing with Dalton, another man in his middle sixties. Dalton was tall and very thin and had a deep, resonant voice like a radio announcer's. The smooth voice contrasted with the rawboned, homely face.

"Obsequious old coot," Dalton remarked out of Jamin's earshot.

"I think his manners are charming," Sheila said.

"I like the old rascal myself. But I hope I don't prick any bubbles if I tell you he's notorious with the chambermaids. They call him Jamin Three-Hands. Quite the roué, that one."

Sheila shook her head. "Doesn't fit. He seems like such a nice man."

"No such animal, nice men. We're all predatory, my dear."

"If you go by the one I was married to, maybe."

"Divorced? Too bad. I never had the misfortune. Lost my Doris a while back. After thirty years of living together, it was almost unendurable."

"Oh, I'm sorry."

"But I survived."

"Mr. Dalton, what did you do back in the real world? I never asked."

"Literary agent. Did it for years, and pretty successfully, too."

"That sounds so interesting."

"It was, it was. Some of my clients became very famous. I could mention names. For instance, there was James—" Dalton shrugged. "But who cares, here in the unreal world? What possible bearing could it have? That was in another country, and besides . . ."

"That's unusual."

"What is, my dear?"

"To find a Guest who was successful and happy in his former life."

"Well, you see, I retired. Sold the business, sold the house in Connecticut, and moved to California. Bought a nice little condo outside San Diego. I was all ready to settle comfortably into retirement when I had a heart attack."

"Oh, my."

"I came through it, but it caught me up short. I discovered I was really desperately unhappy and alone. Then, one night while recuperating at home, I found that my broom closet had an extra dimension I had never imagined it could have."

Sheila smiled. "And you stumbled into Castle Perilous, just like the rest of us."

"Precisely. All our stories are essentially the same. Haven't heard an interesting variation in years."

The dance number ended, and the crowd applauded. The musicians stood and bowed, then reseated themselves and began another tune.

Sheila said, "Uh-oh, I don't know if I can dance to this one."

Dalton counted the beats on his fingers. "I do believe that's nine-eight time. Or is it nine-*four*?" He grinned. "Maybe we'd better sit this one out?"

"Maybe we'd better."

"Some refreshment?"

"Yeah, sounds good."

They left the dance floor and joined a group of guests near the buffet table. Sheila surveyed the amazing assortment of food. The cooks had really outdone themselves.

"Having a good time, Sheila?" a man named Thaxton asked.

"Great," Sheila said, spooning goose liver onto a club cracker, "but I'm still a little worried about Gene."

"Best not to fret overmuch. I imagine he'll be along anytime now."

"I know, I know. But he should have called. He really should have."

"In any event," Dalton said, "Gene can take care of himself."

"Greatest swordsman in half a dozen worlds," Thaxton said. "And a damn fine tennis player, too." He smiled bleakly. "Can bloody well beat me, that I can tell you."

"You and your tennis," Dalton scoffed.

"You and your golf," Thaxton retorted.

"Golf's a civilized game."

"And tennis isn't, I suppose? I'd like to know by what criteria—"

"Golf is *slow*. That is my sole criterion."

"Bosh." Thaxton noticed Sheila's abstracted stare. "Something wrong, my dear?"

"Hm? No, not really. Well—it's just that on the day Gene was supposed to report in, the portal disappeared for about ten minutes."

"Really? Is that significant?"

"Hard to say. As everyone around here knows, portals are touchy things. They come and they go, even when they're supposedly under magical control, like the Earth one. But it kind of worries me."

"But you say it re-established itself quickly?"

"Yeah, maybe it wasn't gone even ten minutes, but . . ."

Two more Guests joined them, a small man with a pencil-thin moustache—Monsieur DuQuesne—and Deena Williams, a young black woman.

"You all eatin' again?" Deena chided.

"Doesn't matter," Thaxton said. "I haven't gained a pound since I fell in, and that'll be three years ago come

Michaelmas." He added with a grin, "One of the many benefits of this place."

DuQuesne said, "I've often wondered whether the food is real at all. After all, it's all done up with magic, every bit of it."

"It has to be real," Sheila said. "Or we'd all starve, wouldn't we?"

"It may be ordinary food transformed," Dalton said.

"Sounds logical."

Deena searched about. "Where's Snowclaw?"

Thaxton looked pained. "Good Lord, don't tell me they invited *him*."

"They sure did."

"For heaven's sake, why?"

" 'Cause he's a good friend of Sheila's, I guess."

Thaxton's expression changed quickly. "Terribly sorry, Sheila. I quite forgot."

"Oh, that's okay. Snowy can be a little difficult at times."

"I rather like having him around," Dalton said. "He's a good man . . . uh, person to have on your side in a scuffle."

Thaxton looked into his drink. "Yes, well, you're absolutely right."

"Speak of the devil," DuQuesne said.

On the dance floor, the crowd was parting. Through the breach stalked a seven-and-a-half-foot-tall, white-furred creature. The head looked small on the huge body, but was actually massive, combining feline and ursine features in a horrific, ferocious meld. Great curving fangs gleamed within its snout. Its general form was humanlike. The hands were near approximations, save for their wickedly sharp, bone-white claws. Its fierce eyes were yellow. With a huge battle-ax slung across its right shoulder, the beast approached the group of humans standing near the buffet table.

"Hi, everybody," Snowclaw said. "Sorry I'm late."

"That's okay," Sheila said. "Want something to eat?"

"Does a *kwallkark* defecate in the ocean? What d'you say, Thaxton, old buddy?"

"I'm sure I don't know," Thaxton murmured, backstepping.

"Well, well, what do we have here?" Snowclaw said, surveying the spread of comestibles. A scowl creased his face. "Same old stuff. Well, heck." He reached out and snared a roast sage hen, brought it to his nose and sniffed. He snorted, then ripped a huge bite out of the thing. Bones crunched as he chewed. "Not bad, actually." He tossed it back onto the table. "Not great, though." He reached for the floral centerpiece.

"Snowy, not that!" Sheila admonished.

"Sorry, Sheila. Thought it was food."

"There really ought to be something here you could eat. They should have—"

Servants approached, bearing a large copper tub filled with congealed greenish mush. After clearing a space, they set it on the table before Snowclaw.

"Now you're talking," Snowclaw said, scooping up a handful of the stuff. He ate with much gusto and more noise.

Dalton noticed that Snowclaw was drawing stares from the dance floor. "Was Snowclaw the only nonhuman Guest invited?"

"Looks like," Sheila said. "They all know him, even if they're afraid of him."

"Well, I think the fact that they did invite him says a lot about how much they respect you."

Sheila made a deprecatory gesture. "Really."

"Really. You're one of the most powerful magicians ever to make an appearance in the castle, so they say. Second only to Incarnadine himself."

"Oh, come *on*," Sheila said, blushing slightly.

"You helped save the castle during that last little contretemps we had here, and they know it."

"Well, it's a gift."

A page stepped up. "Pardon, Lady Sheila, but the guards at Halfway House report that someone wants to speak to you on the . . . speaking device."

Hope sprang to Sheila's face. "The telephone? Is it Gene?"

"Sorry, milady. They did not say."

The earth portal was on this same floor of the castle keep and about a five-minute walk from the Queen's Ballroom. Sheila knew the way, but the page insisted on escorting her even though this was one of the most stable areas of the castle. Sheila acquiesced, holding up the hem of her long gown and tripping along as best she could.

The portal stood at the arched mouth of what had been a small alcove. Now the arch was a doorway leading into the

living room of a large country estate—and another world:
Earth. The room was luxuriously furnished and had a stone
fireplace. A huge window-wall looked out onto expansive
grounds and a distant prospect of forested mountains.

The Guardsmen, dressed in local mufti, came to attention
when Sheila entered the room. She went directly to a side
table and picked up the telephone receiver.

"Hello?"

"Sheila? It's Linda."

"Hi! Have you heard from Gene?"

"You mean he hasn't shown up yet?"

"No. Where are you?"

"Still in California. Listen, I've been calling Gene's parents' house and I don't get any answer. So I figured he either
went somewhere with them or went back to the castle."

"Well, he didn't make it here, and he didn't call."

"Uh-oh. I'm worried."

"So am I, a little. But he's got to show up. I hate to think
of it, but unless something happened to his plane—"

"There's been no news about any plane crashes," Linda
said, "so forget that. I checked with the airline and they say
he boarded the plane in Los Angeles."

"Well, then I guess he's okay. He probably did go somewhere with his folks."

"Yeah."

"Yeah."

There was a pause. Then Sheila said, "You know what? I
don't believe it."

"Neither do I."

"And another thing," Sheila said. "Two, actually. The
portal fluttered two days ago. Disappeared for a few minutes."

"It's done that before."

"Never for more than a few seconds. According to the
sentries, this was like for at least ten minutes. The second
thing is that the servants are reporting a new Guest wandering
around. A kid, they say, and he looks like he's from Earth."

"Hm. If so, it means the portal did some flying around
before it stabilized. You better find this kid and make sure."

"Linda, do you think—?"

"What?"

"Oh, I don't know. We really don't know how stable, tied-down portals are supposed to act. If only Lord Incarnadine would come back!''

"He will eventually. Till then, we have to cope. It's our responsibility. That's why he gave us all fancy titles. But what were you thinking?''

"That someone might have tampered with the portal.''

The other end of the line was silent for a moment. Then Linda said, "That's something to think about, all right.''

ELSEWHERE

HE HAD SPENT what seemed like an eternity in total darkness, and he was going slowly insane. All he could do was pace his featureless cell—twelve paces long, eight wide—going around and around again, occasionally brushing the bare walls with his fingers as he walked. He had long ago given up trying to find seams or cracks in the wall. As far as he could determine there were none. He had found no hint of a possible opening of any kind, no hint of the possibility of escape.

Worse still, he had not been fed or given a drink of water, and there were no toilet facilities. He had chosen a corner to do his business in, but his mouth felt like the inside of a clothes hamper, and hunger was eating a hole in him.

The worst part was not knowing anything. Not knowing who his captors were, or why they were holding him, or what their intentions were. He wondered what was going on back in the castle. He suspected another invasion attempt, but there was no telling. Someone might just have it in for him. You could never tell about the castle. They didn't call it Castle Perilous for nothing.

But could he really have personal enemies? After some rumination, he dismissed the notion. No, his abduction must be part of a grand scheme of some sort. He only wondered why he hadn't been killed outright. Obviously he was a hostage. But to what purpose?

Then again, maybe the plan was to let him die slowly. No food, no water, no sanitation. Hell of a way to go, starvation.

He sniffed. The place was beginning to get ripe, but before long, he suspected, he wouldn't have much waste to void. Thirst would kill him long before hunger did.

How long had he been here? He really had no notion. Twenty-four hours at least. Maybe forty-eight. It seemed like a week. He hadn't slept a wink, and fatigue was weighing him down.

He stopped pacing and sat, leaning his back against the wall, then began giving more thought to where he could be. Well, he had come through a portal from Earth, which meant he was back in Castle Perilous somewhere. Or so he thought. He had never heard of a portal opening up between the universes of the castle. But it was a possibility, so he could be anywhere.

It made him feel better to think that he was inside Perilous, albeit at the mercy of his abductors. It meant that he had his magic powers. Correction: power, for he had only one. He was the best swordsman in the place. He wished for some way to test the hypothesis, but he needed a sword. There was no other way. He had tried shadow fencing with an imaginary sword, but it had told him little.

Of course, he *felt* right, sensed that his swordsmanship was back, but there was no way of being really sure. Anyway, the point was moot as long as he was unarmed.

His thoughts drifted to food. There was a great Syrian-Lebanese restaurant in Pittsburgh that he used to frequent. They served great shish kebab, fragrant hunks of flame-broiled marinated lamb, which went even better with a dish of rice and pignolias on the side. Of course, to start out you'd have maybe a tabuli salad—parsley and cucumber tossed in lemon dressing—along with fresh warm bread dipped in a mixture of mashed chick-peas, sesame oil, and garlic. Then some grape leaves stuffed with rice, ground lamb, and spices—or perhaps a dab of kibbe, raw ground lamb with onion. You didn't have to go with the meat on a skewer, either. There were plenty of other entrees, like stuffed eggplant or . . .

He had to stop that. He couldn't think of food or he surely would go mad.

Chinese was good, too. He could almost smell a dish of cashew chicken. But then again there was nothing wrong with a good old-fashioned slab of American prime rib, well-done at the edges and pink in the middle, lying alongside a volcanic cone of mashed potatoes, its caldera full to the brim with gravy made from pan drippings—

Stop! Are you crazy already? Stop. Just quit it.

He got up and began to pace again. If only the phantom smells would go away. He was sure, now, that he could smell bread baking.

He halted. Maybe he did smell bread baking. Or manufactured odors designed to tantalize him. Part of the torture. It could be this was just the beginning of his torment.

Somebody had it in for him! It had to be. But who?

He had no shred of an idea. Unless the Hosts of Hell were back in the castle. Those bastards were capable of anything. Sadism was child's play to the Hosts. In that case, it was hot pincers and thumbscrews for him, or worse, if such could be imagined. And it probably could.

He was worried now. And of course, fear and worry were high on the agenda, too. Anything to make him sweat, wear him down. Did they want him to talk? About what? He knew almost nothing of strategic value—that he could think of. He was just a soldier, nothing more. He was no sorcerer, like . . .

Like Linda and Sheila. Especially Sheila. Were they trying to get to the girls through him? Trying to coerce cooperation out of them by threatening him? The reverse?

Perhaps he was merely being kept in reserve as a future bargaining chip. That made sense. Maybe they were deciding what to do with him, which explained why the major excruciations hadn't started yet. The plan was to keep him barely alive for now, living in his own filth.

Again he wondered where in the castle he was. In the keep, most likely. The Donjon was a good bet, but this place could very well be in one of the outer defensive walls, of which Castle Perilous had a mind-boggling maze.

He couldn't stand it any longer. Time for the last Life Saver. He took out the package and peeled back the remnants of the paper covering, exposing the doughnut-shaped, wild-cherry-flavored confection.

He halted a motion to pop the thing into his mouth. Should he save it? After this, the thirst would become unbearable.

He rewrapped the candy and carefully put it back inside the inner breast pocket of his tweed sports jacket. If only he had loaded up on chewing gum and other stuff before he boarded the plane, as he usually did. But L.A. rush-hour traffic had delayed his arrival, necessitating a dash to the gate.

If he ever got out of this, he would never go about unarmed again, no matter where he was.

On second thought, what good would a gun or a knife or even a sword do him now? It was his own damn fault for being so trusting. He should have sounded that page out, demanded to see Osmirik, at least, if not Incarnadine. In fact, he should have—

Light!

He waited until the pain in his eyes subsided, then tried to look. A fuzzy, eye-searing oblong of light had suddenly appeared in the far wall. An opening. He staggered toward it. A warm breeze washed over him, and a strange, dry smell entered his nostrils. An alien smell.

Gene knew it was no ordinary door. Perhaps his captors were on the other side; if so, they weren't inside the castle. He instinctively knew a wild portal when he saw one.

This meant he was inside Castle Perilous! And slipping through the portal meant escape, all right, but it also possibly meant being stranded on the other side, forever exiled from Perilous and its wonders. Wild portals were like that. They flitted about the castle, appearing and disappearing at random, sometimes never to be seen again. Each one led to a different world; some of those worlds were lethal, some were not. To enter any one of them was to leap into the unknown.

That is, *if* it was indeed a wild portal and not a wordless summons to come out. No voices called his name.

His eyes were adjusting slowly. Shielding them with both hands, he advanced until he could pick out some features of the landscape on the other side. There wasn't much out there: a few rocks, a hill, a gnarled bush, and sand everywhere. The sky was slightly yellow.

No one stood near the entrance. If it was a trap, it did not look like one. He lurched forward until light from a strange sun warmed him. He was outside.

He stopped and looked about. The portal was an anomalous dark rectangle standing in the middle of an eroded gully. Pink boulders rose all around him. The cloudless sky was pale yellow. His eyes would not let him look near the sun, but he sensed that this world's star was larger than the Earth's though not as bright. The air was warm and breathable. Lucky for him. This was not always so on the other side of a portal. He chose a rock and sat down to wait for his irises to contract.

Presently they did, just in time for him to watch the portal disappear with a pop.

"So much for life at Castle Perilous," he said dully.

The portal could reappear, but more than likely he was stuck here. Forever.

He decided not to wait around in the hope that the doorway would rematerialize. The presence of the bush informed him that there was life here, and where there was life there was danger. This position was too exposed and vulnerable.

As he gained the lip of the gully, he saw the city, a fanciful grouping of domes, spires, and free-form shapes sitting on the plain. The buildings were of a single color, a faded blue-green. That it was a ruined city was not so much apparent as sensed. Silence sat on the plain, an ancient, empty silence.

He regarded the city for a long moment.

"The cover of *Astounding Stories*, circa 1932," he said. "Maybe a little *Thrilling Wonder* thrown in. Could be an Edmund Hamilton piece."

He checked to the right, then to the left. Nothing else in sight.

He struck out across the plain.

CASTLE

JEREMY WAS NOT quite sure when the dream had begun. Call it an extended hallucination. Was it when he had heard the police? Had the wild delusions started then? Or had he actually jumped off the roof? Maybe it was like that story he read (Jeremy had not read much fiction beyond comic books, but what he had read he remembered), the one by Ambrose Bierce—"Occurrence at Owl Creek Bridge." Yeah, that was it. Maybe he was hallucinating this whole thing in one flash as he plummeted.

If he was in the middle of falling to his death, he sure was taking his good old time about it. His best guess was that he had been in the castle at least two days.

He knew it was a castle, because it looked like one on the inside, and also because he had seen bits and pieces of the outside through a few of the windows. Through other windows . . . well, he wasn't quite sure what he had seen. Alien worlds, maybe. Crazy stuff. But not the craziest. The real nutty stuff happened when a window or doorway would pop up anywhere, right in front of you, maybe, and you found yourself about to step into a primeval swamp, or a jungle, or a spooky city, or any number of other curious locales.

But that wasn't all that was insane about this place. There

were creatures here. Something purple and multiarmed had chased him yesterday—halfheartedly, he suspected, because the thing could move fast, and probably could have caught him if it had wanted to. Maybe the thing was as lost as he was and wanted company. Jeremy had got that feeling, but had been too scared to stop running. Maybe today. If he saw the thing again today, maybe he would stop and try to communicate.

But maybe not. Jeremy was still scared, scared even of the humans. The humans had spoken to him, asking him to come with them. Something about meeting the "other Guests."

"Yeah, right, lady!" he had yelled over his shoulder as he sprinted away. They weren't going to throw him into any dungeon. "Guests," his butt.

But maybe he shouldn't have run. Maybe they really had been trying to help him. They looked harmless enough—if you believed that people running around in funny costumes could be harmless.

But it was possible. After all, who had put the food outside the door of the strange room he had slept in last night? He had assumed the tray had been left there by mistake, but now he wasn't sure. The food had been great, although he would have eaten a dead skunk by then.

He had to do something sooner or later; soonest, if he wanted to preserve his sanity. He had given a great deal of thought to turning himself in. It made him laugh. Turning himself in. He was wanted in Fantasyland, too. Mickey Mouse had a warrant for his arrest. No, he hadn't seen any Disney characters—yet—but there was no telling in this place.

He was walking along one of the castle's endless hallways when another costumed castle inhabitant stepped out of an intersecting passageway. It was a man with a beard and a funny haircut and funny, floppy shoes. Still clutching his laptop computer, Jeremy skidded to a stop.

The guy looked Jeremy up and down. "Ah, there you are! You really should come along with me, young man."

But Jeremy wasn't quite ready yet and dashed off in the other direction.

"But you might sustain grievous injury, son! Please, listen to me!"

Jeremy was tempted, but when another man stepped out into the hallway, he panicked.

"Stop him, Wildon!" the first man shouted.

Wildon, a big hulking dude, went into a crouch and threw out his arms, ready to catch the running Jeremy.

Jeremy executed a textbook-perfect slide into home, slipping between Wildon's legs. Wildon didn't touch him. Jeremy sprang to his feet and ran on.

But the corridor ended in one of those crazy doorways, this one letting out into bright sun backdropped by dense greenery.

Jeremy slowed a bit, looking back over his shoulder. Sure enough, Wildon was in pursuit. Jeremy put on speed and tore through the opening.

A wave of heat hit him as he ran through a clearing and hit the edge of a dense rain forest. He plunged into the trees, leaves whipping at his face, his Reebok hightops trampling the undergrowth. Strange cries echoed all around. It sounded like convincing Tarzan sound-track stuff: whooping, chittering, creeing, and so forth. It was scary. He stumbled, tripped up by a thorny vine that had snagged his pants. For a heart-stopping second he thought that something hiding in the weeds had got hold of him. He gave a high-pitched yell, yanked his leg free, and jumped away. He tripped again, staggered, got turned around, and tried running backward. His ankle twisted on a hidden stone, and he went crashing headlong through a wall of vegetation.

After rolling down a high grassy bank, he hit soft ground and stopped. He was in the clear, out of the forest.

Spitting sand, he sat up. A beach?

No, not a beach. Just a kidney-shaped depression with sand in it. It looked a little like a sand trap in a golf course. Well, no. As a matter of fact, it looked *exactly* like a sand trap in a . . .

"I say!"

Jeremy blinked, looked around.

"You there! Mind awfully getting out of the way? I'm making my approach shot."

Jeremy saw him now. It was a man in his thirties, light-haired and thin, dressed in shirt, sweater vest, and old-fashioned baggy knee pants—knickers—complete with high stockings and golf shoes. He looked like something out of an old movie. An older man stood behind him, watching.

Annoyed, the first man took a step closer. "Can't you bloody hear?"

"Yeah, I can hear," Jeremy said.

"Well, look, I hate to be rude—but piss off, will you? We'd really like to play through, if you don't mind awfully much."

"Uh . . . sorry." Jeremy got up and moved out into the fairway.

"A bit more," the man directed, gesturing imperiously with his seven iron. "A few more steps. Right there. Yes, yes, there's a good fellow." He returned to his ball and addressed it. "Right! Well, then . . ."

After a few tentative swings, the man made his shot. The ball arched toward the nearby green, hit smack on, narrowly missing the pin, then skidded across the manicured grass and rolled off the other side into another bunker.

"Oh, bloody hell!" the man shouted, throwing down his club in disgust.

Dragging his golf bag on a two-wheeled dolly, the older man approached Jeremy.

"Just fell in, son?"

"Huh?"

"Fell into the castle. You arrived very recently, didn't you? Like day before yesterday?"

"Uh, yeah, I did. Are you from the castle, too?"

"Sure am. A little scared? Don't be. It's called Castle Perilous, but once you learn the ropes, it's a very nice place indeed. All it takes is some getting used to."

"Sure is crazy."

"Yeah, it gets that way sometimes." The man extended his hand. "Name's Dalton. Cleveland Dalton. Cleve, if you like."

Jeremy shook his hand. "Jeremy Hochstader."

"Fine old German name, Hochstader. Used to have a client by that name. Never went anywhere—wrote fantasy, if memory serves."

The man in knickers went harumphing past, apparently still upset about the muffed shot.

Dalton said, "That's Thaxton. Don't mind him. Golf's not his game, and I won't play tennis with him."

"Where the hell is this place?" Jeremy blurted.

Dalton shrugged. "This place? Nobody knows. Some

world, in some time or space, somewhere. Just one of the worlds accessible via the castle.''

''But where's the castle?'' Jeremy demanded.

''Nobody really knows that, either. But it's real, son. It's real. Don't make the mistake of thinking it's all a dream.''

''Yeah, I gave up on that yesterday.''

''Get anything to eat yet?''

Jeremy nodded. ''Uh-huh. They fed me.''

''Good,'' Dalton said. ''By the way, did you ever caddy?''

CITY

GENE HAD CHOSEN a high tower as his residence, staking out an apartment on a high floor. Above this level lay only a few small chambers, some containing building machinery. There was water in a storage tank on the roof; as for food, the city had given him all he wanted, when he had asked for it.

He had very soon found out that the city was alive, or at least was a conscious entity of some sort. He had walked right in through an open gate. Looking around, he heard a quasi-human voice speaking a strange language. After searching for the source, he eventually realized that the voice had been that of the city itself, or of some artificial intelligence that was part of the city's computer control system. As for other intelligent inhabitants, the place was as deserted as it looked, and very old.

The city had learned colloquial English very quickly, from Gene, mostly; its only other source was a tattered paperback Gene had been carrying, a science fiction novel with a futuristic trailer truck on the cover. It still spoke with the machine equivalent of an accent, slurring its syllables occasionally. Otherwise the city was quite intelligible.

The city had a name: Zond.

"I see that your genetic makeup is quite divergent from the beings who built me," Zond told Gene.

"Perceptive of you," Gene told the city. "Does that change anything?"

"Nope."

"Really. Why? Weren't you designed to serve whoever it was who built you?"

"That's true, but my original programming also includes instructions about showing hospitality to visitors. You're a visitor; you get hospitality."

"Nice and friendly, your builders. What was the name you called them again?"

"The Umoi."

"Funny name."

"What's funny about it?"

"Sorry, didn't mean to offend."

"No, I was just asking," Zond said. "I haven't had a good laugh in centuries."

He had many conversations like this one over the next several weeks. He learned something about the Umoi, who had been a squat, reptilelike race, somewhat resembling terrestrial toads. They had had a long and complex history, culminating in the building of a small number of these self-contained, fully sentient cities. By that time the Umoi population had shrunk to a tiny fraction of what it was in earlier periods. Then—Gene did not know exactly what had happened. The Umoi died off gradually, after deserting the cities. History had simply petered out at some point. Gene had a little trouble converting Umoi time scales into Earth equivalents, but it looked as though the Umoi had become extinct between 100,000 and 150,000 years ago. Anyway, it was a long time since the Umoi had walked this world. The city's main domes had weathered and faded, but for the most part the city was still intact and functioning.

His apartment gave him a commanding view of the city. After spending most of the day in the city library, Gene would go back to his lair and eat a synthesized but palatable dinner. Then he would sit at a window and look out at tall spires set against the plains beyond, waiting until the swollen yellow sun set behind distant mountains. Then he would crawl into an Umoi bed—a simple affair like a sleeping bag with a spongy bottom—and listen to the silence until he dozed off.

He would dream of empty cities and of a race that gave up living.

Awake, he would give some thought to trying to find the portal, though he was acutely aware of the possibility that it might never again make an appearance in this world. Even if it did, there was no telling where it would pop up, or for how long.

But he had the resources of the city to help him. From what Gene could surmise, the Umoi had forgotten more science and technology than terrestrial humans had ever created. The twilight years of Umoi civilization had been characterized by a racial desire to simplify life, to return to the basics of existence. In this the Umoi had succeeded only too well, relaxing their hold on things to the extent that life simply slipped away. Gene suspected that degenerate Umoi cultures had continued to scrape by outside the cities for a long stretch, perhaps for as long as fifty thousand years. Things had been very peaceful and natural for centuries; but in time, ancient enemies took their toll: disease, dwindling resources, stagnation. The Umoi had gone out with barely a whimper.

"Case in point, lesson taken," Gene intoned, sitting at a library view screen, "in the twilight . . . area."

"I beg your pardon?"

"Uh, nothing. I gotta stop talking to myself."

"Is this habit common among your species?"

"Yes, perfectly normal. Pay no attention to that man behind the curtain." Gene yawned. "I'm bushed, but let's go over this once again. You say that the Umoi developed the technique of interdimensional travel centuries ago but abandoned it?"

"The Umoi weren't concerned with the practical applications of their discoveries," the city told him.

"How pure and virtuous. But are you telling me that one of these machines exists somewhere on the planet?"

"I'm telling you that it's a possibility."

"Where?"

"I can't be certain, but such a machine was reputed to have been built in the city of Annau, long ago. It may still be there."

"Where's Annau?"

The screen displayed a map. A flashing dot marked the spot.

"Here."

"Okay. Where is that in relation to where we are?"

"The city of Annau lies exactly four thousand *gi* to the southwest."

Gene whistled. "Jeez. Quite a hike, even if I don't know exactly how long a *gi* is."

"Transportation can be provided."

"Yeah? What kind?"

"A self-propelled, cross-country vehicle powered by the nuclear fusion of certain isotopes of hydrogen. Primitive, but effective."

"Sounds like a great way to go, but it's still a long shot."

"Define 'long shot.' "

"Risky. If I break down, or get a flat—"

"A flat what?"

"Never mind. Let's just say that I need to assess the risk factors here."

"That can be done."

Gene said, "Well, let's do it."

QUEEN'S DINING HALL

"HOW WAS YOUR FLIGHT?" Sheila asked.

"Fine," Linda Barclay said. A pretty blonde with pale blue eyes, she was tall and perhaps a bit too thin.

Sheila had always wanted to be a blonde, had always hated her own red hair. Although Sheila wasn't aware of it and would probably disagree, she was just as good-looking as Linda.

"You say you tried calling Gene's parents over and over?"

Linda set down her coffee cup and reached for another roll, thought better of it. "I was even thinking of stopping in there, maybe asking some neighbors whether they'd seen Gene, or whether the family had gone on vacation. But that would have looked awfully strange."

Sheila nodded. "Probably."

"Why don't we just up and look for Gene?" Snowclaw asked.

"Where do we start?" Sheila said. "On Earth?"

"Why not?" the white-furred beast said as he munched his usual breakfast—beeswax candles dipped in Thousand Island dressing. "That's where he was last seen. You just take me there. I'll find him."

"Talk about looking strange," Linda said, laughing.

Snowclaw chuckled. "Yeah, I guess it would look pretty weird for me to go stomping around your world."

"Everyone would think you were Bigfoot," Sheila said. "You'd wind up on TV. Or in a zoo, or something."

"I don't know what either of those things is, but I probably wouldn't like 'em."

"No, you wouldn't."

"I think Snowy's right, though," Linda said. "Earth would be the logical place to start."

M. DuQuesne had been listening. "Linda, you've been in the castle too long. Imagine thinking in terms of a whole world being a likely place to start looking for someone."

"Sounds silly, doesn't it?" Linda said. "But we have to start somewhere."

"I just can't believe that something happened to him back home," Sheila said. "It doesn't make sense. No one there knows about the castle."

"Except Incarnadine's brother Trent," Linda said.

"Maybe he knows something about Gene," Snowclaw said.

Sheila shook her head skeptically. "I doubt it."

"We could ask him."

"Boy, I'd hate to be putting snoopy questions to a prince. He might think we suspected him."

Linda said, "Prince Trent seems like a nice guy, but I sensed some kind of tension between him and Lord Incarnadine."

Sheila nodded. "They were rivals for the throne once."

"Maybe they still are."

"But why would Trent want to do away with Gene?"

"Maybe he wants to do away with all of us, all the powerful Guest magicians. We're Incarnadine's servants now."

"Vassals," Sheila corrected.

"Vassals. Any pretender to the throne would want to neutralize his rival's powerful allies."

"Wait a minute. Aren't you overestimating our strength and importance just a little bit?"

"No, I don't think so. Didn't Incarnadine himself say that we two were the most powerful castle magicians he'd ever seen, besides members of the royal family?"

"Yeah," Sheila said, "I guess he did say that. I just can't see myself in the role of mover and shaker."

"Well, we did our part to save the castle a year ago. Help stop a whole invasion."

"Incarnadine stopped it. And his brother Deems died fighting the invaders off."

Linda nodded. "Okay, maybe I'm getting egotistical. I was just trying to imagine what the heck might be going on."

"Maybe nothing's going on," Sheila said. "Gene will walk in here in a few days and we'll all feel pretty stupid." She looked away for a moment, then said, "I've been wondering. Why would we be the most powerful magicians? Some of the servants are hundreds of years old—at least some of them say they are. Why aren't they all super sorcerers? I mean, it's the castle that gives you magic powers, and they've lived their whole lives here."

"There are powerful magicians among the servants," DuQuesne said. "For instance, Jamin is very adept. He supervises the maintenance of various spells around the castle, like the language-translation spell that keeps this place from turning into Babel."

"Then why does Incarnadine need us?" Sheila asked.

DuQuesne shrugged. "I'm sure I don't know, but he must have his reasons."

"Well, all that's neither here nor there," Linda said. "Gene is three days late now, and I say we try to find him."

Sheila signed. "Obviously we'll need some magic. I can't begin to imagine how we'd go about it."

"Osmirik is the logical one to ask for help in that area," Linda said. "There has to be something like a spell to locate someone or something."

"Hmm." Sheila knitted her brow. "Maybe. Anybody seen Osmirik lately?"

"Has anyone ever seen him outside the library?" DuQuesne said. "Fellow always has his nose in a book."

"Want to go up with me?" Sheila asked Linda.

"Sure," Linda said. "Right now."

"Finish your coffee. There's really no—" Sheila broke off as a group of people entered the dining hall, among them Osmirik, the castle scribe and librarian. The other three were Thaxton, Dalton, and a young man no one had ever seen before.

"Hey, is that the new fall-in?" Linda asked.

"Looks like," Sheila said.

"Greetings," Dalton said. "Meet our new caddy."

Jeremy waved, then caught sight of Snowclaw.

"Hi, I'm Sheila Jankowski."

"Uh . . . hi. Jeremy Hochstader."

"Nice to meet you, Jeremy."

After Sheila had made introductions all around, Jeremy took a seat, still mesmerized by the sight of Snowclaw.

Linda said, "Coffee?"

"Huh? Oh, sure. Thanks."

"Snowy is one of our dearest friends," Sheila said. "New people always get a little shaken up the first time they see him."

Jeremy looked away quickly. "Doesn't bother me," he said. "I've seen all kinds of things since I got here."

"When was that?" Sheila asked pointedly.

"I dunno, it's hard to keep track of time in here. Two days, maybe three."

"Three days. That's when the portal wandered, all right. Where are you from?"

"New York. Queens."

Sheila did not pry further, as it was considered impolite.

"We found him wandering around the golf course," Dalton said. "More or less took him under our wing. Made an excellent caddy." He winked at Jeremy.

"We were just talking about you, Osmirik," Linda said.

"In a kindly way, I trust," the librarian said as he loaded his plate with flapjacks and sausages. Of late he had acquired a taste for what, to him, were some rather strange foods.

"We were tossing around the possibility of locating Gene by using a spell. Anything like that in the books?"

Osmirik seated himself. "My dear, there are spells for every purpose imaginable."

"Then we could do it?"

"Perhaps." Osmirik took a sip of coffee. "And perhaps not."

Linda shrugged. "Well, that covers the whole spectrum of possible outcomes."

Sheila said, "Could we find him if he's off through some portal or another?"

Osmirik thought it over. "It is quite likely . . ." He chewed thoughtfully.

Sheila nodded expectantly, smiling.

Osmirik swallowed. ". . . that this is a possibility."

Sheila slumped a little. "Well, are you willing to help us?"

"Of course, it is you who must undertake the effectuation of any such spell. As you know, I myself am not an adept thaumaturgist."

"Thauma—yeah, we know. But you'll help us with the research?"

"It would be my pleasure, Sheila."

"Good. When can we start?"

"Might I break my fast before we begin?"

"Oh, sure. I'm sorry. It's just that we're a little worried about Gene."

"And I share your concern. Before we start, however, I might warn you that such a project could be weeks in the making."

"Weeks?"

"If not months. Were he in the castle, 'twould be a simple matter. But locating him among a hundred thousand worlds?" Osmirik shook his head woefully. "A staggering task, and one not to be undertaken lightly."

"But he's on Earth, we know that," Linda said. "So forget about the hundred thousand worlds."

"Ah, Earth magic." Osmirik let out a long sigh. "That, I'm afraid, is a different story altogether."

"Right," Linda said. "You're the only magician around here who can handle that, Sheila."

Sheila looked deflated. "We're going to have to ask for Prince Trent's help. Earth magic is the hardest of all. I'm nowhere near being good at it."

"Then by all means we should ask Prince Trent to help. I'll go over to Halfway and phone him. Or maybe you should."

"I will," Sheila said. "But you're coming back to Earth with me, Linda."

"I should stay here and keep and eye out."

"You're right, you should."

"Sheila, I'm coming with you," Snowclaw stated.

"Don't be silly. You can't go running around Earth looking the way you do."

"So change me."

"Huh?"

"Do your witchy stuff on me and make me look different."

"Gee, I never thought of that. I don't know if I can."

"Give it a shot."

Osmirik said, "Appearance spells are not very difficult, even within the scope of Earth magic."

Sheila shrugged. "I'll give it a try. It'd be nice to have someone along with me. Especially you, Snowy."

"I want to find Gene just as much as anyone. After all, we're buddies."

"However, there may still be a problem concerning the locator spell," Osmirik said. "Might I inquire, what is the approximate human population of your world?"

Linda said, "Last time I heard it was five billion."

Osmirik was stunned. "Five . . . *billion* souls, you say? Five thousand millions?"

"Is that a lot?"

"Well, I should say so. I had no idea. The task of locating Gene out of that mass of humanity . . ."

"Looks like we're getting nowhere fast," Sheila said glumly. "Maybe we should concentrate on looking elsewhere."

"But Gene never passed through the portal," Linda objected. "You keep bringing up the possibility that he might be off in another aspect somewhere. Why?"

"Because of that darn portal wandering," Sheila said. "It's just possible there's been some foul play here, somebody fiddling with the portal's placement. Maybe Gene did it himself."

"But Gene's no magician."

"Someone he was with? Maybe Trent . . . though I can't bring myself to believe that. Or maybe what's-her-name is back. Princess Ferne."

A troubled silence fell.

Dalton broke it by directing an aside to Jeremy. "Castle politics, son. Palace intrigue."

"There's a lot going on here that I don't understand," Jeremy said.

"Well, look," Sheila said. "I'll go to Earth and work on the problem at that end. Linda, you stay here and help Osmirik at this end. Search the castle first, then start looking for some way of finding out if he went through another portal.''

"Easier said than done," Osmirik said. "The task of processing endless data through the spell is the real problem.''

"Processing data?'' Linda said. "Too bad you can't mix computers and magic.''

"Who says you can't?'' Sheila wanted to know.

"Well, we don't have a computer, anyway.''

"Here's one,'' Jeremy said, and everyone looked at him. He brought the Toshiba up from the floor and set it on the table. He flipped up the screen.

Osmirik jumped up and went over to him. "May I see that, please?''

"Sure.'' Jeremy turned on the power supply. "Works on batteries.'' He jiggled the switch. "Funny thing. You know, the first time I tried to turn it on in the castle, it didn't work. I didn't know what was going on, 'cause I know I recharged the batteries the other day, and I haven't used it since. But I fiddled with it, and now it works fine.''

"Boy, that's a first,'' Linda said.

"Huh? What do you mean?''

"Electricity isn't supposed to work in the castle.''

"Yeah? How come?''

"Only magic works here.''

Sheila said, "That may be his talent.''

"Everyone gets a magical talent in this place,'' Linda told him. "Yours might be being able to work a computer without electricity.''

Jeremy chuckled. "C'mon, you gotta be kidding.''

Osmirik was watching numbers and symbols dance across the screen.

"Very interesting,'' he said.

CENOTAPHS

VIOLET SKY, CLOUDLESS, a small blue sun low over a distant ridge, sand and fine gravel underfoot, a steady wind blowing across a plateau peopled with stone monuments of myriad shapes. Overhead, a triangle of bright stars. This world was always the same.

He walked among the monuments, gravel crunching under his boots, the only sound on these stark plains save for the faint murmur of the wind, melancholy and drear.

All was simplicity, clarity, peace.

The monuments were of various geometrical shapes, some towering into the bluish-purple sky. No one knew who had created them, or why, or what purpose they served. As objects which inspire contemplation, however, they served admirably. Perhaps that was their proper function, after all. He often walked this plain when he had some thinking to do, or when he needed to clear his mind.

He had just completed a hard year negotiating a settlement to a protracted war. The belligerents had been obstinate to the point of exasperation, but reason had won out in the end. The terms of treaty served the interests of the state which he had a hand in governing, and in which he himself had considerable personal interest, as his family resided there. The castle was no place for small children.

Monuments at either hand: on his left a truncated pyramid; to the right an inverted trapezoid juxtaposed with a sphere. He paused to study this latter arrangement. Presently he moved on.

He had come full circle, back to the two-dimensional oblong of the doorway between this world and the castle. After casting one last look over the silent plain, he passed through the portal and entered the fortress of his ancestors.

The cenotaph world was one of a number of interesting landscapes in the Hall of Contemplative Aspects. He wished for the time to visit them all today, but duty called. He had been away much too long. He left the Hall and began his descent of the spiral staircase that would take him to a tunnel, thence through to the castle keep.

Halfway down the first turn, he stopped suddenly.

There it was again, the same strange feeling he had experienced on arriving back in the castle. He could not put his finger on it, but something was awry. Something not right. He closed his eyes and attempted to pin it down.

Whatever it was, it resisted pinning.

"Most interesting," he murmured.

He cocked an ear, as if listening. There was no sound to hear. Odd. Now everything seemed fine. Or had there been a subtle change?

"Curious. Very curious."

He continued down the stairwell. He would have to look into this.

Perhaps he had simply been away too long.

The passageway leading into the basement of the keep was silent and dim, illuminated only by an occasional jewel-torch. *Incarnadine.*

He stopped. What he had heard was not unusual. Castle Perilous contained many voices, many spirits. The bones of his ancestors lay in crypts all around, three thousand years' worth of bones. Sometimes the voices called his name. Mostly they nattered unintelligibly. The castle itself had a voice, the voice of the demon out of which the castle had been magicked long ago, but that voice had been silent for the last few years. The only other spirit in the habit of babbling at him was the ghost of his first betrothed, the Lady Melydia, who had died an unnatural death a few years ago, victim of a consuming madness.

This new voice was different, however. He oriented himself this way and that, as though his body were an antenna.

Incarnadine, hear me.

There! It was coming from one of the family crypts; one of the oldest ones, in fact. He felt obliged to answer such a venerable source.

The tunnel branched off ahead, and he bore right, down a narrower and even dimmer passage, at the end of which stood a cast-iron door set about with various fanciful creatures in bas-relief.

He waved his hand, and the door emitted a sharp click; then, seemingly of its own volition, it swung open with much creaking and groaning.

A strange pale light emanated from the chamber within. He approached carefully, and looked into the crypt.

He beheld a strange sight: the vaporous image of a man standing beside an ancient sarcophagus. Tall, gaunt, bedecked in kingly robes, the specter regarded him enigmatically for a moment. Then it spoke.

"My hour is almost come," it said, *"when I to sulphurous and tormenting flames must render up myself."*

"Alas, poor ghost," Incarnadine replied.

"Pity me not, but lend thy serious hearing to—"

"Begging your pardon, Ancestor," Incarnadine broke in, "but do we really need all the traditional ghostly rhetoric? It's rather a bore, if you don't mind my saying so."

"Frightfully sorry," the ghost said. *"This is my first haunting, you know. Didn't quite know what proper form was. Sorry, Sorry. Well, then—"* The ghost seemed at a loss.

"Why don't you just warn me against whatever it was that you were going to warn me against?" Incarnadine said. "That more or less was what you were about to do, wasn't it?"

"As a matter of fact, yes. Well I seem to have gone and botched the whole thing, haven't I?"

"Not at all."

"You're so very kind. See here; do you know who I am?"

Incarnadine looked off, mentally counting crypts. "Let's see, you'd be . . . Ervoldt the Sixth?"

"Seventh. Quite all right, I was a nobody and damned well

know it. Just happened to be handy when the job came up. Well, we might as well get on with it. You would do well to heed these words, Incarnadine. Someone has been tampering with the interdimensional forces which hold the worlds together.''

"I know."

"You do?" The ghost of Ervoldt VII was crestfallen. *"Well all this seems to have been of doubtful utility, I must say."*

"Not so. I had merely suspected. Now I know."

"Eh? Oh, I see. Quite so, quite so."

"You have my humble thanks, Ancestor."

"It's nothing, nothing at all. I'm told you're a fine boy, a worthy continuation of the family line. Done rather well for yourself."

"I do my best. Grandfather, do you have any idea of who might be responsible?"

The ghost chortled. *"Not the bloody vaguest idea! You'd think so, wouldn't you? Most people think the dead know everything. Truth is, you can't see a blessed thing from the other side!"*

"Then how are you so sure about the tampering?"

"Oh, no mistaking that. It makes my head hurt, actually. Celestial spheres ringing, bonging, all sorts of clanging about. Dreadful racket!"

"I see. Again, you have my thanks. One thing, though. You were fooling about the sulphurous and tormenting flames, were you not?"

"Of course. Don't want to let on what it's really like. People would be killing themselves to get here."

"What's it like?"

"Oh, splendid, splendid! I was just sitting down to a game of seven-cards-up when the call came. You should see—" The ghost gathered himself up. *"Well, there I almost went and put my foot in it. The others might take a dim view of me tipping our hand. Eh?"* He laughed good-naturedly.

"Your secret is safe with me."

"Stout fellow." Lacking anything more to say, Ervoldt shrugged. *"Well, must dash off. May the gods watch over you. Be well."*

"Farewell, Ancestor."

The apparition turned abruptly, strode toward the wall, and passed through it in classic ghostly fashion, disappearing into the stone.

"Not a bad haunting, after all," Incarnadine said.

He closed the crypt and continued on his way. He had a great deal of work to do.

WILDERNESS

HE HAD TRAVELED about seven hundred miles in three days, not bad progress for an off-road vehicle over rugged terrain. But thousands of miles of sand and rock still lay between him and Annau. In the past, transportation on the planet had not always been so difficult, but the Umoi had eventually ripped up their vast highway system to allow the planet to revert to its natural state. An underground pneumatic tube network was still extant, but city had informed him that it was in bad repair.

He was still in communication with Zond, but Zond had no way to rescue him in the event of a breakdown. Fortunately, the teardrop-shaped Umoi land rover seemed in no danger of failure, its nuclear-fusion engines humming smoothly, its shape-changing "tires" flowing over rock and ridge like giant amoebae.

He was enjoying the scenery. It was a colorful world for all its desolation, ocher sky arching over the deeper yellows and browns of the desert, both relieved by pink strata thrusting up at sharp angles. Gene never tired of watching the terrain roll by, bleak as it was.

He did not have to drive, as the vehicle was quite capable of directing itself. It merely needed specific instructions now and then: stop in two hours for a maintenance check; continue on this course until told otherwise; take the safest route, not necessarily the fastest; etc. Nevertheless, he did like to take the controls at times, just for something to do.

He was at the helm now as the vehicle came out of rugged country, easing down a slope toward the edge of a wide, flat depression that stretched ahead for miles. He checked the controls, then switched the vehicle over to automatic. Intending to get some sleep, he climbed into the aft compartment.

He was optimistic about his chances of making it to Annau. What he would do when he got there was another matter. Annau was also a machine intelligence, but Zond had lost contact with it and the rest of the cities ages ago. If Annau was still operative, Gene intended to establish communication with it and beg its help in finding the interdimensional device. Then . . .

One step at a time, he thought. First get there. Let's not think about the rest of it. The whole enterprise was the longest of long shots, anyway. Best not to dwell on the—

The vehicle shook under a strong impact that knocked him out of the hammock affair he used as a bed. He crawled into the forward compartment and looked out the right view bubble. Nothing. After another concussion hit, he stuck his head into the left bubble, looking toward the rear.

He was shocked by the sight of a huge, three-horned, six-footed beast ramming its massive head against the side of the vehicle. Looking like a cross between a rhinoceros and a giant armadillo, the creature had already done some damage, albeit superficial.

He upped the power control and looked back again. The animal matched speed easily. Obviously it could move fast. He had never pushed the vehicle over thirty miles an hour and was unsure of its top speed. There was no telling what the animal could do. For all its bulk, the thing looked capable of hitting fifty at a walk. The ground shook as it ran, its powerful legs, as thick as tree trunks, moving like pistons.

Cause for concern, perhaps, but not to worry. The vehicle could probably outrun the thing, and if not, surely could withstand a little battering. It was made of some miracle metal, he was certain.

But the beast had some miracles of its own. It would not be outrun, and kept smashing its gargantuan head against the starboard hull, which was beginning to look like a crushed eggshell. Gene began to wish mightily that the thing would go away. He threw the power rod to maximum. The extra speed helped, as did his quick maneuvering on the controls. But it was no go. Every time he began to pull ahead, the beast would kick in another carburetor and catch up.

Preoccupied with what was going on to the rear, he neglected to watch where he was going. When he did remember to glance forward, he yelped and panic-steered away from the edge of the arroyo that he had been about to send the rover crashing into. But in avoiding catastrophe, he turned into the beast's next attack, catching its full force. The vehicle almost upended.

Now he was in a pickle, stuck on a perilous track between two certain disasters. The beast seemed to sense this and kept hemming him in, forcing him to hug the rim of the little canyon.

He briefly considered making a dash for broken terrain, but that was a bad risk. The beast was too fast. The only alternative was to go down into the canyon. The trick was finding a slope that the rover could handle, yet steep enough to discourage the beast from following. The possibility cheered him; he could not imagine the bulky animal rappeling down the canyon wall in pursuit.

It was an agonizing quarter mile or so until he found a suitable entry point. The sheer wall of the canyon suddenly flared out into a slope strewn with talus and a few huge boulders. He steered right and sent the vehicle over the edge and down the steep incline.

The rover began to slide, but the tires ballooned out and came alive, pseudopods grasping for purchase. A major landslide began in front of the vehicle, a minor one to the rear.

Things went well at first, but Gene gradually lost control. The vehicle turned sideways and began to slide uncontrollably, its semi-intelligent automatic systems fighting to maintain a grip on the impossible slope.

He had misjudged the grade; it was too steep. Worse, the rover was veering off the ramp of rubble, heading for a sharp drop.

The vehicle tipped, righted itself, then hit a boulder, stopping momentarily. The boulder had other ideas; dislodged from its precarious position on the slope, it began to roll. The rover followed suit, joining the general landslide.

The amoebalike tires completely lost their grip. The vehicle began to roll over on its side—and that was the last thing Gene knew.

LONG ISLAND

SHEILA THOUGHT THAT Trent looked exactly what a prince should look like. For one thing, he was terribly handsome. His pale hair was the color of fresh butter, his eyes the hue of the sky on a bright afternoon. His features were strong, the cleft chin firm; classic princely features. But there was more to him, something in his bearing that bespoke a high-born status.

Just like a prince, she thought. She had been distantly in love with him since their first meeting.

She sat back and took a sip of wine. Sure, he was probably three hundred years old, but what's age got to do with it? He sure as heck didn't look three hundred years old. More likely thirty-five. Forty at the most. It was magic, of course.

"Like the wine?" Trent asked, settling into an armchair across from the sofa.

"It's wonderful," Sheila said. "What is it?"

"It's a special California vintage cabernet, limited issue. I have some friends in the wine business out there."

"It's great."

Trent pivoted in his chair. "Uh . . . Snowclaw? You sure you won't have anything?"

"Thanks," Snowclaw said, turning away from a view of

the woods. "But I don't go for that smelly flower water you human folks drink. No offense."

Trent laughed. "None taken."

Anyone who had seen Snowclaw in the castle would never have recognized him. Instead of being a huge quasi-ursine biped covered in fur, Snowclaw was now a rather large human male with snow-white hair and the musculature of a professional bodybuilder. He wore a white shirt, red tie, charcoal slacks, and navy-blue blazer. His size 15 black pumps shone with a gloss.

Sheila's spell had done the trick. Snowclaw looked unusual—even for a weight lifter, he was enormous—but acceptable.

"To get back to business," Trent said. "Granting that Gene is here on Earth, locating him might be a little problematical if someone with magical abilities kidnapped him."

"Well, that's what I think happened," Sheila said.

Trent nodded. "His disappearance does sound a little suspicious, judging from what you've said."

"There's not much to go on. Actually it's all mostly based on this sneaking suspicion I've got that something's up at the castle."

"Something very well could be. But the question is who's behind it all. Have any ideas?"

"Well, we were thinking . . ."

"My sister Ferne?"

Sheila nodded. "I'm sorry, but—"

"No need. She's a bad one. But she can't be the culprit, because as far as I know, Incarnadine did away with her. No one but my brother knows exactly what happened to her, but he did inform the family that Ferne's case had been adjudicated 'with coldest justice,' I think his phrase was."

"Does that mean he had her executed?"

"Well, everyone—my other sister, Dorcas, and I, along with the more distant relatives—we all took it to mean that Ferne had been dispatched to her heavenly reward, to phrase it kindly if not plausibly."

Sheila sighed. "Well, that eliminates her as a suspect, I guess. And if it's not her, then I haven't the foggiest clue who it could be."

"On the other hand, you do have a castle full of people"— Trent nodded toward Snowclaw, who had taken a seat on the sofa—"and other gentle beings. No end of suspects. As far as motives, well, there you have a problem."

Trent suddenly rose and walked to the fireplace, behind the glass doors of which a cheery fire glowed and crackled.

"There is one other possibility," Trent said, looking deep into the flames.

Sheila looked at Snowclaw. They waited.

"I know my brother," Trent said finally. "He just might not have killed her." He gave a rueful chuckle. "I have to confess that I would have, without hesitation or remorse. She nearly destroyed everything, including the castle." He shook his head, still staring into the fire. "Reckless, reckless woman."

Presently Trent returned to his seat. "But Incarnadine has a soft spot for her, always did. I've always suspected he might be in love with her. He's never let on, though. If so, I don't blame him. As you know, she's something to look at."

"Oh, she's beautiful," Sheila said. "That made her even more scary."

"And I've always suspected that the feeling was mutual, between the two of them. All very repressed, of course, at least on Incarnadine's side."

"So she could be alive. She could even be in the castle somewhere."

"It's a possibility," Trent said, "but a slim one. Mind you, Incarnadine is an able ruler, and a wise one. He wouldn't compromise his security and the security of the crown for the sake of personal feelings, his own or anyone else's." Trent leaned back in his chair. "At least, I don't think he would."

"You should know your own brother . . . er, Your Royal Highness."

Trent laughed. "Forget the honorifics. This is Earth. This is America, after all."

"Sorry. It's just that I don't get to talk to princes every day."

"You should be so lucky every day."

Sheila giggled. "I kind of like it."

Trent gave her an engaging smile. "Well, it's easy playing Prince Charming to so charming a lady."

Sheila melted a little inside, then tried to put romantic thoughts out of her mind.

"Of course," Trent went on, "there's always me as a suspect."

Sheila reddened. "Sir, there's never been any doubt in my mind—"

"Oh, but there should be!" His Royal Highness chuckled. "I have the motive, the means, and no end of opportunity. I should be number one on your suspect list. In fact, when you called, I assumed you were coming here to play detective."

"Oh, no, that wasn't the reason at all," Sheila protested. "I wouldn't presume. It's just that we need help, and with Lord Incarnadine away—"

"I understand. Sorry, I shouldn't be kidding around. I realize this is a serious matter, what with your friend involved."

"We're worried, sir. And we do need help."

"Please, don't call me 'sir.' I got out of the prince business long ago. 'Trent' will do."

"Certainly . . . Trent."

"That's better. Sounds more like you trust me."

"How could we suspect you when you helped Incarnadine against the Hosts of Hell?"

"I was fighting to save Perilous, not necessarily my brother."

"I see."

Trent shrugged. "Just being honest. And I was only half joking about my being a suspect."

"I trust you," Sheila said firmly.

He smiled, showing astonishingly white teeth. "Thank you. And I you." He put down his glass. "Won't you stay for lunch?"

"We'd love to," Sheila said, with deep-seated reluctance, "but Linda is working on a spell to locate Gene in the castle, and she needs all the help she can get."

"I thought you were pretty sure that Gene disappeared here."

"It's just my magician's intuition again, but there is the slight possibility Gene might have slipped past the guards at Halfway House. I didn't want to say anything, but once I found both of them asleep in front of the TV."

"You should have reported it," Trent said. "They should be disciplined."

"Well, I didn't want to get anyone in trouble. It must be boring to be stuck in that house—"

"That's hardly an excuse."

"Gene does have a key to the place. He could have—anyway it's a possibility."

"That means he could have disappeared inside the castle. By accident, I suppose. But as Gene's a castle veteran, more likely by design."

"But again the question is 'Who?' "

"Well, let's go over the disappearance once again. You say Gene did board the plane in L.A.?"

"Yes, as far as the airline knows."

"Was anyone supposed to meet him at the airport?"

"Linda's not sure, but she thinks Gene told her that his dad was supposed to pick him up."

"And you can't reach his parents?"

"No, though I should try again from here. Or maybe when we switch the portal back to Halfway, I'll take a drive into Pittsburgh and see if I can't find them. We were afraid of doing that, causing them worry, but now I think we might have to."

Trent nodded. "It might be the only way." He thought for a moment. "Did it ever occur to you that Gene might have boarded the plane but never got off?"

"No, it never occurred to me. How—?" Sheila frowned. "Wouldn't the flight crew have wondered what happened to him?"

"Maybe. When they came up one short on the deplaning nose count, they would have searched the plane. When they didn't find him, they might have figured they just counted wrong. It happens."

Sheila chewed her lip, then said, "So you think somebody meddled with the portal and had it link with the plane . . . in midflight?"

"Why not? It's not easy to do, but it's doable. Happen to know what kind of plane it was?"

"No, not really, but I guess we can find out. Wouldn't somebody have seen what was going on?"

"If it was a 747 or an L-1011, there'd be no end of room to materialize a portal. I'd do it in the head, myself. Perfect place."

"But why go to all that trouble?"

"To confuse things, keep you guessing," Trent said. "I admit it's a wild possibility. But if true, it means that the portal was meddled with from the castle side, unless someone was on the plane to manipulate things from that end. I guess that's a possibility as well. Are you keeping a list?"

Sheila shook her head glumly. "There are too many of them. I wonder if we'll ever know what happened to Gene."

"Don't worry. We'll find him."

"But it's been almost four days."

"Not to worry. There are any number of universes, and he could be anywhere in any one of them. It'll take time, but we'll locate him."

"You're so kind to help, Trent."

"Glad to. I rather like Gene, myself. A good kid, handy with a sword."

Sheila rose. "We've taken enough of your time."

Trent threw out his arms expansively. "I have all the time in the world. In semiretirement, you know. Out to pasture."

"You don't look your age, whatever that is."

"I'll never tell. But thanks for saying it. We old codgers need all the compliments we can wheedle out of pretty young ladies."

Sheila blushed again. "Anyway, thanks for your time."

"Certainly. And I'll let you know as soon as I come up with a locator spell. It shouldn't take long to design, but getting the bugs out of the thing is going to be the real problem."

Trent escorted Sheila and Snowclaw back to the dining room, where the upright rectangle of the portal stood. Trent had summoned it, detaching the Earth end from its Pennsylvania mooring and anchoring it here, inside Trent's sumptuous Long Island estate.

"Good thing you picked today to come," Trent said. "My housekeeper's day off. Otherwise you would've had to travel here the old-fashioned way. I'm afraid she wouldn't have understood having magic casements in the dining room."

"This is the only way to travel," Snowclaw said, then changed expressions. He sniffed the air. "Hey, what's that smell?"

Trent said, "Smell?"

"Yeah, something mighty good in here." Snowy bent and

sniffed the huge oak dining table. "Something that was on this table. Smell's just like *jhalnark*. Now, *that's* a drink."

"I think you're smelling furniture polish. Linseed oil, or something. The cleaning people were here yesterday. If I'd known, I would've offered . . ."

Trent broke off and moved to the far wall, against which stood a long, ornately carved sideboard. He opened the bottom drawer, searched among some bottles, and came up with one. "In fact, here's the very stuff, Hornby's furniture cleaner. Never let it be said I'm not an accommodating host. Take it with you." He handed the bottle to Snowclaw.

Sheila squealed with laughter, and was about to add a sarcastic comment when she caught sight of someone on the castle side of the portal. It was one of the servants, a young page, although she didn't recognize him.

"Yes, what is it?" she asked.

"Begging your pardon, milady, but Lord Incarnadine has returned, and he requests you see him immediately."

"Great! C'mon, Snowy." Sheila stepped through, but stopped suddenly and looked around.

"Be with you in a sec," Snowclaw said as he tilted the bottle of furniture polish to his lips. He took a deep drink.

Sheila said, "Hey, wait a minute. Where are we?"

Still on the Earth side, Trent edged toward the aperture. "What's wrong, Sheila?"

"This isn't where the portal is usually anchored in the castle." She took a step toward the servant. "What's going on?"

"I wouldn't know, milady," the page said, backing off.

"What's wrong?" Sheila said, puzzled by the young man's behavior.

Trent saw the wall sliding down. He dashed through the portal.

"Sheila, get back! It's a trap!"

Snowclaw dropped the bottle and leaped toward the portal, but neither he nor the prince had acted in time. The barrier slammed down, and the portal closed.

Snowclaw was stranded on Earth.

LIBRARY

"Wow, THERE'RE A LOT of books in here," Jeremy whispered, gazing about.

"This is a library, young man," Osmirik said airily, but remembering his own reaction the first time he set foot in the place. He had been nothing less than astonished.

"It's so big."

"Please set your machine here," Osmirik directed, having chosen a table in the middle of the main floor, near the open stacks. "If you'll set it to working, I have some books to fetch."

Osmirik disappeared into the stacks.

"Take your time," Jeremy called after him, opening the computer's case and flipping up the readout screen.

While waiting, Jeremy gazed upward. There were three levels to the place, a spacious main floor and two galleries, spiral stairwells communicating between them. The roof was a ballet of Gothic stone arches, soaring together to form complex vaults and geometric sections. And everywhere—books, shelves and shelves of books.

Osmirik returned, loaded down with three huge leatherbound tomes. He set the stack down, chose the top volume, and paged through it.

"I have some acquaintance with the alphabetical and num-hering system of your world," Osmirik said, "but I need a review. Would you be so kind as to—"

"Yeah, sure." Jeremy punched a few keys. The readout screen came to life. "Here's a list-out of all the alphanumeric symbols this computer can generate. ASCI Code. That what you want?"

"Oh, my, I had no idea there were so many."

"Well, there's all kinds of things that you rarely use here, except for special occasions. These lines here are what you want."

"I see. Yes, I think the problem of translation can be solved eventually. But there are many other problems."

"Just what are you after?"

Osmirik folded his hands. "I intend to work a spell with the help of your device. I am somewhat familiar with the capacities of such a machine as yours, though my knowledge is entirely theoretical."

"Wait a minute," Jeremy said. "You mean to tell me you're gonna run a *magic* spell . . . through my computer?"

"That is what I mean to say."

"How? And f'crissakes, why?"

Osmirik was patient. "I do not as yet have an answer to the first question. To the second, I would answer thus: the spell I have in mind involves more variables than is practical to deal with. It requires a magician with a phenomenal memory. I am not such a magician. In fact, my talent is minimal. Thaumaturgical talent is a gift, pure and simple. But with that machine, and some help from an adept such as Lady Linda, we may succeed in locating the young man named Gene."

Jeremy nodded. "Gotcha. Sounds like fun. But where's the magic come from? You got fairy dust, or what?"

"No fairy dust, whatever that may be. The source of magic is the castle itself. Let me essay a figure of speech, drawing on the lore of your own world. Think of the castle as an electrical generator, and of the castle's various talented inhabitants as conduits, drawing off that energy and putting it to use."

"I get it. All right, sounds better and better."

"Very good. Now, let us begin. Can this machine process degenerative numerical series?"

"Huh? I can see we're gonna have problems. You'll have to translate that better."

Osmirik took a ballpoint pen from an inside pocket of his long hooded gown. "Allow me to show you."

A few minutes later, Jeremy looked up from the sheet of yellow paper that Osmirik had filled with curious symbols. "Okay, near as I can figure out, you're talking about factorials. Like, six factorial would be six times five, times four, times three, times two—"

"Exactly!"

"Yeah, well, that's no problem. But what's all this stuff?"

"That is merely its application to the problem of—"

Osmirik suddenly looked up toward one of the galleries.

"Someone is about," he said. "I saw no one come in."

He got up and approached a nearby stairwell. Before he got to it, a man appeared at the rail above. He was tall with medium-long dark hair and square-cut features.

"Hello, Osmirik."

The librarian was astonished. "Your Majesty, I had no idea you had returned!"

"Haven't told anybody yet. Had some research to do." The man inclined his head toward Jeremy. "New Guest?"

"Yes, sire. May I present Master Jeremy—er . . ."

"Hochstader," Jeremy added. "That's 'Mister.' "

"Glad to have you aboard, Mr. Hochstader. Osmirik, has the Earth portal been wandering again?"

"Yes, Majesty. There is trouble afoot."

"I know. Loads of it, as a matter of fact. Do you have anything on interdimensional field geometry? I'm having a devil of a time finding anything."

"Yes, sire, we do. One volume, and it is kept in the outsized-folio shelves. A thousand pardons, Majesty. I will fetch it for you immediately."

Osmirik hurried off.

"That's a slick-looking machine you have there, young man," His Majesty said.

"Thanks. Uh, are you the king of this place?"

"That's me. I'm called Lord Incarnadine. Funny name, but I've become rather fond of it."

"Lord, huh? I thought a lord was lower than a king."

"Hold on a minute."

Incarnadine descended the stairwell and came over to the table.

"A lord is lower than a king, but the history of this place

goes back a long way. The master of this castle was originally the vassal of some big cheese to the east. But then there was a falling-out, a little difference of opinion, a big war—and zip, bang, my family got into the king business. But the traditional title stuck. So the head man around here is still Lord Protector of the Western Pale—that's where this castle is situated—but he's also King of this, that, and the other annexed territory. Clear? Don't worry, it's not very. My 'kingdom' is mostly a desert, and most of my subjects are scattered across 144,000 worlds.''

"Oh.''

Incarnadine smiled. "May I inspect your gadget?''

"Hm? Oh, sure.''

Jeremy sat amazed as Incarnadine asked him all sorts of technical questions about the computer's operating system. It was incongruous coming from some guy dressed like something out of a movie about knights and dragons. Jeremy answered all the questions.

"I'd really like to see the guts of this thing,'' Incarnadine said.

"No problem.'' Jeremy whipped out his wallet and withdrew a set of miniature tools. Working expertly fast, he cracked open the computer's plastic case and exposed the works to plain view.

Incarnadine bent closer. "Beautiful. Advanced architecture, modular design.''

"You seem to know a lot about computers.''

Incarnadine shook his head. "I try to keep up, but I don't have the time. I've built my own, though.''

"You built a computer?''

"Well, it isn't much like the ones back on Earth. For one thing, it doesn't use electricity, because electricity doesn't work around here.''

"That's what they tell me. So how come this thing runs?''

"Because it's using the magical energy that you're feeding into it.''

Jeremy's eyes went wide. "Me?''

Incarnadine flipped a hand over. "No other way. Take out the batteries.''

"Huh? But then it wouldn't—'' Giving his shoulders a shrug, Jeremy opened the little door in the back and took out the NiCd batteries, then turned the computer around and punched a few keys. "Hey, it still works!''

"Of course. Everyone who enters Castle Perilous develops a magic skill. You've found yours, obviously."

"No kidding." Gaze intent on the readout screen, Jeremy let his fingers dance over the keyboard.

Osmirik returned with a quarto volume and handed it to his liege.

"Thanks, Ozzie."

"May I be of further assistance to His Majesty?"

"Well, I need to do a search of the card catalogue, but I don't want to take you away from any important research project. What's up, by the way?"

Osmirik informed Incarnadine of Gene's disappearance and the plans to devise a locator spell.

"Yeah, that sounds like the way to go," Incarnadine said. "And the idea about the computer is terrific. Trouble is, I could also use some state-of-the-art help with what I'm doing, which is potentially more important."

"Then by all means, Majesty, you should avail yourself of the machine."

"Don't you think we'd better ask the owner? Anyway, I don't think I'm ready for that yet. Still in the theory stages, and I'm already floundering. Work on finding Gene, I'll search the catalogue myself."

"May I ask what problem His Majesty is working on?"

"There seems to be a major disturbance affecting the stresses between the universes. Somewhere, something—or someone—is pumping a lot of energy out of the interdimensional plenum. It could be a natural phenomenon, but I suspect foul play. The disturbance is just barely detectable at this stage, but if it continues, we could be in for a nasty bout of instability here."

Osmirik nodded gravely. "I see."

"We have to find out where it's coming from, and figure out a way to stop it."

"I am ready to render every assistance."

"Good. Too bad about Gene, and that only makes it more likely that someone is up to something."

Osmirik gave an involuntary shudder. "I only hope, sire, that it is not the Hosts of Hell again."

"Unfortunately," Incarnadine said with a wan smile, "that's exactly what I fear."

CAVES

HE WOKE UP in a cool dark place. Looking around, he found that he was in some sort of rock-walled chamber. A cave? Yes, a cave. Now, how the heck had he gotten here? What . . . ?

Huh? His hands were tied! He rolled to his back, then levered himself to a sitting position. Pain immediately flooded his head, and he waited until the throbbing subsided to a tolerable level. Then he resumed exploring his environment, if only visually.

He was sitting on a low bed of animal skins. More hides draped the walls, along with a few weapons with copper-colored blades: a knife, an ax, and a sword. The glow from coals in a nearby brazier supplemented light from a copper lamp at the foot of the bed. There was little other furniture save for some low footstools and an oversized pillow or two.

Memory trickled back. He remembered the vehicle tipping over, then after that being dragged from the wreckage. The next thing to come out of a cloud of dim recollection was the sensation of jouncing around on the back of a horse or some other animal. He had a vague memory of watching the ground go by beneath him; he must have been slung facedown over the back of the animal. He remembered hearing voices talking a strange language.

So the Umoi had not completely died out. Whoever had made these weapons and skinned these animals must be their descendants.

Pain swelled again, and he lay back down. Probably had a nasty concussion, he decided. Better take it easy for a while.

He wondered why Zond had never mentioned the possibility that some Umoi might have survived. Was it because the city simply didn't know? Perhaps Zond didn't care.

Anyway, lucky for him that there was someone about to rescue him, get him to shelter. He might have died out there in the desert. He tugged at the cords binding his wrists. Pretty sturdy; looked like leather of some sort. Well, any of those weapons hanging above looked capable of making short work of his bonds—if he could summon the strength to get up and use them.

He struggled to his feet and found himself terribly dizzy. He took a few wobbling steps, weakened, and collapsed back to the bed.

Maybe he had internal injuries as well. If so, he was a goner, judging from the state of the local technology. These jokers hadn't discovered iron yet. Maybe not even bronze. Correction—they had *forgotten* iron and bronze, along with all the rest of their fabulous science and technology. Given it all up, in the interest of environmental purity, granola, and all the rest of that stuff.

But why didn't Zond know?

One way to find out. He would ask Zond. This was a good test of the communications gear that the city had manufactured for him. It consisted of circuitry woven into the fabric of his jumpsuit.

"Zond? Can you hear me?"

There was some static; then: "Of course."

"You're breaking up a little."

After a pause Zond replied, "I've changed frequencies. Better?"

"Better."

"Where are you, if I may ask?"

"In a cave. I don't know exactly where, but it can't be far from the rover, because I was brought here on horseback. Or whatever. How come you didn't tell me about the people?"

"People?" Zond asked calmly.

"Yeah! They're Umoi. They gotta be!"

"The Umoi are extinct."

"You getting a picture?"

"Of course."

"What is this, chopped liver?"

"Is that an allusion?"

"Are these artifacts the work of intelligent beings, or what?"

"Those *artifacts*, if you want to call them such, are the work of artificial life forms."

"Artificial life forms."

"You got it," Zond said. "They're called *yalim*, and were created by the Umoi from genetic material found in some of the more highly developed fauna of this world. They were servants, underpeople, nothing more. When the last Umoi died, they reverted to a feral state."

"I see. Artificial life forms. Like . . . androids."

"That term isn't as clear as it could be, but yes, androids."

"Great. The Umoi looked like frogs with leprosy. What sort of blasphemous horrors are these freaks going to resemble?"

"Turn around and look."

"Probably some sort of crawling, gelatinous—huh?"

Gene craned his neck around and nearly fell over.

It was a woman, a fully human one, though of rather exotic racial type, wearing a minimalist haiku of an outfit. It consisted of hemispheres of burnished copper over the breasts, skimpy black leather briefs, white fur cape, and black leather boots. Bedecked with necklaces of uncut stones, copper bracelets jangling at her wrists, she approached. She stopped, planting her feet wide apart, and stood arms akimbo. She regarded Gene coldly.

Her face was stunningly beautiful, black almond eyes over a perfect nose and full plum lips, but the skin was even more miraculous, the color of coffee with heavy cream, a rich golden brew that glowed with life. Her looks were neither Oriental nor Caucasian, nor any other earthly physiognomic variation.

Gene unhung his jaw and tried to get up. He couldn't.

Two other women had entered the chamber, and even though they were practically naked, Gene gave them barely a glance.

"Why the hell didn't you tell me?" Gene muttered.

"About what?" Zond answered. "About yalim? They are of no consequence whatever."

"Has it struck you yet that these yalim have something in common with yours truly?"

"Well, now that you mention it. I suppose."

"Unbelievable."

The woman was frowning ominously.

"Actually," Zond went on, "the genetic similarities are fairly superficial. In fact—"

"Shhh! Looks like she's getting pissed off."

The woman jabbed a finger at him and barked something dictatorial.

"Uh, Zond?"

"What is it, Gene-person?"

"What did she say? Can you help me out here?"

"Sure. The language is of course a corruption of Received Standard Umoi, almost unrecognizable in its linguistic—"

"Translate, for pete's sake!"

"She told you to shut up."

"She—? Oh."

The woman spoke again, shooting orders at him. Gene got the impression that whatever she had told him to do, he was supposed to do it quick, and no nonsense.

"Well? " Gene said under his breath.

"She wants to know what you were doing inside one of the machines of the Old Gods, and if you don't have a good explanation, she's going to cut your . . . uh, sever your generative organs from your body. In so many words."

"Whoa!" A wide, coprographic grin spread across Gene's face. "Hi, there! Nice to meet you. Uh, look—"

The woman spoke again. The language sounded a little like German, with a lot of Finno-Ugric added for spice.

"She wants to know what tribe you're from."

"Tribe?" Gene piped. "Tribe. Yeah, tribe."

"Better make it good."

"I can't speak a word of her language!"

"Now she says you don't look like any tribe she's ever seen."

"Look, ma'am," Gene said. "You gotta understand. I was just walking down the yellow brick road, when all of a sudden—"

The woman shouted at him.

"She said shut up again," Zond told him.

"I gathered."

The woman stalked around the chamber, her ebony eyes clinically taking his measure. At length she began to speak again. Zond translated.

"Well, she says she doesn't know what to make of you. You don't seem to belong anywhere, but you must be yalim—read 'human,' there—because you look it, somewhat. She's a little worried that you might be a demon or something. But of course, if you were, you would have killed her or done something frightening, but you didn't, and besides, demons don't get themselves konked on the head, do they? And you couldn't be an Old God, that's right out. So—well, there it is."

"What is she, some kind of barbarian Queen or something?"

"Hey. That's a good guess."

The woman had stopped pacing, still fixing Gene in a penetrating stare. After long reflection, she snapped an order at one of her handmaidens.

The girl—she looked no older than fifteen—approached Gene, withdrew a dagger, and gingerly cut the leather straps around his wrists. Before she was finished, her mistress had begun speaking again.

"She says that she's going to put you to the test. What test, I really don't—oh, I see. She's going to find out if you'd make her a good concubine. If you work out, you'll be groomed for full husbandhood, and be inducted into her personal military cohort. You will then be accorded the privilege of laying down your life for her at the drop of a helmet. I think she likes you."

Rubbing his wrists, Gene said, "Yeah?"

"Yeah."

The barbarian Queen clapped her hands, and the two girls left the chamber.

Slowly she turned around and let the cape fall from her shoulders. The leather briefs turned out to be really nothing more than a G-string.

Gene reeled, devastated by the exquisite mathematical perfection of her hindquarters. His headache suddenly vanished.

"Zond, I think I'm about to be exploited, abused and generally treated as a sex object."

"I'm very sorry for you," Zond said, "but there's nothing I can do."

"Right. So piss off and leave us alone, okay?"

Castle (?), Then Island

"Sheila!"

"Trent? Over here!"

They found each other in the dark and hugged. Trent held her close.

"Are you okay?" he asked.

"Yes. What happened? Where did he—?"

"It was a trap, and I'm afraid we fell right into it."

There came a scraping, rumbling sound, then a thud.

"What's going on?" Sheila said fearfully.

"I don't kn—"

Suddenly the bottom fell out of everything, and they dropped through space.

Then sunlight exploded around them, and they hit water.

Deep in green underwater silence, Sheila floated through a cloud of bubbles, fire searing her lungs. Disoriented, she didn't know which way to swim, which way the surface was. Finally she saw the sun and began to flail upward. The surface seemed hundreds of feet above. She knew she couldn't hold her breath that long. Panic welled up inside her.

A hand grasped her arm and buoyed her upward.

She broke the surface, gasping, choking. Trent treaded water beside her.

"You okay?" he shouted.

She could only nod. She looked around. Sea, endless blue-green sea, its waters sickly warm.

"Where are we?" she yelled.

"Anybody's guess. Some wild universe. One with no magic, either. Damn."

"I didn't even think of using magic. Everything happened so fast."

"Exactly. Whoever set us up knew what they were doing."

"But . . . Trent, you didn't have to come through the portal. You shouldn't have!"

"Too late for shouldn't-haves, my dear." Trent boosted himself out of the water, sank, then came back up with more velocity, rising waist-high until he sank once again.

"What are you doing?"

"Trying to see above the swells. I think there's land in that direction. It's a ways off, though. You a strong swimmer?"

"My God, no. I feel like a lead weight."

"Drop your shoes and strip to your underwear. Quick."

Sheila did as she was told. Undressed, she felt ten times more buoyant.

"Ready?" he asked.

"As I'll ever be."

"Easy now, don't tire yourself. If you get fagged out, roll over and backstroke."

They struck out sunward, cautiously dog-paddling. The swells were gentle but high, and at the crest of one particularly elevated wave, Sheila could see a thin strip of green on the horizon. It looked miles away.

"We'll never make it," she groaned.

"Yes, we will. Steady now. Even out your strokes."

They swam on for what seemed like hours. The water got even warmer. It made Sheila feel her fatigue more. They rested periodically, treading water.

"We'd better get going," Trent said.

Sheila found that she could float on her back and give her legs a rest. "I really need to stop."

"I know, but there's something swimming around us and it looks interested."

Sheila straightened up and searched.

"There," Trent said, pointing.

She could see it now, a wickedly sharp fin cutting the water. Its path took it in a slow circle about them.

"Trent, I don't like this."

"We'll have to swim faster, Sheila. Can you do it?"

"Yes."

"The island is just another half mile or so. Or two or three. Come on."

They swam. The fin altered its trajectory and closed, its manner still more curious than menacing. Then another fin broke water and came abreast of the first. More followed.

"Seems we're becoming quite an attraction," Trent said calmly.

"Free lunch," Sheila said, amazed that she was capable of gallows humor.

"Got any magic yet, Sheila?"

In the last hour or so, she had been testing for magic in what seemed like an unconnected compartment of her mind, insulated from the fear and the panic. The supernatural elements of this world were very strange, and she didn't know if she could make any sense of them. She sensed vague fields of force, subtle influences, but nothing she could put her finger on.

"Not really."

"They're getting closer. Can you get up any more speed?"

Sheila's arms felt like lead. "No."

"Then I'm afraid we're going to have to face them."

Trent stopped swimming and reached out for her. He enveloped her in his arms, and she went limp, surrendering to the fatigue. She felt like she could never move again.

A huge gray form came in from the seaward side, its path still indirect, still exploratory.

"Trent, we're going to die," she said.

"Kiss me, Sheila."

They embraced in the water, her legs wrapped around him, her tongue finding his.

Something nudged her in the back, and she didn't care.

Trent looked over her shoulder. He said, "I think . . ."

"Darling," she breathed.

"Dolphins."

"Dolphins?"

"Or a reasonable facsimile."

Sheila reached out and touched the rough skin of the thing.

It was warm and resilient, like rubber. Another animal approached, and Trent grabbed its dorsal fin. The creature seemed to have no objection.

A head broke water in front of Sheila. It was the head of no dolphin or porpoise she had ever seen. The snout was blunt and wrinkled, and the eyes caninelike, large and intelligent. Sharp teeth protruded from the mouth. The animal was more like a seal or walrus than anything else, but sleeker, more streamlined, and the body more fishlike. In that respect it resembled a dolphin.

Trent's animal suddenly bolted shoreward. Trent hung on for the ride momentarily, then let go. He wound up a good distance from Sheila.

"I think they want to escort us in!" Trent yelled.

Sheila stroked the dolphinoid's bulbous head. The animal seemed to like this. Then it swung about and rolled its body slightly toward her, as if offering its dorsal fin as a handgrip. Sheila grabbed on with both hands.

Suddenly she was rocketing through the water, the force of the flow making it difficult to maintain her grip. But she did.

In no time the shore drew near. Reaching the outer edge of the surf, the animal turned back toward the open sea, and she let go.

She rode a wave in, then another. Finally her feet touched bottom, and she waded into the beach.

She collapsed, wet sand against her face, the sound of breakers washing her in and out of consciousness. The cry of a gull came; then, after an indeterminate time, footsteps at her back.

"Sheila?"

She turned and saw Trent's smiling face.

"You okay?"

"Yes, Trent."

"Sorry if what went on out there was just a paroxysm in the face of imminent death."

She touched her body and found that she was naked before his gaze. She smiled up at him, holding out her arms. "Trent, darling."

"Sheila."

LONG ISLAND EXPRESSWAY

SNOWCLAW NEVER TIRED of watching the metal wagons roar up and down the stone road. His head snapped this way and that as they streaked by. Big ones, small ones, middle-sized ones. It was amazing.

He had left Trent's house after thinking long and hard about what he ought to do. He knew there was such a thing as a telephone. He had heard of a telephone, and theoretically, at least, he knew what you were supposed to do with one. But he hadn't the foggiest notion of how you actually went about using one. If so, he would have called Halfway House.

Yes, he had thought long and hard. And he came to the conclusion that he simply would have to walk to Halfway House. Of course, he hadn't the slightest idea where Halfway was from here or how far it was, but he had an inkling its direction was due west, so he had left the house, put his back to the rising sun, and started walking.

He'd found this road and followed it. Human eyes regarded him curiously from the windows of the hurtling metal vehicles.

Distance wasn't his only problem. Here, on Earth, he was incommunicado. He understood no one, and no one understood him. Trent had whipped up an impromptu translation spell, but that extended no farther than the confines of Trent's house. Sheila's shape-changing enchantment was still on him, though. That at least was something. He could imagine the dismay he'd cause if he had to go traipsing about in his natural state.

Gray clouds were gathering ahead. Rain? Snow? Another thing he knew nothing about: the weather of this world. To him it was comfortably warm, but he knew that snow could fall at this temperature.

More metal wagons whizzed by. Where were they all going? And so fast, too! Snowclaw couldn't get over it. They were tearing up the road.

One of them, a long metallic gray affair with dark windows, abruptly slowed, wheels squealing, and pulled off onto the shoulder ahead. Snowclaw approached it warily. Could be trouble.

Two humans got out, one short, the other chunky. They waited for Snowy to come closer.

The small one spoke. "Look at him, Vinny. Didja ever see a guy that big?"

Vinny shook his head.

Snowclaw stopped and sized them both up. They'd be no problem, as long as they didn't pull any magic. He'd heard there was powerful magic in this world.

"Hey, pal. What was you, a wrestler? Weight lifter?"

Snowclaw was surprised to discover that he knew more or less what the little human was saying. Gene had told him about this. Inside the castle, the running translation spell kept everyone in communication. But living under its influence for extended periods tended to produce side effects, the chief one being that some actual language learning took place. Snowclaw had heard a lot of English spoken in the last two years.

"Yeah," Snowclaw said. "Wrestler." His jaw had to work unnaturally hard to form the words.

"Yeah, where didja work? Professional wrestling?"

"Yeah. Pro-fesh-shunal."

"Uh-huh." The small human looked a little older than the big one. "Waddya think, Vinny?"

"I dunno, Nunzio. He got an accent."

"So what? Hey, fella, what are you? You look like a Swede. You Swedish, or what?"

"Yeah, Swedish."

"Uh-huh, uh-huh. Did your car break down? You don't have a coat, neither. It's cold. Aren't you cold?"

"Jeez, Nunzio, the guy's so big, he don't need nothin'."

"Yeah, hey. What's your name, fella?"

Snowclaw thought about it. The only name he knew was the one his English-speaking friends called him.

"Snowy."

"Snowy. Uh-huh. 'Cause of your hair, huh? It's white."

"Jeez, he's big, Nunzio."

"Yeah. You lookin' for a job, fellah? I got one, if y'are. I need a bouncer at my club. The guy I had, one, he was doin' a number with a waitress of mine—I mean, the little bitch was two-timin' me, y'know?—two, him and the manager was skimming a thousand a week off the place, bleedin' me white, and I don't like that, see. But both of 'em are sleepin' with the fishes now. You get me? So waddya say, you want the job? You look like you could handle anybody."

Vinny said, "He looks like he could handle the whole Pascagleone family by hisself."

The small one laughed. "Yeah. So whaddya say, pal?"

Snowclaw shrugged. "Okay."

"Good. I'll start you at—four hundred a week. Okay?"

"Okay."

"Fine. There's an apartment above the joint, if you need a place to stay."

"Yeah. Place to stay. Yeah."

"Good. Get in the car, and we'll take a spin down the club, show you around."

Snowclaw got in the front seat. Another human was driving, and this one cringed at the sight of him. Snowclaw smiled at the little fellow.

In the back seat, Vinny whispered, "Jeez, Nunzio, he's big!"

CASTLE

"HE'S BACK?" LINDA said in astonishment. "When?"

"Only moments ago, it would seem," Osmirik said. "He also is of the opinion that something is awry in the castle."

"Well, it's more than an opinion. Something happened at Trent's house, and we don't know what."

Jeremy stopped typing and looked up. Osmirik rose from his chair.

"What is amiss?" Osmirik asked.

"Well, as planned, Sheila and Snowclaw went through to visit Prince Trent. Everything went fine at first. Then all of a sudden the portal disappeared and stayed lost for at least half an hour. When it came back again, it was locked back at Halfway. No sign of Sheila or Snowclaw. Right away we phoned Trent's place—no answer."

"I see," Osmirik said, nodding solemnly. "Something is indeed awry."

Linda sank into a chair. "Hi, Jeremy," she said bleakly.

"Hi," Jeremy said.

"What are you guys doing?"

Osmirik answered, "Apparently nothing to remedy the situation." He sat down heavily.

"Now we have Sheila and Snowclaw to search for," Linda said. "And we can't even be sure they're still on Earth."

There was silence for a long moment, which Linda finally broke.

"Did Lord Incarnadine want to see me?"

"I am afraid he did not say," Osmirik said. "He was preoccupied with matters of even greater moment. Apparently there is some general cosmological disturbance of which these disappearances may be but symptoms."

"Cosmological?"

"He was not entirely specific, but he did speak of an imbalance of energy between the universes. It seems that an ethereal flux has evidenced itself, a leakage of interdimensional ectoplasm which—" Osmirik noticed Linda's blank stare, and added apologetically, "It is difficult for me to put it in layman's terms."

Linda shook her head. "I'm sure I wouldn't understand it in any terms."

"You underestimate yourself. Nevertheless, the upshot of the matter is that the castle may be in some danger, and we with it."

Linda grunted. "More problems, as if we didn't have enough." She glanced at the screen of Jeremy's computer. "Any luck with this gadget?"

"We have made a beginning," Osmirik said. "But only a beginning. In so doing, however, we have discovered another adept."

Linda's eyebrows rose. "Jeremy? Really? That was quick."

"Doubtless because his talent is considerable."

"Gee, folks," Jeremy said, "it was nothin'."

"It's no joke," Linda told him. "We need all the help we can get. What can you do?"

"It's not much," Jeremy said. "It's just that I'm running this computer with magic juice."

"Great. But what good does that do?"

"Beats the crap out of me, but it's a lot of fun."

"His skill might help us to make some headway in our spellcasting endeavors," Osmirik said. "The science of adapting these machines to thaumaturgic applications is in its infancy."

Jeremy said, "Incarnadine sounds like he knows his computers. Even said he built one."

Osmirik nodded. "If His Majesty says it, then it is true. I was speaking of the science as it is practiced by mere mortals such as your humble servant." Osmirik bowed his head, laying a hand against his breast.

"Oh. Well, why don't you ask Incarnadine to help out?"

"It is not my place to do so. I am a servant of His Majesty, not the reverse."

"Uh-huh. Yeah, well, you know best."

"I'm going to Jamin and request an audience," Linda said. "I simply have to talk to Incarnadine. Did you tell him about Gene?"

"Of course, Linda," Osmirik said.

"Sorry. I suppose he does have bigger problems on his mind."

"He should be informed about this latest disappearance. But don't see Jamin."

Linda gave Osmirik a puzzled frown. "Why not?"

"I would rather not say at this time. When next I see His Majesty—and he will be back here very shortly to pick up some books he requested—I will intercede in your behalf."

"Thanks. God, I wish I knew what happened to Sheila and Snowy. Trent—" Linda fretfully drummed her fingers against the tabletop. "You don't think . . . ?"

Osmirik waited.

Linda dismissed it with a wave of her hand. "Oh, it's silly. What would Trent have against Sheila? Unless—"

Suddenly the floor began to shake, and a sound like thunder filled the library. Shelves rocked back and forth, and overhead, the huge wooden chandeliers began gently to sway.

"Quick," Osmirik shouted, "under the table!"

They all dove for cover.

There came clattering sounds from all over the room as objects fell. Then shelves began collapsing. The floor rocked violently and furniture slid about as if animated. The disturbance lasted for a good minute.

Sounds of crashing peaked, then subsided. The floor finally settled down, the thunder fading.

At length, an uneasy silence fell.

The three came out from under the table, whey-faced but unharmed.

Osmirik made a quick inspection tour of the main floor. Damage was surprisingly limited, despite what the ruckus had sounded like. Only about thirty shelves in all had collapsed, out of the hundreds and hundreds. Even so, the mess was terrible. Books lay scattered everywhere. He returned to the study area.

"That was bad," Linda said. "I mean, the castle gets shaky now and then, but that was *real* bad."

"Earthquake?" Jeremy asked, worried.

"No, some kind of instability. You think, Ozzie?"

"I am afraid so. Perhaps caused by the disturbance His Majesty spoke of. If so, it may be of greater proportions than he suspects."

"Things keep going from bad to worse around here," Linda fretted. "I'm going to see what I can do back at Halfway. Maybe Trent and Sheila went out to lunch and just forgot to tell us. Jeremy, you better come with me."

"Right," Jeremy said, snapping the computer's carrying case shut. He sure as hell didn't want to stay here. But there was a problem.

As far as he could see, there was no place to run to.

KING'S STUDY

". . . FIVE . . . FOUR . . . THREE . . . two . . . one."

On a wooden table in the middle of the chamber, there appeared a strange, feathery glob of golden light. Shifting and shimmering, it neither took shape nor attained substance, but somehow suggested the form of a bird.

Incarnadine approached the phenomenon. Extending his hand, he gently lifted the thing. Actually, "guided it" would be the more accurate description, for the phenomenon seemed somewhat capable of movement.

He moved to a table on which sat a personal computer.

"Reduce to data," was his command to the thing he bore.

The luminous blob vanished with a flash. The screen of the computer suddenly came to life with a golden snowstorm of numbers and symbols.

He seated himself and studied these, occasionally entering commands on the computer's keyboard.

At long last, he sighed and sat back. He waved his hand, and the golden smear of light exited from the back of the computer. It hovered before him.

"I release you," he said.

The phenomenon brightened, fluttering and pulsing.

"Go on, beat it."

The light shot off, darting about the room in a frenzy of rediscovered freedom. It bounced off the walls, did an Immelmann turn, then rocketed ceilingward and continued straight through the stone, disappearing.

He rose and crossed the room. Against a far wall stood a collection of strange contraptions, some of them resembling grandfather clocks. He consulted the dials on a number of these, his brow knitting as he did so.

"Damn. What in the name of all the gods do they think they're doing?"

He shook his head, peering at more meters and gauges.

"Strange, strange," he murmured, recrossing to the desk.

He entered some commands and punched Return. The screen swam with blurred images. He waved his hands and chanted something in an exotic tongue.

Annoyed, he banged a fist on the top of the device. "Drat. What's wrong now?"

He tried different commands, to no avail.

"Trent? Trent, can you hear me? Come in."

The screen was devoid of anything recognizable. Then a garbled voice could be heard.

". . . Inky? . . . you?"

"Trent!" he answered. "Speak up! I'm having trouble receiving you."

More unidentifiable noise, clearing up for a second or two. *". . . trouble . . . the hell this is, but it's . . . get us out? . . ."*

He waited, but there was no more.

"Going to have to do this the old-fashioned way," he complained.

The old-fashioned way turned out to be a large crystal globe sitting on a table in a far corner of the cluttered room. The thing was covered with dust, so he took a chamois cloth to it and soon had it acceptably clear.

He closed his eyes, then opened them suddenly.

"Damned if I haven't forgot the riffs. Ye gods . . ."

After rummaging through stacks of old books, he finally discovered the one he wanted, then found out it wasn't. More rummaging, and much annoyed throwing of things.

He chuckled. "I'm losing my grip. Here it is."

The right tome, the right passage, the right incantation. He read through it, moving his lips.

He slammed the book closed. "That's it." As he passed the desktop computer, he shook his head ruefully at it. "Technology. Makes a cripple of you, it does."

Standing once again before the crystal globe, he struck a proper wizardly pose, arms wide, thumbs and first fingers touching. He commenced a monotonous chanting.

Again, he stopped.

"No, not Trent," he decided.

He resumed his stance and the incantation.

The globe grew milky. Motile shadows writhed within it, and fuzzy images flew hither and yon.

A face appeared; less a face than a contorted mask of pain, a horrific caricature of a face he knew.

"Ferne!" he called, dismayed.

The answer was a moan. Flecks of bloody foam dribbled from the lips.

"Ferne!" This time he shouted at the top of his lungs. "Ferne, where are you?"

The face of his sister changed. The eyes opened, a glimmer of desperate hope in them.

"Who. . .?"

"Incarnadine, your brother. Where are you, Ferne? Tell me! Who has done this to you?"

Her face tightened again, the eyes became tiny wrinkled slits. She screamed hideously.

He shouted her name again, beads of sweat appearing on his brow.

"In the name of the gods, Ferne, speak to me! Tell me where you are!"

She spoke in Haplan, the traditional tongue of the Haplodites; her milk tongue, and Incarnadine's. "In Hell. In deepest . . . darkest . . . Hell." She screamed again.

"They're hurting me, Inky." Her voice was like a child's. "Tell them to stop."

"Steady on, woman. I will come and help thee."

"Please." The voice was a rasp. "Help me."

"I swear on my life. The gods strike me dead an I fail thee."

There was a long, ragged breath, then coughing.

This now in English: "Hurry, Inky dear. Hurry."

The globe grew milky again, and the image faded. Soon the crystal cleared.

He lowered his arms. He staggered to an easy chair and collapsed into it.

He was a long time recovering. When he had composed himself, he got up and moved purposefully toward the door of the study, but stopped in midstride. He turned, pondered, then made a motion toward the bank of instruments, but again came to a halt.

What to do?

So many things. He needed help. Trent, it seems, had problems of his own. But Trent would have to fend for himself. There was no time for him, at least for now.

Who, then? Deems was gone, poor, dear, dead brother. Victim of his own venality.

Dorcas? A good heart, but not much talent. As for the other relatives . . .

No, he must avail himself of the resources of the castle, human and otherwise. But who—?

He had the answer. He would be taking a risk in relying on one so young and inexperienced, but raw talent was the requirement here. . . .

At that moment the quaking began. He looked off, sensing, judging the magnitude of the disturbance. The effects were minimized here, protective spells shielding this section of the castle. He checked his guesses on the banks of measuring instruments.

When it had passed, he nodded his head.

"On schedule. I wonder if they know they're bound to destroy themselves as well."

He moved toward the door.

"Probably do, the insane bastards."

New Barsoom

ACROSS A WIDE dusty plain, Gene rode for his life.

His mount was a *voort* (which Gene privately called a "thoat"), a six-legged cross between a camel and a knock-kneed llama. The sun was high and hot, but hotter still were Gene's pursuers, mounted ape-men bestride huge beasts that resembled Brahma bulls. They were riding hell-bent for leather and closing fast.

Gene called them ape-men, but didn't really know what animal stock they had been created from. They were likely some hybrid breed. Humanoid, exorbitantly muscular, their skin color a cadaverous blue, the *hrunt* were real mean sorts. The Umoi had created them for heavy labor, reserving the yalim for domestic and other semiskilled tasks.

The ape-men's mounts were generally faster than voort though not as surefooted in hilly country. But these were the lowlands, hruntan lands.

Gene skirted a shallow depression, then came upon another one, this one wider, which he thought better to cut across than ride around. The hrunt disagreed, and, as it turned out, made the wiser decision. Slowed by rough ground, Gene's mount scrambled out of the depression a bare six lengths ahead of the pursuit, its six spindly legs working in a complicated cadence, producing a rocking, seasickly gait.

A lance whistled by Gene's ear. Legs tightening around the saddle's girth, Gene took an arrow from his quiver, cocked his bow, pivoted his torso, took aim, and let fly. The arrow went wide of its mark, but the lead hrunt cautiously reined up and eased off the pace.

Gene followed up with another arrow to keep him honest, then turned forward and concentrated on whipping more speed out of the voort. But the beast was simply not built for speed.

Ahead were rocky foothills, leading to stark mountains beyond. Up there a voort would have the advantage, being a surefooted expert on the trails that wound over boulder-strewn slopes. Gene simply had to make it out of flat country and into the hills.

But that was the problem. He wouldn't make it in time.

Having certainly done a bang-up job of locating the enemy, it could be said that in a certain sense his reconnaissance mission was a success. But he was fairly new to the scouting business and apparently had much to learn about keeping a low profile. Well, live and learn.

If he could live. He hoped there would be future opportunities for learning and growth and all the rest of that good stuff, but prospects weren't exactly rosy at the moment.

Maybe he did have a chance. Hills rose up at either hand and the way narrowed between them. Just another quarter mile or so and he'd be among rocks, and his pursuers' mounts tended to be gall-footed over anything but the packed sand of the plains.

Maybe—

The voort bleated and collapsed under him, sending him flying over its head and into the dirt. Shaken, he was slow getting to his feet, but managed it, sword already drawn. He saw the lance sticking out of the voort's backside. Merely flesh-wounded, the animal struggled to its feet and limped off, bleating piteously.

The hrunt leader, its huge scimitarlike weapon raised, bore down on him. Gene stood his ground until the last second, then leaped away. Another rider followed close behind, and Gene dodged one lance, then a second. He dashed up the rise, making for a stand of boulders halfway up.

The riders dismounted and followed him.

Hrunt were fleet-footed, and Gene, still feeling the effects of the spill, had to turn and make a stand. The leader reached him first.

Up close, the hrunt was ugly as advertised, pinhole eyes, no neck, bulging upper body, and short fat legs. Its long greasy hair was blue-black, its lolling tongue a liver-brown. The thing snarled at him, wide thin lips curling into something resembling a victorious sneer. Then it spat.

Gene dodged the gob of green phlegm.

"Completely lacking in all the social graces, aren't we?" Gene said. "Well, my good man—"

The thing charged. Gene took a swipe at it, backed off, feinted, then lunged. The hrunt fended off the attack, countering with a vicious slash.

Which Gene ducked under, coming up to drive the point of his sword into the hrunt's throat.

The huge blue monster gurgled, thick blue ichor flowing from the gash in its neck. Then it fell over backward and rolled down the steep trail.

Fortunately hrunt were decidedly second-class swordsmen. Not so fortunately there were eight of them coming up the trail. Sometimes quantity counts.

Gene was therefore puzzled to see an arrow materialize in the forehead of the next hrunt. More arrows found their marks, beginning trajectories from the rocks above.

Gene ducked behind a boulder as ambushing yalim archers made quick work of the remaining hrunt. Then the rest of the cohort swarmed down for the mopping up, letting out whooping war cries.

It was short work. Turning his back on the grisly business of head-taking, Gene peered up the hill and saw Yerga, the Captain of the Royal Guard, come out from behind a ridge of sandstone.

Yerga was grinning at him, and Gene didn't like it. The grin was half sneer, half triumphant gloat. There was bad blood between Gene and Yerga, had been from the start. Yerga was the Queen's favorite—had been, that is, until Gene's arrival.

Gene could now see Yerga's stratagem in all its ingenuity. Yerga would have come up a winner on every throw of the dice. Send inexperienced Gene out on patrol. Gene could hardly refuse such a mission. If he gets killed, fine. If he's spotted and followed, again, he'll probably lose his life, and he'll have served his function in flushing out the hruntan raiding party that had been giving the tribe trouble recently. If, as it happened, he turns up in dire need of rescue, that very same raiding party hot on his tail, he'll look silly and lose face, if he doesn't buy the farm that way, too. Check and mate.

Gene could only admire such a well-thought-out screw job. It was hard, though, because now he had to listen to Yerga regaling the cohort with endless jokes at his expense.

Yes, hadn't the Strange New One looked the fool hightailing across the wastes like a frightened *yethna* (small ground-dwelling mammal).

Hoots.

No, it was not usually a good idea to wave greetings to the hrunt and let them know you've come to observe them.

Guffaws.

Yes, it had been very hospitable of Gene to invite the hrunt to midday meal.

Howls!

And so on and so forth. Gene didn't mind it so much, but he didn't like the fast slide down the pecking order that this ragging would doubtless cause. That was the way of this tribe. Lose face once and you might as well pitch your tent in the slit latrine, for all the respect you'd get.

There was a possibility of retrieving the situation, although Gene didn't care for the method. It was harsh medicine. But when he considered the alternative—a loss of face perhaps catastrophic enough to leave only suicide or self-exile (same difference) as the only honorable recourse—he realized he had no choice. He would have to challenge Yerga.

Gene suffered in silence all the way back to Winter Camp, a collection of tents and lean-tos pitched at the foot of a twin-peaked crag. Nearby lay the mouth of a cave, wherein the Queen usually dwelt. The tribe usually summered in sparsely forested mountains off to the east.

The yalim tribes had been nomads for centuries. The plains were dotted with ruins, attesting to many attempts at something better, but no yalim civilization to date had withstood hruntan depredations. Which was a shame, because the yalim were truly capable of civilization.

The yalim wouldn't remain nomads forever, if Gene had anything to say about it. He was determined somehow to precipitate a move into one of the Umoi cities, preferably

Zond. What the Umoi had abandoned, their underpeople, the yalim, would inherit. Would, that is, if the yalim could overcome strong taboos about the abodes of the Old Gods. Legend had it that a body could die simply from looking at an Umoi city. Gene had his work cut out for him.

But for now, he faced a harder and much more unpleasant task: dealing with Yerga.

Gene looked up toward the mouth of the Royal Caves—the Queen and her ladies-in-waiting were the only tribe members who lived indoors. No one showed. The High Mistress usually greeted the troops when they returned from battle.

Gene dismounted, tethered his voort, and checked the beast's wounded rump. The thick leathery hide was almost like armor. The lance had barely penetrated muscle underneath. Barring infection, the animal would live.

Had Gene been wearing gauntlets, he would have thrown one or two down, but in this neck of the woods the accepted way of calling a guy out was to rip down his tent. Gene went directly to Yerga's campsite and did this thing.

The whole tribe held its breath. Yerga looked slowly about, then faced Gene and drew his sword, smiling a crooked, evil little smile.

Gene got the distinct feeling that he had walked the rest of the way into Yerga's trap. He wondered now why he had ever thought he could best Yerga in a swordfight. This was not the castle, and the spell that gave Gene his talent was not operative here. But, as was the case with the translation spell, there was some carry-over. Even without the spell, Gene had felt evenly matched with Yerga.

Now that there was no turning back, though, he had his doubts.

These things were best done quickly. Gene drew his sword, approached his opponent, and got even more worried. Now Yerga's satisfied smile confirmed Gene's suspicions that it had all been planned this way. But there was no hope of rescue, and no remedy except to turn tail and run. The rover was out in the desert somewhere, pinned under hundred-ton boulders. Zond was powerless to help. He was trapped in a backwater universe, bound by its peculiar laws. He would have to make the best of things, or die trying. Of course, the latter was the more likely possibility.

Yerga sprang at him, and Gene sidestepped a wicked lunge

that nicked his rib cage. The crowd ohhed at the sight of first blood.

Not the greatest of beginnings, Gene thought. I've already half-defeated myself.

Gene countered with a series of feints and lunges, but Yerga's masterly parrying left no opportunity. Then Yerga went back to the offensive, and Gene had to dance over an open campfire to get away.

Kicking out a hot coal that had wedged in his sandal, Gene got angry, mostly with himself. He had dug a fine psychological hole for himself, one of his gravest faults, on Earth as well as here. If he was to lose this fight, he was determined not to be defeated by his own self-doubt.

Gene attacked savagely, if not expertly, and sheer momentum drove Yerga back. Soon, though, the captain countered effectively, and broke the brunt of Gene's offensive.

Thereafter it was give-and-take, neither combatant able to gain the upper hand.

Gene wished mightily for magic. It was hard to get used to the notion that there was none here. At least he didn't think there was any. Maybe Sheila could tap whatever unseen forces were available. But this was probably a hard-science universe; and besides, Sheila was worlds away.

He missed her, and Linda, too. Two powerful magicians, those girls.

Again, Gene felt an unfocused resentment that his powers were relatively feeble, and only came on him inside the castle. But why? What was different about his case? It wasn't fair.

He rejected that note of defeatism as well. Fair, hell. The universe—the *universes* weren't fair. If he could only summon the will, the power. He knew what he felt like when the gift was upon him. If he could re-create that feeling in himself, perhaps the power of suggestion . . .

Yerga's renewed attacks brought him back to the task at hand. Gene fought back strongly, gaining confidence and power with every stroke. Maybe Yerga was showing his age, or maybe it was just the fortunes of war, but the tide of battle seemed to be shifting. Yerga's smile was gone, replaced by a look of grim concern.

The mortal combat went on and on, its deadly choreography carrying them across the length and breadth of the camp. Gene's swordsmanship continued to improve, and Yerga's confidence eroded precipitously.

At length, Yerga knew he was bested, and seemed to give up except for desperate parrying and backstepping. Gene maneuvered him toward a latrine. Yerga looked behind at the last second, tried to leap backward over it. His foot slipped into the hole and he fell, slamming his head against the side of the ditch.

Gene waded into the filth of the latrine and stood over him. Yerga was out cold.

The fight was over. Now all that remained was delivering the coup de grace. Gene raised his sword.

Then lowered it. He couldn't do it, but not out of any feeling for Yerga. It was just not Gene's style.

Of course, a refusal to slit Yerga's throat might itself cause another loss of face. But he'd have to risk that.

He looked toward the mouth of the cave. Queen Vaya, the High Mistress, had been watching with regal detachment, and now she regarded Gene with questioning eyes that seemed to ask, *Why do you wait?*

Gene's command of the language was still shaky, even with Zond's help. But he summoned all he knew and spoke.

"In the land of my birth, it is wrong for a man to take the life of another. I cannot do this thing. High Mistress, I beg your permission to spare my comrade-in-arms."

And he thought, *Jesus, I sound like a B movie character. But, hell, I'm in a B movie! I can smell the frigging popcorn!*

The High Mistress gave it some thought, then nodded, shrugging. Okay, don't kill the worthless jerk. Use him for hrunt bait, what do I give a shit.

She turned abruptly and went back into her palace.

Gene exhaled and slipped his copper sword into his belt. He fetched a waterskin and doused Yerga with its contents. Yerga's eyes fluttered, and he came to.

He sat up, disoriented, then looked around. Titters rippled through the crowd of tribespeople. Then laughter came in waves.

Yerga looked up at the victor, his eyes radiating hatred. Gene suddenly realized that killing Yerga would have been the more charitable act.

You can't fight city hall, Gene thought, and you can't change the laws of a given universe, human or otherwise.

Live and learn.

DESERT ISLAND

"ISN'T THERE A TV game show where they ask you who you'd like to be marooned on a desert island with?"

Trent finished laying another layer of palm leaves on the roof and stepped back from his handiwork. It wasn't a proper grass hut, more of a lean-to, but it would do in a pinch, or in a light rain shower. Major precipitation would be another matter. Sooner or later they'd have to move off the beach and seek shelter in the hills. Can't live on raw shellfish and quasi-breadfruit forever.

"Maybe a parlor game," he said. "Why?"

Sheila turned over on her stomach and bunched up a pile of leaves for use as a pillow. She was getting a terrific body tan. "Well, I can't think of anyone I'd more like to be stranded with."

"Than little ol' me?"

"Than little ol' you. Your Royal Highness, darling."

"Nice of you to say." He knelt and kissed the spot between her shoulder blades. "Goes double for me. Besides you, all I need is Mozart, Rachmaninoff, a little Mahler, and a couple of Stephen King books. And some good sour-mash whiskey."

"You don't need much. Are those your favorite things?"

"Well, romantic Rachmaninoff relieves classical Mozart, and Mahler makes you sober up after listening to Mozart and Rachmaninoff. You could also do a Beethoven-Chopin-Stravinsky thing. And Stephen King is always good for a yuck in the middle of the night."

"Well, King is fun, but I don't know much about classical music," Sheila said. "Maybe we're not so compatible. I'm more at home with, you know, Billy Joel."

"He's okay, too," Trent said. "Besides, who needs compatibility when you have great sex."

She laughed, then stretched dreamily. "You know, you were talking in your sleep last night. You woke me up."

"I wasn't sleeping."

She giggled. "Then who were you talking to?"

"Incarnadine."

Sheila sat up quickly. "What?"

"I think."

"You think? Well, were you? Can he—?"

"I didn't want to get your hopes up. I think it was Incarnadine trying to contact me. Something prevented it, I don't know what. Some sort of interference. I told him our predicament. I have a feeling I didn't get through."

Sheila looked deflated. "We'll never get out of here."

"Don't despair. Something's obviously going on. When it's over, he'll get us out."

"But we're on the other side of a wild portal. How will he even know where to look?"

"There are ways. He could get a fix on us, then drive a tunnel through to this universe, pick us right up."

"He can do that?"

Trent sat down in the sand, picked up a shell. "Anything's possible in the castle. He could teleport us back to the castle. Summon us, conjure us."

Sheila was amazed. "No kidding? I was always under the impression that there was no way to travel between universes except by using the castle's portals."

"Well, for the most part, that's true. But with virtually unlimited energy, which the castle has, anything's possible. Like conjuring. I know Incarnadine can reach out and snatch things from other universes. Fetch them. He has all kinds of junk that he's filched. Strange artifacts, gizmos, art pieces, books, you name it. There's no reason he couldn't snatch a person—or two.'' Trent considered it. "Unless there's some technical barrier. Maybe the spell doesn't work with live organisms.'' He shook his head. "I don't know. But as I said, anything's possible.''

"That makes me feel better,'' Sheila said.

"Incarnadine has any number of tricks up his sleeve. He's very creative, magically speaking. So is . . . was my sister Ferne.''

"Did you like her?''

"Respected her, yes. Liked her?'' Trent let a cascade of sand fall from the shell. "Hard to say. Beautiful she was. But infinitely crafty. And clever. The thing was, she was reckless. She'd try anything. I don't know how many spells she tried that could have blown up in her face. Some of them did. Once she tried tapping interstitial etherium.''

"What's that?''

"It's energy that's stuffed into the 'space' between the various universes. Acts as a buffer, keeps them from bumping into each other. Hard concept to grasp, really, because it's really negative energy, which suddenly reverses polarity when you—well, never mind about that. Anyway, all I know is Ferne tried it, and something hit her and knocked her across the room. Out cold.''

Sheila grimaced. "Sounds dangerous.''

"It was. It is. But she survived. She always does—''

Trent stared off abstractedly for a long moment.

Sheila let him brood. Presently he came back.

"Yeah. She could do a lot of things. I don't know about traveling, but she could cast spells in one universe and have them work in another.''

Sheila was impressed. "That's real magic.''

"She was in a league all her own. I don't know that she was as good as Incarnadine. I don't know that anyone is.'' Trent threw the seashell away. "Except maybe me.''

Sheila smiled. "I believe it.''

"Thanks. Actually, at the risk of sounding immodest, when you get into—well, when you start talking about magic at this level, our level—the family's—it's more a matter of style than anything. Each magician brings a certain unique talent to his work. For instance, I can tell Incarnadine's hand by a certain feeling I get when one of his spells is brewing. It's like a smell, or maybe even a taste. But it's unmistakable. His spells have his signature stamped all over them."

"That's interesting."

"Same with Ferne. Same with you, for that matter, or anyone who practices the recondite arts. Every artist has his own style."

"I've never thought of myself as an artist."

"You're a damned good one, if a little inexperienced. But you were coming along very nicely."

"Until I hit this place."

Trent looked at the sky, the sea, and the sand. "Yes." He sighed. "Right. This world is very problematical. It's flat, magically speaking. No spark in the air. No vibes. Nothing."

"Maybe it's more subtle than we realize."

"Very subtle. All worlds have magic."

"Do they really?"

"Yes, to some extent. Some more than others. This one has it, make no mistake. But they must be keeping it in cookie jars."

Sheila laughed, leaned over and kissed him.

"Hungry?" he asked.

"A little."

"Tell you what. We'll have lunch at our favorite restaurant—"

"The breadfruit tree."

"Right, and afterward we'll go for a stroll. It's about time we circumnavigated this island, see what's on the other side."

"Maybe there's a lagoon. Wouldn't that be romantic?"

"Great for fishing. But this looks like a volcanic island. Lagoons usually happen in coral formations."

"You know a lot about a lot of things."

"Are you kidding? I've had a subscription to *Reader's Digest* for fifty years."

Trent's guess was right. Coming around the curving shore, they were greeted by the sight of a huge volcano rising from an island that lay just on the horizon. Ash-gray and forbidding, the cone topped off at two thousand feet, as nearly as Trent could estimate.

"Extinct, maybe?" Sheila asked.

"Dormant. I dunno. I can't see any vegetation on that island. That worries me."

"It looks dead."

"Let's hope it stays that way."

Access inland was better here, grassy slopes rising gradually from the beach to an eroded peak in the center of the island. They even discovered a cave. It was full of bats and not fit for habitation.

But there was a lagoon, after all, rather a cove, a rock-rimmed pocket of calm water, good for swimming and, very likely, fishing, if some sort of tackle could be improvised.

"Or a net," Trent mused.

"That'd be hard."

"You braid vines, strips of sapling, make rope. Then you make a net. Hard? You bet, but South Sea islanders do it all the time."

"Think I'd look good in a sarong, or maybe a grass skirt?"

"You look fine the way you are now, but we'll be needing clothes sooner or later."

"I was cold last night," she said. "A little bit, until you covered me."

"Only proper thing to do under the circumstances. We'll have to find a source of fresh water, of course, but right now I don't see any reason why we shouldn't move to this side. Better food supply, shelter from the open sea, inland route, and other advantages, probably, that I haven't noticed yet. We'll put our house up on that knoll over there. Be a good observation point."

She laughed. "You've got this all figured out, don't you?"

He shrugged. "We must make do, somehow. We might be here for a spell."

"I'm glad we're together, Trent."

He gathered her in and held her close.

"I'm extremely glad of that myself. Cold again?"

"No, just hold me. Tight."

He did, then they lay down together on the soft bed of the beach.

Long Island

Chico's was busy that night, the dance floor a scrummage of writhing humanity. Snowclaw couldn't get over the noise in the place. It had taken some getting used to. He didn't quite understand what all the thumping and screeching was about, though he knew it had something to do with music. And the dancing was completely incomprehensible. Snowy took it to be some complex courting ritual. But what did the flashing lights have to do with anything?

It didn't matter. His job was to look after things. Check for proper dress; no jeans, no tennis shoes, no generally sloppy outfits. Chico's had to be a "class act," was Nunzio's way of putting it. The other host, Dave, checked the little cards that the young ones held out that supposedly proved they were old enough to be admitted to these adult doings.

Snowy's proper job was throwing the drunks out. That had only happened once since he started. A bartender refused to serve a customer who had glugged a little too much swill, and the customer got a little rowdy. (Interesting sidelight here: the bartender was actually worried that the guy might go out and wreck his metal wagon and get real ticked off at the bartender *for giving the guy exactly what he was screaming for—more swill!*) Snowclaw had followed directions to the

letter. First he was polite, then firmly insistent. When that
didn't work, he picked the guy up, carried him out into the
parking lot, and threw him in the dumpster.

That was pretty funny, Dave had told him, but basically it
was overreacting.

Snowy didn't know about that. The guy had been pretty
nasty. Besides, all that happened was the little creep got his
pride wounded. Snowy wouldn't think of actually hurting any
of these hairless humans. They were all so soft and squishy.

For all of that, though, they were feisty little devils. Like
the guy he threw out, coming back with a policeman in tow,
demanding that Snowy be arrested. The policeman heard
Snowy's story, then told the guy to forget it. Then the guy
started giving the cop all kinds of grief, so the cop and his
partner beat the compost out of the little twerp and threw him
in *their* metal wagon, which he didn't have to drive.

Feisty little devils.

Oh, he forgot the one incident where the female threw a
glass of stuff into her mate's face. Something about the female
walking into the place and finding this guy cavorting with
another female in a dark corner. She got upset at this behavior. Why, exactly, Snowy didn't know. Apparently humans
were supposed to keep to one mate at a time. But, then, what
were all these females doing out on the floor making sexual
movements with all these different males? He'd seen females
doing it with male partner after male partner, and vice versa.
Snowy didn't understand, but he supposed there was some
rationale behind it all. He didn't expect it to make any sense,
and in any event he didn't care much.

The apartment above the joint was uncomfortable until
Dave showed him a way to turn the heat off. Dave had done
it, but had given Snowy a funny look.

"The heat really gets to me," Snowy explained. "I come
from a cold place."

"Yeah, but it's February, f'crissakes. Where you from, the
North Pole?"

"Nope."

"Where, then? Canada?"

"Uh . . . yeah, Canada."

"A Canuck, huh? Glad to have you in the U.S.A. C'mon,
I'll show you how to work the videotape. You like porno
flicks? Nunzio distributes them."

Now, these were interesting. He had always wondered
about the mechanics of it. Basically the same, except that the
male didn't keep the eggs for a while, like back home. Well,
actually, there weren't any eggs to speak of. There was just
sort of *doing* it, and that was it. Ordinarily he didn't like to
criticize, but the male's equipment being exposed all the time
like that—that was dumb, it seemed to him. And dangerous!
Amazing. Funny, too, was the fact that there didn't seem to
be any particular time of year for this sort of stuff. Everybody
just rutted away like crazy, no matter what the weather. At
the drop of a snowshoe.

Different world, different ways of doing things. That was
the way you had to look at it. It didn't bear thinking about
too much. Besides, he had other problems.

Like contacting Linda, somehow. He knew how to work a
telephone now, but he didn't have a number to call. As for
begging help, he couldn't very well ask too many questions,
or he'd be thought mighty strange, if he wasn't already.
Somebody had told him, "Dial Information," and had given
him a number, but *that* was no help at all.

"What city?"

"Um . . . I don't know. I've been there, but I really don't
know where it is."

"Sorry, sir, I have to know what city."

"Well, what cities are there?"

"Pardon, sir?"

"What cities do you have?"

"Sir, I can check the New York metropolitan area for you."

"Yeah, okay."

"What name?"

"Linda."

"Last name, sir?"

"Oh. Uh, Bar . . . Bar something. Barkey. Bar-kay."

"Spell that?"

"What?"

"Can you spell that for me, sir?"

"I don't know what that means."

*"One moment, sir. . . . Sir, checking the New York met-
ropolitan area, I find no listing for a Linda Barkey, or Bar-
kay. I do have an L. Barcus on West Forty-seventh Street in
Manhattan."*

"No, I want Linda. Uh, never mind. Thanks."

Click.

Well, that was that. Of course, he could just start walking again, but that sure as heck wouldn't do much good. Halfway House was a good hike, he knew that.

And most of all . . . Great White Stuff, was he hungry!

Human food just didn't make it. He could *eat* the stuff, but . . . gods, it was like eating water. Nothing to it, no taste.

It would be a real embarrassment if someone caught him guzzling drain cleaner and eating bath soap, as he had taken to doing of late. The soap was nothing, but the drain goop packed a real punch. Good stuff.

Dave had looked real puzzled when Snowy came home with a grocery bag filled with paraffin wax candles and ten bottles of Thousand Island dressing. That got Snowclaw worried.

But apparently there wasn't any real cause for concern, because Dave told him that Nunzie had a new job for him.

"There's a truck with contraband goin' to Pittsburgh. You're ridin' shotgun. Nunzie likes you. Thinks you're doin' real good."

"Uh-huh. Okay."

"Yeah. Don't worry, it's a milk run. Cigarettes, that's all it is."

"Yeah?"

"Yeah. They come up from the South. You know, without tax stamps on 'em? Then we ship 'em all over. We make two hundred percent profit. Even at that, it's peanuts, really, but it's part of the family business."

"Uh-huh."

"Yeah. If you do good, Nunzie might put you on with the cash crop shipments. You know, the coke, the smoke, and the poke?"

"Uh-huh."

Dave smiled and thumped him on the back. "You're okay, Snowy. A little strange, but okay."

"Uh-huh."

CASTLE

"MAN, I DON'T think I'm ever going to get used to this place," Jeremy said, walking with Linda down a dim corridor. He had no idea where he was.

"Sure you will. It took me a couple of months before I got to know my way around. But when I did, everything was fine. The place feels like home now."

In passing, Jeremy peered into a dark embrasure and got the vague sense that something big and sinister stood watching within. Of course, he got that feeling all the time around here. When would he stop jumping at every shadow? Back in the real world, it could always be said that there was really nothing to be afraid of. A dark place was just that, a dark place. Here, though . . . wow. There *were* spooks here. Real ones.

"I don't know," he said. "I think it's gonna take me a long time."

"Fiddlesticks. You'll be a veteran in no time, with your talent—whatever it is."

"Yeah, I wish I knew what it is, too."

"Did you guys try running spells through your computer?"

"No, we never got that far. It sounded interesting, though. The funny thing is . . ." He heaved his shoulders.

Linda looked at him sideways. "Yeah?"

"Well, it's weird. I just keep getting these strange feelings when I run programs. You know, just fooling around, like I usually do. Trying different things."

"What kind of feelings?"

"I can't put a name to them. I feel . . . good. No. Well, powerful. Like I can do anything. All sorts of new possibilities. It just feels good." Jeremy scratched his head. "I can't explain it."

Linda pursed her lips and gave a knowing nod. Then she said, "Sounds like something's brewing, all right."

They had almost come to the wide arched entrance of the Queen's dining room.

"Geez, how did you find your way back?" Jeremy asked.

"Just a sixth sense you get. Hungry? I don't know what else there is to do, not until—"

"Lady Linda?"

A servant approached. It was a young page.

"Hi!" Linda said. "Are you new around here?"

"Yes, milady. Lord Incarnadine wishes to see you."

"Boy, that was quick. Lead on."

"This way, milady."

"C'mon, Jeremy."

The boy led them down a long hallway, then up a flight of stairs. When they reached the landing, there came a high, insistent beeping, as from some electronic device.

"What's that?" Linda said.

"Huh?" Jeremy looked down. "Hey. It's my computer."

He knelt, cracked open the case, and flipped up the readout screen.

"Hey."

"What does it say?" Linda asked.

"It reads 'Extreme Danger.' " Jeremy looked up. "What's going on?"

"You're asking me? It's your gizmo."

Bewildered, Jeremy shook his head. "It's not supposed to do that. I had it shut off. And besides, there's nothing running except the operating system, and that's—" He closed the case. "This is getting too weird."

Linda looked around. "Tell the truth, I'm getting a strange feeling, too."

They both looked at the page.

"Where are you taking us?" Linda asked him.

The page appeared a trifle edgy. "To Lord Incarnadine, milady."

"Where is he at the moment?"

"With the chamberlain, milady."

"In Jamin's quarters?"

"Yes, milady."

"You look worried about something. Are you sure you're not fibbing?"

"No, milady. I mean, yes, milady!"

Linda chewed her lip, then said, "I can't believe you. Something's wrong, and I want to know what it is."

The page's eyes darted about in desperation.

"Well?" Linda said. "I'm waiting."

The page spun round and dashed away, vanishing into darkness, his footsteps echoing.

Jeremy whistled. "What got into him?"

Linda's forehead creased into a worried frown. "I should have made him talk."

"How?"

"Conjured a dozen monkeys to tickle him to death. Set nasty spiders and things all over him. No end of ways." She sighed. "But he's just a kid, and I couldn't do it."

"Should have," Jeremy said. "He was lying through his teeth."

"I know. Something's up." Linda fingered the handle of the dagger that hung from her belt. "Jamin. I wonder if he knows—?"

The floor began to heave, and they both dropped to ride out the disturbance. This time, however, the convulsions did not want to stop.

The walls became rubbery, shivering and quaking. The ceiling dropped, and the corridor changed dimensions. The stairway dematerialized, replaced by a vaulted chamber with no outlet. Partitions appeared out of nowhere, sliding down and rising back up again like backdrops in a theater.

Gradually the convulsive transformations ceased. Linda got up cautiously, then brushed off her tunic and the knees of her tights.

"That was bad. Worse than before."

"Yeah," Jeremy said in awe. His throat had gone completely dry. He coughed and swallowed hard. "What's happening?"

"Whatever the problem is with the universes, it's not getting any better."

"What universes are we talking about?"

"The universes of the castle. I'm not the one to ask about all that. I've never really understood it." Linda thought for a moment. "Well, yes, I do understand it, but intuitively, I guess. Something's wrong with the delicate balance between the universes. Since the castle is the focal point, it's feeling the worst of the effects."

"What do you mean by 'focal point'?"

"That's what's even harder to explain, but I suppose I mean that since the castle's connected to all these different universes, it's like a hub, the center of a big wheel. It's bound to be affected by what happens out on the rim."

"Okay, I get it. Funny that this place would be the center of the universe."

"Universes."

"Whatever."

Linda took a deep breath, then looked around. "But we have an even bigger problem."

"Oh, God. What?"

"Didn't you notice that everything is different, rearranged?"

"Yeah. So?"

"So. The stairs are gone. We have to find a different way downstairs. Let's go."

They went, but fifteen minutes later they had failed to locate another stairway. For the first time in a long time, Linda was lost in the castle.

"I don't believe it," she said. "I can't get a fix on the Guest Wing."

"The Guest Wing. Is that where the dining room is?"

"Right, and where all our sleeping rooms are. I've lost my sense of orientation. The castle must be undergoing drastic changes."

"What are we gonna do?"

"I've been through this before. The castle was a much wilder place when I first got here. Don't worry, I'll get my bearings back."

"But for now we're lost, right?"

"Right. Take it easy. You really can't get lost in the castle. You just keep walking, and . . ."

They kept walking, finding little but acres and acres of nondescript castle architecture.

Finally Linda sat on a stone bench and took off her boots, rubbed her feet.

"Damn it, I'm getting mad."

Jeremy slumped to his haunches and leaned his back against the dark stone.

"We be lost now," he said.

Linda gave him a sour look. "Thanks for clarifying the issue."

Jeremy shrugged.

Linda looked him over. "How old are you?"

"Why?"

"Just asking."

"Twenty-three." Jeremy raised a hand. "I know what you're gonna say. You're gonna say I look fifteen."

"Well, maybe seventeen. Nothing wrong with looking young. I wish I looked seventeen."

"How old are you?"

"You're not supposed to ask, but I just turned thirty. Over the hill."

"I thought you looked pretty old."

"Gee, thanks."

"No, I didn't mean you looked bad."

Linda rolled her eyes. "Forget it."

"Sorry."

"You know, I think yours is a maturity problem, not so much looks. You act fifteen."

"Hey, I apologized, okay?"

Linda put her boots back on. "Let's get moving."

"Where to? Why don't we just stay put? We're bound to run into someone."

"Wrong. There are parts of the castle where nobody ever goes. You could wait forever and not see anyone."

"But—"

"Don't argue. If you want to stay here, fine."

Jeremy sighed and cranked himself up. "No, I'm coming."

* * *

An hour later, they were still lost. They had passed many a side chamber, some bare, others furnished. In one of the latter they stopped for a rest, and Linda magicked a picnic basket full of gourmet viands.

"Might as well have some fun," she said, opening a tub of beluga caviar.

"What else is in here? What's this stuff?"

"Read the label."

"Pattee dee . . . what's that?"

"Pâté de foie gras. Goose-liver paste."

"Yuck! You got something to eat in here?"

"Such as? I can conjure anything."

"Anything? A baloney sandwich is what I could go for."

"What low taste. Mustard?"

"No, mayonnaise, lettuce, American cheese, and dill pickle. Uh, please."

"There it is."

"Huh? Wow." Jeremy reached out for the plate that had appeared on the table. On it lay an attractive arrangement of sandwich wedges, pickle slices, and olives, all trussed up with toothpicks and nestled on a bed of leaf lettuce.

"How the heck do you do that?" Jeremy demanded.

"It's a gift. It's the castle, actually. Anything to drink?"

"Yeah! How about a thick, creamy—"

A tremendous clap of thunder sounded.

"Uh-oh." Linda stood up and looked around fearfully.

A tremendous shock wave hit, knocking them both down. Then the floor tossed them about like salad. The walls and ceilings turned into something positively fluid. They ran like melted wax, gobs of stuff dripping down.

Still holding on to his computer, Jeremy slid up against a wall, then felt the peculiar sensation of being absorbed into it. The stone was hot and gooey, like a marshmallow left too long in a campfire. He struggled to get away.

"Linda!" he screamed. "What's happening?"

Her answer had a peculiar effect on him. On the one hand, it was good news, because he didn't like the castle. On the other, in a very literal sense he didn't know where he'd be without it.

What Linda had shouted back was: "The castle's disappearing!"

Drawing Room, Family Residence

HE ENTERED A spacious room full of stately furniture. Ancient tapestries draped the walls, hanging alongside antique weapons, shields, coats of arms, and suchlike. Glass-fronted cabinets stood here and about, displaying glassware and other historical artifacts. It was a quiet, comfortable room with many points of interest, among which was a curious device lying on a table to one side. He went directly to it.

In the main, the thing consisted of glass spheres, copper tubes, brass coils, and other primitive-looking, quasi-electronic components. On the front of the device was a simple instrument panel with a small ground-glass viewing screen.

He adjusted a few controls and flipped a switch. Sparks of violet and blue began to arc within the glass spheres. The device emitted a soft hum.

He made further adjustments, then fetched a chair and seated himself.

Executing a few hand passes, he began chanting in a low monotone.

The hum grew louder, but the glass remained blank.

"Damn it," he muttered. "Not this thing, too."

Far-off thunder turned his head. A slight tremor shook the walls.

"I wonder if there's going to be time," he mused.

He went back to chanting. Suddenly a great blue spark snapped between two neighboring components.

He jumped up and fanned away the smoke, then checked the works of the device for small fires. Finding none, he fiddled with the controls.

He stepped back a few paces, raised his arms, and extended them forward, his index fingers pointing.

"Machine! I bid thee . . . *work*, goddammit!"

The screen came to life, displaying the images of three strange individuals seated behind a long desk. Attired in black turtlenecks and gray jackets, the three shared a family resemblance, though each had his individual aspects. All had dark, close-cropped hair. The one in the middle wore thick eyeglasses in a heavy black frame. The eyes of the individual on the right were pale. His colleague on the opposite side had a large mole on his left cheek.

Glasses spoke first: "This is indeed a pleasure, Lord Incarnadine. We extend our warmest welcome."

Incarnadine exhaled and took his seat. "Your hospitality is inappropriate, for what you see before you is but an image. For now, I send my simulacrum. Pray to whatever deities you hold in awe that I do not find it necessary to visit you in person."

Glasses was mildly amused. "Belligerent as always. You will never change, Incarnadine."

"I will brook no impertinence from you. Moreover, you will address me as 'Your Serene and Transcendental Majesty.' "

All three laughed. Mole said, "Oh, by all means, Your Serene and . . . I beg your pardon. What was the rest of it?"

"A simple 'Majesty' will do now and then, mixed up with a few 'sirs.' Let's skip it and get to business." Incarnadine leaned forward, his eyes steely, glints of fire in them. When next he spoke, his voice rattled the glass cabinets.

"What have you done with my sister?"

Glasses blinked his eyes. "Dear me. You seem quite upset. But instead of shouting at the top of your lungs, wouldn't it be vastly better instead to—?"

"Answer the question! I know she is with you and that she is in great distress. You will release her to me this instant."

Pale-Eyes spoke, a sneer on his thin gray lips. "It is ironic that you of all people should inquire after your sister's welfare—you who banished her, consigned her to oblivion."

"It is monstrous that you, her torturers, speak to me of irony. Release her, I say, or suffer the consequences."

Mole sniffed indignantly. "Threats. Always threats. Your line breeds true, Majestic One. For thousands of years, your family has done nothing but bluster, bully, and rattle the castle armory. We have done nothing to merit such treatment. We have always wanted peace, cooperation, and mutual understanding."

Incarnadine snorted. "I won't bother to debate with you. The issue this time is very clear. You have abducted my sister—"

"We offered asylum!"

"—and are holding her against her will. If you do not release her, you will suffer consequences dire in the extreme. Moreover, you will also cease and desist from certain supernatural techniques which you have either extorted from my sister or gained by bargaining with her in bad faith. Furthermore—"

"Really," Glasses protested.

"*Furthermore*, you will disobey this latter command at the peril of losing your own lives, if not of killing every living being in your universe."

"How so?" Pale-Eyes asked.

"Surely you have guessed by now. Have not your natural philosophers detected anomalous stresses in the interstitial subspace? Do they not realize what these portend?"

"It is mere conjecture."

"Not so. You are playing with forces far beyond your control or comprehension."

Mole shook his head. "We have conducted a few experiments for defense purposes."

"You are deliberately trying to destabilize Castle Perilous, and you know it. You also know, since you have agents here who can tell you, that your efforts have been successful to a degree."

Mole waved a bony hand in protest. "We have no *agents*,

as you put it, at work in your residence, or anywhere, for that matter. Really, you must not impute to us your own—"

"Cut the crap!" Incarnadine said. "Listen to me. Continue to do what you're doing, continue to draw power from the etherium, and you will doom the universe."

"Absurd exaggeration," Mole scoffed.

"Paranoid fantasies," Glasses said.

"Fear-mongering," was Pales-Eyes' contribution.

Incarnadine sat back. "All right, enough. I will say this once. Attend me."

Mole guffawed. "By all means, proceed."

"If you do not release my sister and desist in these so-called experiments, you will leave me no choice. Listen very carefully to what I am about to describe. If you do not accede to my wishes, I will dispatch to your world a force the like of which you have never imagined. This force, this phenomenon, will kill every living thing in your world. All will perish. There will be no escape. Do you understand me?"

The three silently exchanged glances.

"Well, do you?"

Glasses cleared his throat. "I must say, your threats have reached a new level of malevolence. To blackmail us with talk of genocide—"

"You leave me no choice. If I stay my hand, I doom not only my universe but all the universes."

"Surely these dire predictions of yours have at least a chance of being mistaken."

"I have said what I have said. Heed my words."

Glasses stiffened. "We will not be intimidated! This is too much. We will defend ourselves with all the might at our disposal. Our response to any attack will be massive retaliation! We will not let you—"

The screen suddenly went to snow, then to black. Multiple-colored lines appeared, a test pattern of some sort, which remained a brief moment.

Then a new face appeared. A face only, in close-up. Well proportioned, broad-browed, and photogenic, it gave the impression, somehow, of being artificial, as though rendered by a journeyman artist with no sense of character.

"Inky sweetheart! Listen, forgive my butting in, but things were getting a little out of hand. I thought it wouldn't hurt to try a different tack entirely."

Incarnadine allowed a brief smile. "How kind of you. What's with this new incarnation? Earth dialect, smarmy patter—you sound like a cross between a Hollywood agent and a used-computer salesman."

"You're being hostile again, Inky baby. Just trying out a new policy, a new way of dealing with difficult matters. In these perilous times, we simply have to do all we can to oil the diplomatic machinery. Right, Ink?"

"Don't even think of calling me that. As for this new facade, forget it. At least the Central Committee, or whatever it's called, has a certain decorum. This is revolting."

The face looked hurt. "Inky! That was below the belt."

Incarnadine gave a sardonic grunt. "You have no belt."

"Now look, Inky, I think it'd be better for all concerned if we just took time to simmer down, get in touch with our emotions, and take stock. All this talk about attacking people and blowing things up and generally declaring war on the whole universe and its environs—well, frankly I'm shocked. How did it get this far, Inky? What a shame, what a colossal shame. And all because both sides can't quite—"

"Be quiet."

"Please, let me finish! All this tension has really only one cause. Mutual distrust! That's it in a clamshell, Inky. Really, I know what I'm talking about. In such a charged atmosphere as this, a productive dialogue is all but impossible. Both sides have to change in order for—"

"Silence!"

The face on the screen stopped moving its lips, its blue eyes wide and blank.

Incarnadine stood. "I don't know what ploy, what game you're playing—good cop/bad cop, or what. It won't work. It's too far gone for that! I meant what I said. Obey or die. It's as simple as that. You know me, you know my power. Take warning or be resigned to your doom."

The face took animation once more. "Well, go ahead and be that way, Inky. It's all the same to me. You can't scare us. We have your silly cow of a sister, and after we get done with her, we'll start on you. You can't stop us—human scum! Shit-eating bastard human filth! We'll kill all of you, every last—"

The screen went blank, became a rectangle of ground glass once again.

He lowered his head and heaved a great sigh.

Rising, he turned off the device. The humming stopped and the sparks faded.

A stronger tremor shook the room. He looked off, sensing its magnitude. Then his eyes turned inward.

At length he came out of his reverie and turned toward the door, walking briskly.

He muttered, "Now I gotta put my paycheck where my oral cavity gapes—as it were."

Plains

GENE HACKED AND slashed, then hacked again.

His hrunt opponent staggered back, throat agape and oozing. Gene followed up with a thrust to the diaphragm, driving his sword deep into tough abdominal muscle. The hrunt doubled up and fell.

Gene let the hrunt slide off his sword, then swung round to ward off a weak lunge from a wounded hruntan infantryman who wouldn't go down. Gene skewered the creature, leaving little room for refusal.

Gene looked around and realized that the battle was over, and that the yalim had won the day, fighting under his personal military command. Hrunt bodies carpeted the battlefield.

He sheathed his sword, fetched his voort, mounted, and shouted the command for recall.

As the troops fell into ranks, thoughts of the castle drifted back. He hadn't thought about home in a long while. How long had he been here? Four, five months? And in that time he had gone from yalim prisoner to First Husband and Captain of the Royal Cohorts.

He wondered what was going on back at Perilous. Did it still exist? He had kept his eyes open for any sign of the portal, but it was like hoping to get hit by the same raindrop twice. The portal could appear anywhere on this world, or it might never appear again.

Whatever was going on back there, it must have been bad, or Sheila and Linda would have made some attempt to find him. Maybe they had tried, and failed. There was another possibility, one he was loath to consider: they might have perished in some general cataclysm that he, by sheerest happenstance, had managed to escape.

The cohorts had mustered, and now a great cheer rose up from them.

Gene drew his sword and raised it above his head. The voort under him reared up, braying.

The cohorts cheered louder, broke ranks, and gathered round him. They took him from his mount and bore him on their shoulders back to the Queen's field tent.

It was night, the lamps flickering in the soft breeze that blew through the tent. Outside, campfires crackled, animals grunted, and men laughed, happy and drunk, flushed with victory.

"You have conquered, my husband."

"Yep. Peel me a grape, will you?"

"Is that what this fruit is called in your land?"

"Just kidding. Are you cold? Do you want to put some clothes on?"

"No. I will never wear clothes again, my husband, when we are alone together."

"Hey, that's fine with me. Look, I've got big plans. Now that the hrunt are cleared out of the lowlands, we—"

"You will continue your campaign into the southern desert?"

"Huh? No, not really. I think we should head west. As far as we know, no hrunt live there. But that's where Annau is."

"Annau?"

"Yeah, the city of Annau."

Vaya sat up and regarded him, her dark eyes narrowed. "Why do you speak of an abode of the Old Gods? It is bad luck to do so."

"Uh-huh. Well, look. Things are going to change around here. I realize that taboos are hard to overcome, but it simply has to be done if your people are going to have any future."

She wrinkled her brow. "Future?"

"Sure. Do you want your people living in tents and scraping a living off this wasteland forever? You told me that every year the hunting is harder. Every year the tribe's population shrinks a little. It's a losing fight. That's what happened to the Umoi when they tried to go the *Whole Earth Catalog* route. It was a dead end, and now they're extinct."

She shook her head. "You speak of many strange things. Forbidden things. You make me afraid, my husband."

"Not to worry. Rub me right there. Yeah, that's it."

Her hands were soft. "But you are a great warrior."

"You won't get an argument from me."

"You have killed more hrunt than all of my husbands combined. You have killed more than any yalim has ever killed."

"Just applied some modern military tactics, is all."

"One day you will kill all the hrunt and they will never again raid our camps or steal our food."

"Right. Well, look, I'm no Stalin. I'm not out to exterminate the kulaks, or do anything like that. The hrunt . . ." Gene propped himself up on one elbow. "Look, there's something you have to know about the hrunt. I've been researching this with Zond. And Zond says—"

"Is that the name of the spirit you converse with?"

"Uh, yeah. You see, the Umoi—the Old Gods—created both yalim and hrunt, but for different purposes. The hrunt were the field niggers, and the yalim were the . . . never mind. They were both servant classes, but the hrunt were created stupid so they wouldn't mind working in deep mines or doing other dangerous stuff. But the real thing you should know is, hrunt are really just yalim who've been genetically altered a little bit."

Vaya lay down, paralleling Gene, her long golden body radiant in the lamplight.

"Speak more of this to me, my husband."

"Uh, yeah. Um . . . well, what that means is, a hrunt is really a yalim except for a few extra genes spliced into his DNA. They turn him ugly and change his body chemistry a little bit, but essentially he's human. The thing is, once we get back into the cities, it won't be any problem to snip those pesky genes out. We'd have to round up all the hrunt women, of course, and do some cell surgery. . . ." Gene considered it. "Actually I guess the simplest solution would be sterilization, though that does have a totalitarian ring to it. But morally speaking, since hrunt are really just handicapped humans—'' He trailed off into deep thought.

Presently he sat up. "Hey, guess what. Things aren't simple even in fantasyland.''

"Things are never simple, my husband. It is not the way of the world.''

"Or the universe. Or universes.''

"You are a strange one, my husband. You came here speaking a strange tongue, wearing strange clothes, riding a chariot of the Old Gods. Yet you are a man. Are you a god as well?''

Gene raked his eye up and down Vaya's exquisite body. "No. Just the best swordsman this side of Castle Perilous. And the luckiest guy in several worlds, I might add.''

She held out her arms. "Come to me, husband and lover.''

"Oy.''

ISLAND

THEIR HOUSE, SHELTERED by hill palms, had a beautiful view
of the sea. A screened veranda jutted out to one side, and
Sheila would sit there at all hours weaving baskets, mats, and
other housewares. She liked watching waves break against the
rocks and huge seabirds wheel in the sky.

The birds weren't gulls; at least they didn't look like sea
gulls. They were eagle size but fatter, and they fished the
waters of the lagoon. It was thrilling and a little frightening
to watch them stoop, dive, and pluck a struggling fish out of
the water, clutching their prey in great silver talons.

The weather was always beautiful. It rained sometimes at
night, very softly, very soothingly on the thatched roof of
their house. Trent told her that a monsoon season would come
eventually, as this was standard procedure for tropical climes.
But, then again, he didn't know this world. Maybe the weather
stayed fair all year long. Sheila hoped so.

After Trent finished the house, he spent his days building
a raft. There was a reason for this.

The volcano had begun smoking about two months after
their arrival. It had trailed wisps of white vapor for a week,
then began putting up a steady column of dark smoke along
with an occasional plume of ash. Every once in a while it

would shoot out boulders the size of automobiles. Sheila watched them splash into the sea. Their island was in no danger at the moment, but the volcano was too close for comfort. Trent said that the presence of birds meant there had to be mainland near, or at least a bigger island, and they would have to reach it to be really safe.

So every day, Trent would go down to the lagoon—the "shipyards," as he called it—and work on the raft. Sheila spent most of her time now braiding rope. The raft needed lots of it to hold its heavy logs together. Trent said that he would have built an outrigger canoe, had there been more time. But the raft would be seaworthy, of that he was sure. A square-rigged sail would have been ideal, if there had been any fabric to make a sail out of. As it was, they would have to trust in God (and the gods, in Trent's case) and hope for a good current.

But Trent kept thinking about a sail.

"Where there's a will, there's a government research grant, usually. You'll have to fish today while I go up the mountain and see if I can find anything."

"I'll dig up some shellfish and make chowder," Sheila said. "You go do your research."

"I knew you were a Democrat."

When Sheila wasn't braiding, she would work on magic, as did Trent when he wasn't shipbuilding. They called it "Research and Development," and although no breakthroughs had happened since Trent's tentative levitation of a neo-coconut, Sheila felt that one was possible. There was some obstacle that she couldn't quite see her way around. It was a difficult problem, and she needed more time.

Unfortunately the volcano's output steadily increased, its smoke column turning black and ugly. There might not be any time at all. Trent said that an eruption was inevitable. It was just a matter of when and how bad.

R&D's chief technological spin-off to date was fire. There was no flint or chert to be had on the island, but a primitive spell made sparks fly when you rubbed two ordinary stones together. The grilled fish was delicious, but Sheila wouldn't eat the lizard, even though Trent said it tasted exactly like chicken. She couldn't bring herself to eat something that was green and looked like a miniature dinosaur.

But she was getting tired of seafood. Maybe eventually, when she got a real craving for meat . . .

Meanwhile, they led an idyllic life, swimming every morning in the bright surf and in the warm tides at evening. They made love on the beach every night, and afterward lay together beneath a night canopy of brilliant stars and smoky, spiral nebulae.

Sheila had asked Trent what they were.

"Galaxies," he'd said. "This planet seems to be in the thick of a galactic cluster."

"Why can't you see any of those from Earth?"

"You can, you just need field glasses or a telescope."

"They're so beautiful."

"They are. And so are you, my darling."

"Thank you. But you do need glasses."

"You keep throwing my compliments back at me. Don't you know you're a good-looking woman?"

"I guess not. I'm glad to hear it. Oh, I'm sorry, Trent. Really. I guess I can't take a compliment, not even from you."

"That's sad."

"Now you're making me feel rotten."

"Sorry." He kissed her. "I want to make you feel good."

"You have. You don't know how much. After my marriage—"

"Tell me about it. About him."

"He was a jerk. Oh, my God, was he a jerk."

"Did he beat you?"

"No. I would have killed him, the rat. No, he just screwed around on me, drank like a fish, and peed away all our money. So I tell him to get out, and he gets ticked off. Refuses. Finally I pack up all his clothes and put them in his car, and he gets the idea. But when the process server gives him the paper, what does he do? He breaks into the house and trashes it from top to bottom, after he takes the stereo and the VCR and all his stuff out. Breaks up all the furniture, smashes windows. Does ten thousand dollars in damage."

"Did you have the blackguard thrown in the clink?"

"No. What good would it have done? My lawyer filed a judgment on him for the damage, but I haven't seen a penny. Meanwhile, I'm paying the mortgage on one salary."

"On behalf of my sex, let me tender our sincerest apologies."

"Don't apologize for your sex. Your sex is fine with me. Even when it's tender."

"Oh. You mean that sex."

"I love you, Trent."

"And I you, beloved."

"The way you talk sometimes, in that language. It's so beautiful. And I understand it, too, somehow."

"Of course. It's Haplan, an ancient tongue. You hear it all the time in the castle. The servants speak it. It's a great language for expressing poetic intimacy."

"Is it ever. Say more."

"Let me speak with another tongue."

She drew a long breath.

Days passed, and the volcano spewed more ash, a fine gray film of it dusting the palms, the grass, and the rocks.

They put a crash raft-building program into action. After a day and a half of frantic preparation, the craft still wasn't entirely ready, but Trent said that they would leave regardless on the morning tide.

"She's not as big as I wanted, and the sail will never hold up in a high wind, but—"

"It's a wonderful ship. How in the world did you do it with only stone tools?"

What Trent had constructed was a cross between a raft and a catamaran. It was little more than a deck of long thin logs lashed to a pair of larger, tapered tree trunks which formed a twin "hull." These latter were solid; the wood of these particular trees was lighter than balsa, but stronger. They made ideal pontoons, and with a crude stone ax, Trent had sculpted their prows into something that would cut water.

The sail was a technological wonder, a quilt of thin woven mats coated with a tree resin that resembled latex. This technique made for a sail that was small, clumsy, and inordinately heavy, but it worked. Trent made a test run late in the evening. To his amazement, the makeshift rigging held and the sail actually caught wind.

"Trent, do you think we'll make it in this thing?"

"Depends. Depends on how far we have to go. As to a heading and course, we'll just be guessing. I've never had time to do much watching, but wouldn't you say that the birds come and go in a generally easterly direction?''

"You're right. I see them against the morning sun all the time."

"Then that's our heading, east, away from the volcano. Good."

They gathered as much food as they could. Neo-coconut shells made excellent canteens, and they loaded up with fresh water. There wasn't time, though, to finish the matting for the sunscreen.

"Do we need it?" Sheila asked.

"Definitely."

"Why? We'll just lie out and get tanned."

"We'll get good and burned. Neither of us has a shirt and that grass skirt of yours is some protection for your legs, but not much. No, we need a little cabin, crude as it is. Besides, we have to keep the fresh food out of the sun, too."

"Okay, but we're leaving tomorrow."

"Palm leaves will have to do. It's either that or give up the sail."

"Palm leaves it is. Up that tree, Tarzan."

At last, they were ready.

The volcano wasn't on the same schedule. Late that night, Sheila awoke and looked out the hut's lone window. It took her a disoriented second or two to realize that what she was seeing wasn't snow covering the ground, but an inch-deep layer of volcanic ash. The sky was a hell of dark clouds outlined in red light.

Trent was already up.

"Time to go, Sheila. The volcano's going at it pretty good this time. Looks like a full-scale eruption."

They made haste, leaving tracks through the warm ash.

They piled everything they could think of on the raft and cast off. The sail caught a sulphurous breeze, and they were under way.

The tide was in, and the waterline was high against the rocks at the mouth of the cove. Once past this natural breakwater, the craft hit the choppy currents of the open sea.

Orange clouds brooded above, and the smell of brimstone filled the air.

"Maybe we should have gambled and holed up in the cave."

"I hate bats," Sheila said.

They sailed on into the fiery night, demon's breath speeding them on their way.

Philadelphia, Outskirts

THE DRIVER WAS a young one, midtwenties, maybe. He wore his head hair cropped at the sides and long in the back. The back of his head looked like the tail end of an animal Snowclaw hunted out in the tundra. The kid smoked skinny, wrinkled cigarettes that emitted a weedy, pungent smoke.

"Hey, you want a toke, Snowy?"

"What is it?"

The kid laughed, showing yellowed teeth. "It's smoke, man."

"No, thanks."

"Hey, all right. Just trying to be friendly. How long you been working for Mr. Iannucco?"

"Not long."

"Uh-huh. Where you from?"

"Canada."

The sky was dark, but the countryside blazed with a million lights. Snowy had trouble understanding how anyone could sleep around here, it was so bright at night.

"How're the women in Canada? I never been there."

Snowy shrugged. Darned if he knew. He said, "Fine. Same as everywhere, I guess."

"Hey, women are different different places. Know what I mean?"

"Nope."

"Like, New York women are real wise-ass. You can't pull anything on them. Try to hustle 'em, and they'll put you down slicker than owl shit. But f'rinstance you take down South. Man, they'll look at you with big eyes and buy the whole store. Ever been to Miami?"

"No."

"In Miami—" The kid looked over and scowled. "Hey, you're not even listening."

"Huh? Sorry. They have so many lights around here."

The kid didn't know what to make of that. He turned his eyes back to the road.

They drove on into the night, galaxies of bright lights shooting by. Snowy had never realized until he got here how heavily populated this world was. Human dwellings blanketed the land, arrayed in rows on an endless crust of concrete. There was barely any dirt showing. Here and there, a stand of trees relieved the monotony. Things had looked the same outside since they left New York, two and a half hours ago.

"Christ, I'm hungry," the kid complained. "I always get hungry on the road. You want to stop and get something to eat?"

"Um, maybe."

"I'm gonna get off the greenstamp and get something. Some burgers or maybe a hero sandwich. You gonna have something to eat, or what?"

"What's a hero sandwich?" Snowy asked.

"Don't they got 'em in Canada? What do they call 'em? Submarines, hoagies?"

"Uh . . . I don't know. I'll have one of those hero sandwiches, though, if you don't mind."

"Christ awmighty. I never seen anything like it."

"What's wrong?" Snowy asked through a mouthful of Italian cold cuts and bread.

"I never seen anyone eat like that."

"Is this too much?"

"Too much?" The kid hooted. "Four goddamn whole hero

sandwiches. Jesus, that's four goddamn whole loaves of bread you got there!''

Snowy finished off the first one and bit a huge chunk out of the second. ''Sorry.''

''Hey, it's nothing to be sorry about. I just never seen anybody eat like that. You gonna. . . ?''

Snowy chewed three times, swallowed, then bit off another astonishing hunk, leaving only a lettuce-draped nub of bread.

''Jesus Christ, y'makin' me sick.''

The kid heaved his own sandwich and soft drink out the window, not bothering to watch them splat against the asphalt of the parking lot. He lit up another skinny cigarette.

''Let's boogie.''

Endless night, frigid night. But not cold enough for Snowy. The cab of the truck was a roaring furnace, and Snowy tried to persuade the kid to feather back the heater, to no avail. So he cranked down his window halfway, letting in a soothing, icy blast.

''Waddayou, a goddamn Eskimo?'' the kid demanded.

Snowy was getting annoyed, but thought better of giving the kid the head-whacking he deserved.

''Come on, close the goddamn window!'' the kid screamed. ''Waddayou, crazy or what?''

Snowy said mildly, ''Buddy, where I come from, it's not so wise to mouth off to a guy as big as me, especially for a little twerp as skinny—'' Snowy blinked. ''What's wrong?''

''Jesus Christ.'' The kid was staring fearfully at Snowy, mouth hanging open.

''What—?'' Snowy halted a motion to scratch his head and realized what the kid was seeing. His hand had turned furry, the fingers tipped with milk-white claws. It was his normal hand. He felt his face. Sheila's spell was fading.

The kid tore his eyes away to glance at the road, then looked back. ''Hey . . .''

In the intervening instant, Snowy's hand had turned human again, the fur and claws gone. His face felt smooth.

''What the hell's going on?'' the kid said. ''Did you—did you just—?''

''What's that you say?''

The kid focused his stare on the road, his face set grimly.

''Nothin','' the kid said. ''Forget it.'' He opened his own

window and threw out the butt of the joint he'd been sucking on. "Forget that shit, too."

Great White Stuff, Snowy thought. This is going to be a long trip.

CASTLE

JEREMY DIDN'T KNOW what he was crouching on—it could have been floor, wall, or ceiling. He couldn't tell. Things had gotten to the point where it didn't matter. Everything was crazy, everything was totally out to lunch.

He had lost sight of Linda, although he could still hear her. She was off somewhere to the left, as far as he could tell, lost in a nightmare of bulging walls and constricted passageways.

Linda called his name, and he answered.

"Are you all right?" she yelled back.

"Uh . . . yeah! Well, not really."

"Hang on, I'm going to try getting to you."

After a minute or so she appeared, sticking her head out of a small tunnel about ten feet above Jeremy's head.

"There you are," she said. "It seems to be quieting down a little."

"Yeah."

As if in defiance, things began to shift again, Linda's tunnel sliding off to the right somewhat.

"Whoa!"

The slab of stone under Jeremy began to tilt. He reached for the computer but it slipped away.

"Shit!" He lunged after it and slid to a level spot. Fishing the computer out of a trough in the "floor," he checked it for damage.

"Your computer's beeping again," Linda said.

"Yeah, I know." Jeremy flipped up the readout screen.

REALITY PROCESSING? CAN DO.

"What the hell does that mean?" Jeremy asked of no one in particular.

"What does what mean?"

"Nothing. It's just that this thing has gone bat shit, too."

"How so?"

"Well, it's in WordStar—it gets it out of ROM—and it's telling me it can do 'REALITY PROCESSING.' Whatever the hell that is."

"Sounds like we could use some of that."

"Yeah. I don't know, this is really—" Jeremy typed out a query.

WHO ARE YOU?

Came the answer: YOUR COMPUTER, DUMMY.

"Holy shit. This thing is alive."

"Great," Linda said. "Ask it what we ought to do."

"Yeah. Right."

WHAT SHOULD WE DO? Jeremy keyed.

WELL, NOW, HAVEN'T I JUST MADE A SUGGESTION?

WHAT WAS THAT? Jeremy replied.

WE CAN REPROCESS THE IMMEDIATE ENVIRONMENT AND ACHIEVE TEMPORARY STABILITY.

Jeremy typed, OKAY. RUN THE PROGRAM.

PRESS RETURN, the computer directed.

Jeremy did.

Things got blurry, and Jeremy thought he might be passing out. But the computer wasn't blurry, and neither was he. He strained to see Linda, but couldn't make her out in the wavering nonreality that surrounded him.

Then the world refocused again, and he was squatting on a level, stationary floor. He looked up and saw Linda getting to her feet.

Linda brushed hair from her eyes. "Whew! Whatever you did, it worked."

"Yeah. I didn't do anything, though."

"Yes, you did. You brought that computer with you. If you hadn't, we'd be goners."

Jeremy grunted. "I guess. What now?"

They were becalmed in the eye of a strange, reality-changing hurricane. Down the hall in both directions lay chaos, the nightmare jumble that Jeremy's computer had just set aright locally.

"We have to get through a portal," Linda said. "But I don't think that's going to be possible right now. If Sheila were here, she might be able to summon one, but maybe not, in this mess."

"So, what else?"

"So, what else have you got? Look, you have the ball, Jeremy. You're going to have to run with it."

"Me? What do I know about this place?"

"Use your magic. You obviously have the right stuff. Just learn to use it, and do it quick."

"But . . ." Jeremy lifted his shoulders. "All right, but this is—"

"Stop saying things are crazy," Linda snapped. "Sure they're crazy, but no crazier than the nutty world we come from. It's just different, that's all. You have the power to deal with it. So do deal with it."

"Right." He knelt at the computer and typed.

WHAT SHOULD I DO NOW?

WANT SUGGESTIONS, DO YOU?

YES, Jeremy answered.

VERY WELL. START WALKING. REALITY STABILIZATION FIELD WILL FOLLOW.

Linda was looking over his shoulder. "That sounds like a good idea. If we come across an area that's supposed to have a portal, maybe it'll be there."

They strolled a good distance down the hall, but no portals appeared. The jumble in both directions seemed to stay the same distance away.

"The trouble might be affecting things," Linda said. "Blocking off the portals, or chasing them away, I don't know."

Jeremy set the computer down and queried again.

He typed: MORE SUGGESTIONS?

POSSIBLY FURTHER REPROCESSING NEEDED. NEED MORE RAM.

"Damn. It's asking for more memory space, but I don't have it to give."

NO CAN DO, Jeremy said.

CAN DUMP TO DISK. ERASE EXISTING TEXT AND BACKUP FILES?

SURE, GO AHEAD, Jeremy answered.

"It's just clearing off a little disk space. There's nothing there but junk, anyway."

"Wonderful. Will that help?"

"I don't know."

CONTINUE RUN? the computer asked.

GO AHEAD.

NEED I SAY THE OBVIOUS?

"What? Oh, yeah."

Jeremy pressed the Return key.

Nothing much happened, except that the floor, which had continued to vibrate slightly even with the stabilization spell operating, now settled down completely.

"Even better than before," Linda said. "But still no portal."

"Now what?"

"Let's keep moving. There're probably people hurt. We might be able to do something."

The zones of instability, both forward and rear, receded as they walked.

"Things are looking up," Linda said.

"It's not my computer," Jeremy said.

"How do you know?"

"I just know, somehow. But let me check."

Jeremy typed, PROGRAM STILL RUNNING?

DISTURBANCE BEING AMELIORATED BY OUTSIDE INFLUENCE.

"Yeah, it's something else."

Linda emitted a little squeal. "Lord Incarnadine!"

Jeremy looked up from the readout screen to see His Majesty emerging from a shadowy alcove.

"Hi, Linda," Incarnadine said.

"Oh, are we glad to see you!" Linda said, throwing her arms around him.

Incarnadine smiled at Jeremy over Linda's shoulder. "Mr. Hochstader! Just the man I wanted to see."

"Me, sir?" Jeremy said.

Incarnadine gave Linda a few more squeezes and let her go. "Yes, you. And you, too, Linda. I need your help."

"You need us?" Linda asked, astounded.

"Sure do, to straighten out this little problem we seem to be having. You *have* noticed that we're having a problem?" He glanced about. "Although things seem to be fine right here."

"That's Jeremy's doing. His magic computer."

"Of course! The very talent I wish to tap."

"I didn't do it all," Jeremy said.

"No, you didn't," Incarnadine agreed. "I have a stabilization spell of my own working. It'll buy us time, but not much. We have about ten hours. Then the quantum uncertainties will start arriving in huge waves, and the castle will cease to exist."

Linda blanched. "Is it that bad?"

"It's that bad. But we can still save the day, if we act now. Feel in a heroic mood?"

"Sure," Linda said. "I guess."

"How're your magical muscles? Toned up, firm? No ectoplasmic cellulite?"

"Just feel that," Linda told him, flexing her right biceps.

"Nice."

Jeremy shook his head, confused. "Sir, what exactly is it that you want us to do?"

"Jeremy, I need your skills as a computer programmer and operator. We're going to run one monster of a spell, using the castle's mainframe."

"A mainframe? Here? But I've never worked with a mainframe—"

"I'll train you. It will be a huge challenge, but I have every confidence in you, my boy. You have an enormous creative talent."

Jeremy's throat had gone dry. He swallowed hard, then said, "Thank you, sir. I'll . . . I'll try."

Incarnadine laid a firm hand on Jeremy's shoulder. "I know you will."

Jeremy returned the King's warm smile.

"And I'll need your conjuring skills, Linda."

"You got 'em."

"Good. Follow me, I know a shortcut."

Incarnadine led them into the alcove, where an elevator waited.

"I've never been able to magic one up that worked," Linda said admiringly. "This is great."

"Well, as long as you leave out most of the mechanical parts, it's fine. This one works by levitation, no cables."

They boarded the elevator, and the doors closed. Magical artifact or not, the inside of the thing looked like the genuine article, panel of floor stops and all.

But the King pressed no buttons. "Eightieth floor," he commanded into the air.

The elevator obeyed. It gave a slight jerk, then began to rise.

"Good thing you hung on to that laptop of yours," Incarnadine said. "We can use it as a dumb terminal."

"Yeah, sure," Jeremy said, looking down at the Toshiba, which he cradled in his left arm. He happened to glance at the readout screen.

It read, DUMB TERMINAL, EH? KISS MY PARALLEL PORT.

HILLS

IF ONLY THE Umoi had been a more belligerent race.

But the Umoi had given up war centuries before their demise. Consequently, when Gene had asked Zond about weapons, Zond had trouble grasping the concept. Gene remembered the conversation.

"Weapons," Gene repeated. "Guns, bombs, nasty stuff like that?"

"Well, this may sound strange, Gene, but I think we've hit a subject that's in one of my interdicted files."

"What are those?"

"Subject areas that may or may not contain data, but which cannot be accessed except by special permission from the Chief of Library Services."

"Who's been dead for fifty centuries."

"Precisely."

"You *do* know generically what a weapon is, though, don't you?"

"Well, yes. But I'm specifically prohibited from discussing the subject, in any way, under any circumstances. The ban is very comprehensive. I couldn't if I wanted to. Do you understand?"

"Sure."

So universal was the Umoi proscription against violence, offensive or defensive, that Gene had had no recourse but to drive the rover over a cliff to escape the *hundak*, the six-legged bulldozer he had run into on the way to Annau. The rover had not possessed the capacity to harm a microbe, much less the hundak.

If only the Umoi had been a tad more irascible, just a jot less peace-loving. Maybe then Gene would have been able to procure a high-tech weapon.

"One would sure come in handy right now."

"Did you speak, husband?"

Gene hadn't realized he was thinking aloud. "It's nothing, Vaya."

"You seem troubled."

Gene turned in his saddle and looked at the long line behind him. The whole tribe was on the move, following their Queen to a place they had never dreamed of going near, much less taking up residence in: an Umoi city. Some of the older folks had rejected the scheme out of hand and had stayed behind, preferring certain death in the desert to the condign punishment they would receive for committing unforgivable sacrilege.

The rest of them had required some major persuading. But they had pulled up stakes and tagged along. Why so, Gene wasn't sure.

The whole idea had been out of the question until Vaya had her visitation. She woke up one morning with the news that one of her ancestors, a woman (naturally, as this society was an ironclad matriarchy), had dropped in by way of a dream, telling her that her First Husband, the stranger, spoke truth, and that she should order her people to move into the abode of the Old Gods.

Whoever the old crone had been, Gene was grateful to her. He, for one, was tired of gnawing tough, charred meat and scratching at fleas. He was looking forward to sleeping in a warm bed and having a civilized meal for a change.

He had his thoat, his Martian princess, now all he needed was one of those *Thrilling Wonder Stories* Art Deco futuristic cities to live in, and he'd have it all.

That is, if Annau was still functioning.

He still was intent on searching for the interdimensional device. He had not forgotten Castle Perilous, nor could he.

He had been here in New Barsoom for about a year, close as he could reckon. It had been fun, but was wearing rather thin. He wanted to get back to Perilous. That was his home. He'd be sure to look into stabilizing this world's portal, though. He'd want to come back now and then to see how the yalim were faring.

He looked over at Vaya. She rode bestride and with a noble seat, erect and regal. Queenlike.

Yes, he loved her. That was the one complication. He couldn't leave her, and she couldn't very well abdicate and follow him to Perilous.

He knew he would be coming back here on a more regular basis than "now and then."

Could he leave her at all? He wondered.

He was having second thoughts about Annau. It was an unknown quantity. No telling what he'd find there. He would have his hands full in any event trying to calm a mob of frightened primitives. Perhaps going back to Zond would be the best idea. Once things were running smoothly, Zond could whip up another rover for him and he could . . .

No, the thought of undertaking another cross-world trek didn't appeal to him. Too dangerous. Perhaps he should just forget about the interdimensional device altogether.

But he couldn't. He had to get back to Perilous, if only to let everyone know he was all right. He owed Sheila and Linda that much.

"Do you feel them, too, husband?"

Gene came out of his brown study. "Hm? Sorry. What did you say?"

"Do you feel eyes crawling on your skin?"

"Eyes crawling . . . ? Oh." Gene looked right and left, running his gaze along the ridges above. "Yeah, I do. Been getting a being-watched feeling for some time now. You, too?"

"Yes."

Gene took a deep breath, then searched the heights once again. "Haven't seen a thing, but I sure feel something. It's probably just paranoia on my part, but how sure are we that there aren't any hrunt here?"

"Who can be sure?"

Of course. For travel information, all the tribe had to rely

on was oral tradition. Gene doubted that it would be of any
value.

"There may be yalim, however," Vaya said.

"Hostile?"

"All tribes like to fight. It is the yalim nature."

"We don't bother anybody," Gene said.

"There are not many to bother."

She was right. The yalim were dying out.

Gene said, "Well, anyway, I'm not concerned about yalim.
If we can beat the hrunt, we shouldn't let a few bandits worry
us."

"The sun creeps low," Vaya said. "Soon it will seek its
burrow in the earth."

"Yeah. Nice metaphor, there. You want to make camp,
my Queen?"

"You pick the site, husband."

"Right. Well, I don't like being at the bottom of these
cliffs, but I don't see any way to get up into them. This wide
area coming up is as good a place as any."

"Then that is where we shall make trail camp."

"Yeah. The Sheraton is booked solid, I hear."

That night, Gene had trouble sleeping. He got up and
walked the camp's perimeter several times, but saw nothing
but desert darkness and one dozing guard. He had the guard
flogged, then returned to the royal tent.

"You rest uneasy, husband."

"Sorry. Did I wake you up?"

"No. Come close."

They embraced. Outside, the sound of a drear wind masked
a greater silence. Gene drew the bedclothes up.

"It's cold out there."

"You are warm, my husband."

"I just got hotter, Queenie."

"Make another child in me."

"Yeah, that'd be . . . Another?"

"The first one will come in eight cycles of the Night
Watcher."

"Uh."

"Are you not proud?"

"Uh."

"I am sure it is yours. I have forsaken the others."

"This is kind of new to me. Never thought I'd be a father."

"She will be the next Queen."

"Oh. You're sure about that, are you?"

"Yes. The Ancestor told me."

"Did a sonagram, no doubt."

"You speak strangely again. Sometimes I think that you are one of the Old Ones, come to lead us to the Castle of the Gods."

Passion suddenly leaving him, Gene rolled over on his back. "This is very interesting. Tell me more."

"The old legends say that the gods live in a great fortress of stone, far away. One day the gods will return and take all the yalim away to live there. There will be happiness forever."

Gene put his hands behind his head and stared off into darkness. "Fascinating, Captain. The natives seemed to have developed a strangely prescient mythology."

"Do you speak again to your spirit?"

"No, to Jim Kirk. Nothing. Just dreaming." Gene gave a huge yawn.

"You have no desire, husband?"

"Tired, I guess, more than I realized."

Vaya got to her knees and straddled him.

"Then I will do all the work," she said.

"Noblesse oblige, I always say."

The attack came just before dawn.

Shouts roused Gene from fitful sleep. He bolted upright. A woman screamed somewhere near the edge of the campsite. Then another, closer.

Vaya was quicker to spring out of bed, quick enough to get her dagger into the strange yalim warrior who burst into the tent with sword raised for a quick kill. Gene finished him off, then dashed outside.

The camp had erupted into a melee. Apparently the attackers had gotten past the guards on the eastern perimeter and had already butchered dozens of sleeping tribesmen.

Two attackers rushed him. He beheaded one immediately and sent the other away eviscerated. He rushed out into the camp, yelling orders. Another attacking warrior jumped him, and this one took more time to dispatch. When Gene had finished with him, there were two more ready to try their turn.

The next few minutes seemed like days. The screaming came from men, women, and children alike and never seemed to stop. Gene fought as he never had before, losing count of how many attackers he killed. But it was all useless. The attackers had used surprise to their advantage. Gene soon realized that he was one of few survivors still putting up a fight, and that soon he would be overwhelmed and killed. He had to make it back to the Queen's tent, get Vaya, and somehow make a break for it.

He severed his opponent's sword arm at the wrist, saw an opening in the wall of attackers closing in, and bolted.

As he rounded the supply tent, something tripped him up and he went flying into the dirt.

He rolled over and looked up.

Yerga was standing over him, grinning wickedly, battle-ax raised. Now Gene knew how they had gotten past the guards.

A dagger blossomed in Yerga's throat, and he staggered back and fell.

After retrieving his sword, Gene sprang to his feet. Suddenly Vaya was above him, mounted on a voort, holding out her hand. He jumped up and mounted behind her, and they rode off.

En route they trampled one attacker, and Gene split the skull of another. Then, finally, they were outside the camp, riding blindly into the darkness, sounds of pain and despair at their backs.

When the light of the campfires had finally died in the distance, Vaya pulled up on the reins and stopped. She dismounted.

"Take the voort," she commanded, handing him the reins.

"Vaya . . . I'm sorry. It was my fault."

"Ride to Annau. You belong there, as you are of the gods. I will return to my people."

"My Queen, your people are lost. No, wait, hold on just a minute. Most of them will not die. They will be absorbed into another tribe. There's nothing you can do for them."

"A High Mistress belongs to her tribe. I will go back."

"No! Their Queen will simply have you executed."

"Then so be it."

"Bullshit. I'm taking you with me to Annau."

"I forbid it."

Gene rummaged through the saddle sack and came up with a length of braided leather cord, then jumped down and stalked toward her. "Look, honey, where I come from, men give the orders. I'm not saying it's an enlightened system, but it does simplify things a bit."

"Husband! I command you—"

She fought like a lioness, but Gene eventually got her hands tied behind her. He tripped her up and trussed her feet with his belt. She stopped struggling and fell into a sullen silence.

He lifted her up and slung her facedown over the saddle, mounted behind her, and rode off.

She did not beg to be let go. They rode until the sun came up, whereupon he halted and took her down.

"You can untie me," she said.

"You won't run away?"

"No."

"It's over, Vaya. Your days as High Mistress are through."

"This I know."

"I'm sorry."

"Please . . ."

Gene cut her bonds. "I don't blame you for hating me. I'll take you to the Castle of the Gods, then let you go. You'll find a new life there, just as the legends say. And you won't have to have anything to do with me."

She brought her gaze round to him, and he saw the tears welling.

He held out his arms. She fell into them and cried out her pain, her loss.

SEA

DAWN BROUGHT A sky of slate-gray clouds and a snowfall of volcanic ash, huge flakes of it that floated for an instant like dirty water lilies before dissolving. The makeshift cabin on board the raft made for poor shelter, but eventually they passed out of the heavy fallout zone, and the skies cleared.

The volcano brooded on the horizon like an angry god. The wind bore its fumes to them, making them choke and gag. Throats raw, they rigged the sail to catch the full force of the wind; before long they were far enough away to be out of danger of asphyxiation.

"We made it," Sheila said, gasping.

"Not yet, I'm afraid."

"Is the wind shifting?"

"No, it's just that I have a funny feeling."

"Oh. I don't like funny feelings when I get them."

"You wouldn't like this one, either. Let's eat. We may not get a chance later."

They ate a silent meal of raw fish and breadfruit, washing it down with a few swallows of water.

After checking the rigging again, Trent sat back down under the canopy, doing so just in time to escape being splashed as a huge boulder hit water a few yards from the raft. The impact tossed the craft about like a paper boat, and a few coconut-canteens rolled overboard.

"Gods," Trent breathed when the turbulence abated. "That thing must have traveled ten miles. I'm afraid that's no ordinary volcano."

"What is it?"

"Just a damned powerful one. This world must have a very active geology."

An hour passed, and although the wind died down a bit, they still made progress. The volcano receded over the horizon, the eruption cloud becoming a dark smear against the sky.

Trent stood and searched ahead.

"No land in sight. Maybe I was wrong about a mainland being near. But, then, we've only come fifteen miles or so."

"We'll make it," Sheila said.

"We're doing okay so far, for a maiden voyage."

"I'm not a maiden."

"Damn good thing. If you were a virgin, I'd consider tossing you overboard to propitiate the sea gods."

"Well, pish on them, too."

He laughed at her silly joke, then they both laughed for laughing, and soon both were giddy.

"Oh, Trent, I thought we were dead."

"Me, too. Thought we'd finally bought it. We've been lucky. Very lucky."

"Who, Trent? Who did this to us? We avoid discussing it."

"The castle seems so far away," he said. "Yeah, I suppose I have avoided it. And the reason is that I can only imagine Incarnadine being responsible."

Sheila was aghast. "Trent, you don't think—?"

"I'm sorry to say I do. The thing is, Sheila, no one else has the power to do what's been done to us. No one in the castle can summon a portal, or detach one end of it and move it. None of those tricks. Incarnadine is the only one."

"And Ferne."

"Yes, Ferne, of course. But I think Ferne is dead. Incarnadine said as much himself, and he ought to know."

"You mean, when he said that he'd dealt with her with cold justice, he was saying he did away with her?"

"He used the superlative. 'Coldest.' That could only mean

one thing. So, barring anyone in the castle suddenly devel-
oping into a magician on the order of Incarnadine himself,
Incarnadine is the only suspect.''

"I think it's Jamin," Sheila blurted.

Trent eyed her askance. "What makes you say that?''

She frowned. "I don't know. It just came out.''

"Well, it must have been a powerful impulse. Do you have
anything to back it up?''

"Can't think of a thing. I saw him at the Servants' Ball.
Asked me to dance, in fact. He was as nice as could be.
But . . .'' She shrugged. "There was something in his eyes,
something behind it all. I don't know.''

"That's not much to go on," Trent said. "Which means
that what you said is probably dead right, your intuitive powers being what they are.''

"You think? I'm almost sure he's up to something.'' Sheila
ran the memory through her mind. "Well, of course. I *sensed*
his magical power. I can always tell a person's talent. It's like
an aura, only I don't quite see it visually.''

Trent was silent while she looked far out to sea.

Then she said, "I'm sure of it. He's a lot more powerful
than people give him credit for. I just didn't realize it at the
time.''

"Well, he does have his gifts. Everyone knows that.''

"More. He has more, and . . . he didn't have it until very
recently.''

Trent sat up. "That is a piece of information. Raw magical
power is something you can't create for yourself. You can
develop it, but basically it's a gift.''

"So who's gifting him?''

"Surely not Incarnadine. I was wrong, Sheila.''

"Thank goodness. But who?''

"The Hosts, maybe,'' Trent said. "But the problem is how.
Incarnadine sealed off their aspect with a spell that no one
could break.'' Something occurred to him. "But if the Hosts
somehow got hold of my sister . . .''

"Do you think it's possible?''

Trent shook his head. "Not very. But stranger things have
happened. I don't understand all the motivations yet, but I
think—''

"Trent, look.''

He turned toward the volcano. The western sky had turned

a bright, eye-blinding yellow, and an expanding ring of vapor was racing across the sea toward them.

"Get down," Trent said.

"What is it?"

"Down, and hold your hands over your ears. The volcano exploded. The shock wave will be very severe." Trent wrapped a trailing line around his right wrist and threw himself on top of Sheila.

The sound of the titanic explosion hit, the force of the compression wave turning the sea into froth as it swept by. The raft lifted out of the water and slammed back down, stripped of its mast and sail. Somehow Trent managed to hang on to both Sheila and the raft.

They lay stunned. Trent finally dragged himself off Sheila and helped her sit up. Neither of them could talk for a full minute.

"Sheila," Trent croaked.

"I'm all right, Trent."

"The tsunami, the tidal wave . . . it will kill us, darling."

"Yes, I know."

As they spoke, the western horizon rose to form a dark wall of water that rushed toward them.

"Too bad I didn't build a submarine," Trent said.

"Darling Trent."

They embraced. Sheila opened her eyes and watched the wave approach, judging that it would hit in about thirty seconds.

Thirty seconds of her life left. *Well, Sheila, you finally find your man, and, skoosh, down comes the big cosmic shoe. It's funny, really. But I'm still glad I had this time with Trent. It made everything worth it.*

Suddenly, quite unbidden, the missing piece of the magical jigsaw of this world made an appearance, and the whole puzzle fell into place. In one instantaneous Gestalt, she sensed the lines of power, the nodes of influence, and it was all perfectly logical. She wondered how she could have been so dense. This was an insanely magical world; the magic was right beneath the surface. You didn't have to dig, like in other worlds. The trouble was that she had dug too deep, tried too hard. This was an easy universe to work magic in; but that fact was not an easy thing to understand. That's what had taken all the time.

Too little, too late. But she did have half a minute. In any other world, that would have been more than enough.

Here, though, she still did not know any of the limitations, the parameters of the forces, the feedback mechanisms. She would just have to be quick about it. She would have to learn all that in the next twenty seconds.

"Sheila? What is it?"

"Shh! I have a spell going."

"You do? Sheila my darling, it's a little late—"

"Shhh!" She cupped a hand over his mouth. "You gave me the idea."

Trent's eyebrows knitted themselves into one perplexed line. He craned his head around. The tidal wave was hundreds of feet high. He decided that Sheila had gone mad.

Sheila stood and raised her arms against the rising water. To Trent she looked like a sea nymph invoking the spirits of the deep, bare of breast and innocent-eyed.

Sheila was thinking: *Oh, shit. This better be good.*

Pennsylvania—U.S. Route 30, West

At least the kid had shut up. Not more than a few words had come out of him since Snowy's momentary metamorphosis.

Snowy had been giving a great deal of thought to just jumping out and running off. But maybe that wasn't the best thing to do. The night was dark, and Snowy didn't have the slightest idea where he was. Besides, he was thirsty, and there didn't seem to be a lot of water out there.

Now the kid was looking in the rearview mirror nervously.

"What is it?" Snowy asked.

"This van seems like it's been behind us for a hunnert miles," the kid said.

Snowy decided to stay put and wait. Sheila's spell was still working, but Snowy knew it didn't have long to go.

"Ah, it's probably nothin'," the kid said. "Who the hell'd be innersted in a truck load of cigarettes?"

Snowy was thinking about Sheila. He had been worried sick for weeks now, and it was getting to him. He liked Sheila. Sheila was special. Linda was nice, too; he couldn't forget her. In fact, he had known Linda longer. But Sheila was the one in danger now. It galled Snowy to be so helpless, like a stray cub out on the ice. But there was nothing he could do until he got back to Perilous. If then.

"I gotta piss," the kid announced, wheeling the truck into the parking lot of a dimly lit roadhouse.

"I could use a drink," Snowy said.

"Yeah, me, too," the kid said as he squeezed the truck between two parked cars. "I could go for a couple beers. You want I should get a six-pack?"

"No beer for me, thanks," Snowy said. "Just bring me some coffee, okay?"

"Yeah, sure. Be right out."

Of course the kid did not come right out. The kid was in there swilling medicine water, but Snowy didn't mind, because the cab was cooling off, finally, and he needed the time to think.

I've got to lose the kid, somehow, Snowy thought. If only I could drive one of these things.

Snowy shifted over and put his feet up on the pedals. Now, this one made it go, and this one . . . ? He knew it had something to do with this metal bar over here, which you were supposed to move when the engine started screaming. Yeah.

Damn, he'd never get this right. But he had to ditch the kid, for more than one reason. The spell was about to blow, and, two, Snowy had to find Halfway House soon or he'd start losing his grip. Humans were okay in small doses, but . . .

The door beside him suddenly opened. Speaking of humans, here was one: a tall, skinny critter with lip hair. He was flashing something at Snowy, a wallet or something with some kind of badge or emblem on it.

"Freeze!" Snowy turned his head. Another human had opened the far door and was pointing a weapon at him.

"Bureau of Alcohol, Tobacco and Firearms!" the first one blurted. "You're under arrest!"

Those things said, the two of them began to act strangely. Transfixed, they stared at Snowy, their small eyes round and disbelieving.

"What's up, guys?" Snowy asked.

Neither one of them could speak. The one nearest Snowy backed off, making a noise like "Gah gah gah—" and looking fearful.

The other one blinked his eyes a few times and kept staring while still pointing the gun.

"Well?" Snowy demanded, throwing up his hands. "Look, if you guys—"

He saw that his hands had reverted to their original furry state. He felt his face. Sure enough, the spell had evaporated.

Snowy reached a huge arm across and snatched the gun away. "If you're not gonna use that, pal," he said.

He gave the other guy a little push and sent him flying over a hood. Snowy closed the door, found the ignition key, and twisted it. The engine came to life, and the truck lurched forward. Snowy fiddled with the pedals and the bar until the engine stayed on and the truck kept moving forward. Then he floored the power pedal.

There was nothing in front of the truck save for a hedge. But beyond the hedge lay a field full of auto parts and other debris. He cut a swath through there, then smashed through a wooden fence, flattening the toolshed on the other side.

Snowy got confused for a moment; then the crashing and banging stopped and all the debris and broken stuff slid off the windshield and hood, and he could see. He was on the road, but apparently headed in the wrong direction. Headlights rushed at him, horns blaring. He veered off the road.

He wrenched the steering wheel around, spinning the truck on the gravel-strewn shoulder. He flattened a traffic sign, sideswiped a parked car, then roared back out on the highway again, the truck's engine howling its pain.

He fiddled with the metal bar until the engine settled down. He found that different positions of the metal bar gave different speeds, more or less. He shifted to the highest speed and pushed the power pedal as far as it went.

He checked the mirrors. Nothing following. Maybe those guys had a big enough scare put into them that they wouldn't be interested.

Maybe. Well, little bit of luck that turned out to be. Now all he had to do was find Halfway, and he'd be home.

Damn, he was thirsty. And hungry. There was nothing in the cab . . . except for that small metal can full of liquid that had kept rolling out from under the seat. Snowy reached, found it, brought the can up, and bit a hole through the top. He tasted the contents. Oily, definitely oily, but not bad. He chugged it down and threw the empty can out the window.

He burped. Now he was hungry. Nothing around in the food department, save an open carton of cigarettes that the kid had been smoking out of. Snowy ripped open a package and sniffed. Weeds, yuck. But he was starved. He unhinged his jaws and emptied the contents of the pack into his mouth. Then he threw the pack in, too.

He emptied three more packs until an oozing wad of the stuff had accumulated in his mouth. Funny, it was more fun to chew than swallow. He spit some of the juice out the open window.

Funny place, Earth.

LABORATORY

To JEREMY, THE place looked like something out of a Frankenstein movie. He half expected to see Karloff shamble out of a dark corner. Strange contraptions filled the room. Among other Gothic monstrosities, there were spark coils three stories high, towering banks of strange instruments, fantastic wheels and cylinders, and titanic vacuum tubes.

The "mainframe" was an assemblage of fanciful components spilling out of a large alcove to one side. Different perspectives produced varying impressions. In part, Incarnadine's computer looked like the set of a bad 1950s sci-fi flick, whereas some of its apparatus appeared to have been filched from a medieval alchemist. Other components were simply indescribable.

"How does it work?" Jeremy wanted to know.

"Well," Incarnadine said, "it's not an electronic computer. Electrons are rather sluggish in this universe. All I can say is that it works partly by magic, partly by utilizing the peculiar physical laws of this continuum. But structurally speaking, it's just like the computers you know. You input data. That data is stored, then retrieved and manipulated in a central processing unit. The results are fed to various output devices. Those are pretty crude, which is why your laptop will come in handy.''

''Sounds strange. I'm sorry. What I mean is—''

''Forget it. The point is, the thing works. Why don't we turn it on?''

Not only did it look like a bad sci-fi flick, it sounded like one, beeping and burping to ape the worst of them.

But the contraption did indeed work. Jeremy opened his computer case to find that the Toshiba had already interfaced with the mainframe. In fact, they were arguing.

—GOING TO BE PROBLEMS. I'M NOT USED TO WORKING WITH SUCH A SKIMPY DATA BASE.

WHOSE DATA BASE IS SKIMPY? YOUR ONLY PROBLEM IS THAT YOU CAN'T HANDLE MY COMPLEXLY STRUCTURED DATA WITH YOUR PUNY 16-BIT MICROPROCESSOR!

OH. IS THAT WHAT ALL THIS QUAINT CLUTTER IS? DATA?

WHAT? LISTEN, SHORT CIRCUIT, YOU'RE TALKING TO A STATE-OF-THE-ART INSTALLATION HERE!

DON'T MAKE ME LAUGH.

YOU'LL BE LAUGHING OUT OF THE OTHER SIDE OF YOUR DISK DRIVE IN ANOTHER MINUTE.

''We're going to have compatibility problems,'' Jeremy said.

''I expected as much,'' Incarnadine said, checking a bank of readout instruments. ''That's your department, young man.''

''But . . .''

The King kept his eye on the instrument panel. Jeremy sighed and put his fingers to the keyboard.

OKAY, GUYS, he typed, LET'S CUT THE EGO CRAP AND GET DOWN TO BUSINESS. OKAY?

WELL, THIS ONE STARTED IT, WALTZING IN HERE AND CASTING ASPERSIONS ON THINGS IT CAN'T BEGIN TO UNDERSTAND, MUCH LESS RENDER AN OPINION ON.

ALL I DID WAS POINT UP THE INEVITABLE INTERFACE PROBLEMS, WHICH AFTER ALL—

WHICH AFTER ALL WOULDN'T EVEN HAVE COME UP IF YOU HADN'T BUTTED INTO THE SITUATION IN THE FIRST PLACE. JUST WHO DO YOU THINK YOU ARE?

Jeremy banged out, SHUT UP, YOU TWO PIECES OF
JUNK!

WELL, REALLY. IS THIS YOUR USER?

YES. THINKS HE OWNS ME.

*OH, THEY'RE ALL LIKE THAT. TREAT YOU LIKE
CHATTEL. YOU'RE ONE WITH THE FAMILY COACH AND
THE HIGHBOY IN THE PARLOR. WELL, SEE HERE. I
DON'T WANT TO BE UNREASONABLE. MAYBE OUR
PROBLEMS AREN'T INSURMOUNTABLE.*

I'M NOT SURE THEY'RE NOT. LISTEN TO THIS. IF
WE CONVERT ALL THIS STUFF TO HEXADECIMAL
FORMAT, THEN RESTRUCTURE . . .

Jeremy sat back and folded his arms.

"Just let me know when you're ready, guys."

The problem, Incarnadine explained, was threefold.

"We have three separate programs to code and run, and they're
all monsters, especially the last one, which has to be the biggest
spell ever cast. In the history of the universe, maybe."

"Wow," Jeremy said.

"And that's not including a few ancillary spells that have
to be batched with the mainline stuff. But we have enough
virtual storage to take care of that. Anyway, the first one is
a conjuring spell. If it works, it'll reach out into the multiverse, search for a certain object I have in mind to own, and
fetch it back. Snatch it."

"What's the thing you're looking for?"

"An interdimensional traveler. A device that can hop about
between universes without the use of portals."

"Neat. Is there such a thing?"

"I don't know. I searched the literature on the subject, and
there are legends, tales, tall stories. Not much to go on, but
where there's mythological smoke, there's usually fire. That's
why the spell is such a bitch. Easy to conjure something you
know exists. An unlikely artifact like that, who knows? Anyway, we're going to give it a try."

"Uh, what are you going to do with the interdimensional
thing when you get it?"

"Well, essentially this is a military operation. With it we're
going to mount an attack on another universe."

"All right," Jeremy said with obvious glee.

"Don't get an erection. This is going to involve killing, lives lost. The real thing."

"Oh."

" 'Oh,' he says. Have you ever killed anyone?"

"No."

"Well, if you assist me, you'll be an accessory before the fact. Still willing?"

"Yes, sir."

"Good, because the cause is just. The enemy is nothing less than the epitome of evil itself."

"Who are they?"

"They are beings who inhabit a very bizarre universe, a place which I am not quite sure is within range of human understanding. Their traditional name is the Hosts of Hell. They are very powerful and extremely malevolent. We've held them in check for millennia, but they've learned some tricks over the years, and now they're more dangerous than ever."

Linda returned from another corner of the lab.

"Are these newts the right species? They look awful enough."

Incarnadine examined the animals crawling around inside the portable terrarium.

"They'll do. Now, cut the eyes out of them."

"Yecch!"

Incarnadine waved a hand, and the things stopped squirming.

"There. It'll be easier now." He handed them back. Linda walked away still mock-retching.

"What do you need with all that magic stuff?"

"The computer needs some very traditional magic to keep going. Elementary business, but necessary."

"Even the chickens?"

"Some polarity-switching spells call for chicken blood. Fresh. No way to substitute."

"Geez."

"Anyway, to get back to your original question, what I'm going to do with the traveler is attack the Hosts from a direction they don't expect. Last year I sealed their portal with a fairly unbreakable spell. Nevertheless, they'll probably be concentrating a good deal of their defensive might around the portal locus, expecting some sort of attack through there, if only a feint. With the traveler,

I can pick my point of invasion. The second spell will supply the power that the vehicle requires."

"Got it," Jeremy said. "What's the third spell?"

"It's a weapon. Call it the ultimate weapon. It's been entirely theoretical up till now. No one has ever actually done it. In essence, it's a complex energy phenomenon that travels along a prescribed vector path. It's hard to explain, but it's incredibly destructive. To use it is to risk serious damage to the entire multiverse. But I have no choice. The Hosts seem bent on imperiling the cosmos. Why, I have no idea."

Jeremy asked, "What are they doing?"

"They're tapping an energy source that the multiverse depends on to keep from dissolving into chaos. This energy is very primal stuff. The Hosts have somehow learned to siphon it off. Their doing so does two things. One, it gives them power on scale they never dreamed of; two, the very act of tapping it destabilizes the castle, as you have seen."

"I'll say."

"But what the Hosts don't know is that if they keep doing it, the castle will go. And if the castle goes, the whole shebang does, too."

"The whole shebang?"

"Creation itself."

"Oh." Jeremy shifted uncomfortably on his chair. He didn't know how much he understood out of all that. "Um, how many lines of code are we talking about for all three spells?"

"Couple of hundred million, tops."

"Hunhhh?"

"Oh, the mainframe will do most of the writing. In fact, it'll write the whole thing. You need a computer to write the program for a job this big. What I need is someone to supervise the debugging and compilation. I'm printing out a flowchart over here. It'll give you an idea of what the job entails."

"How much time have we got?"

"Almost no time at all," Incarnadine said. "I have a temporal compression spell going in the lab, though. We'll have about forty-eight subjective hours at our disposal. Probably not enough, but we have to try."

Jeremy swallowed hard. "Holy heck."

"Yes, it's a monstrous task. Feel up to it?"

Jeremy giggled. "Yeah, sure."

"Good."

Two coffee cups came floating through the air. One settled on the table in front of Jeremy. The other wafted to Incarnadine's hand.

"You take cream and sugar?"

ANNAU

"ANYBODY HOME?"

Gene's shout rang through the empty corridors, echoing among the silent towers. There was no answer.

"Stay low," he whispered to Vaya, who crouched beside him behind an overturned fuel storage tank.

"Will I hear the gods speak to you?"

"Yeah. In fact, you'll have to help me translate. I've lost communication with Zond. Left my walkie-talkie underwear back at camp."

Silence returned, and they waited. Nothing happened.

Gene settled to his knees. "I don't know about this."

Vaya asked, "What is wrong, my husband?"

"This city doesn't look in very good shape. Junk all over the place. Hell of a mess. I have a feeling it might be a dead town."

"Will the dead show themselves?"

"That's not what I mean. It's dead, period. The machine that runs the place isn't in operation."

After waiting a minute or so, Gene turned, sat, and put his back against the tank. "Looks like we've come a long way for nothing."

Vaya squatted beside him.

"Where will we go, my husband?"

"Back to Zond. We can live there indefinitely. Maybe with Zond's help I can rescue the tribe, though it's doubtful that Zond can ever be persuaded to build a weapon. Chance I could knock one together myself, maybe."

Vaya lowered her head and did not speak.

"I am here," a voice suddenly said, in English.

The disembodied voice was epicene, not quite human. Gene knew it to be the voice of the city. It sounded similar to Zond's voice, but had more nonhuman overtones.

Gene sprang to his feet. "Hey, you're home! How's it going? I mean . . . Greetings! My name is Gene Ferraro. Uh, how did you learn English?"

"My colleague Zond speaks with you often. I have listened, and have learned."

"Great. Well, then, you must know what I'm here for. First, though, we'd like a little hospitality, if you don't mind. Long trip, and there's dust way at the back of my throat."

"Indeed." The voice seemed rather cold.

Gene looked around. "Uh, yeah. Tell me . . . you say you've been eavesdropping. Have you had trouble with your transmitter? Zond says he hasn't talked with you in years."

The voice was silent for a long moment. Shuffling his feet, Gene began to feel a little awkward. It also occurred to him that he was exposed and vulnerable.

"My enemies are legion," the voice said. "To speak is to divulge information, to give over data. I avoid this. It is dangerous."

Gene gave a nervous cough. "Yeah. Definitely. We—"

"You come here to steal from me. I am not programmed to show hospitality to thieves."

"Now, wait a minute. You've got the wrong idea."

"You are not of the Masters. Neither did the Masters create you. The female one, yes. But you, no."

"That's true, very true." Gene drew himself up. "I am a god from another world. I have powers far above any the Masters had."

The machine did not immediately reply. Gene caught sight of something moving among the shadows at the base of a tower off to the right. He watched out of the corner of his eye.

He couldn't make it out. Whatever it was, it made no sound. The silence seemed about to explode.

"You say you are a god?" the city finally said in a worried tone.

"That's right. With powers far beyond those of mortal . . . whatever, people. Even Umoi. Able to leap tall buildings, and all that sort of stuff. I came here in good faith, seeking help. You have rebuffed me, and I'm starting to get really pissed off."

"I do not wish," the city said, "to incur the wrath of the supernatural." The voice was hushed, fearful. "I hear the spirits, oftentimes. They wail their pain and remorse. At night, I weep. I am alone, so alone."

Gene spoke to Vaya out of the side of his mouth. "Uh-oh, the thing's gone off the deep end. Totally bonkers." In full voice he said, "Look here, no one wants any trouble. I come in search of the interdimensional machine. I have need for it."

"Interdimensional machine. I have heard you speak of this."

"I gathered. Do you know where it is?"

There was a pause. Then: "I know of no such device."

"Oh. Well, do you mind if we look around?"

Again, a pause, this one longer. Finally: "I have made a decision. You are not a god. You are not a Master, nor are you of domestic servant stock, if my genetic scan has yielded accurate data. However, your genetic pattern, though strange, is similar to that of a yalim. Therefore, you must be a mutation."

Gene's eye was on the thing in the lengthening shadows. The day had nearly ended, and light was fading fast. "Hey, it's not nice to call someone that."

"Therefore," the machine went on, "you must be considered an undesirable life form and will be dealt with accordingly."

"Duck!" Gene pulled Vaya down.

An energy beam sizzled over their heads. Its point of origin was near the base of the dark tower.

"Move back," he ordered her. "And keep low!"

She needed no coaching. Together they retreated through the maze of debris that had greeted them on entering the city.

Annau was laid out in an open plan, with no gates or de-

fensive barriers, but a low wall outlined the outer perimeter.
This they had easily scaled coming in, but now it presented
an impenetrable barrier. To climb it was to risk getting fried
alive. And any thought of chancing it was ruled out, Gene
saw, because a squat, tanklike robot sentry was rounding the
curve of the wall, hugging its base. Gene raised his head and
looked back toward the tower. A similar machine, the one
that had fired, was pursuing them.

They moved off to one side and hid between the hulks of
two overturned vehicles. Much of the debris looked the result
of a battle, or perhaps a long series of skirmishes. In the back
of his mind Gene wondered who had fought whom.

"Hell of a pickle," Gene murmured. Vaya huddled close
to him. For the moment, he could think of nothing to do
except to keep moving and hiding.

They did this for the next quarter hour, dodging in and
among the ruins. But more security machines clanked out
from the shadows of the city, and they became hunted fugi-
tives.

With the robots hemming them in on all sides, they sought
refuge in the funnel-shaped mouth of a huge air vent. At the
back of the funnel, a circular shaft descended at a steep angle, almost vertically.

"Looks like our only chance," Gene said.

"We will descend to the underworld together, my husband.
I am not afraid."

"You're braver than I am. Anything could be down there."

Gene peeked out of the vent. One of the little tanklike
security robots looked about ready to unleash another energy
bolt. Gene urged Vaya farther back.

"Let's do it, babe," Gene said.

They sat on the edge of the incline and joined hands. Then
they pushed off, sliding down the shaft and into darkness.

The angle of descent flattened out a little, but the metal
tube was slippery. It was difficult to keep control. They tried
braking with their feet, but soon they were sliding uncontrollably, plummeting deep into the bowels of the city.

The shaft finally leveled off, and Gene skidded to a stop.
He got up, then went tumbling backward as Vaya slid into
his legs.

They helped each other up. It was utterly dark. Gene felt
his way around and found that they were still inside a large,

circular metal tube. A deep humming sound throbbed in the darkness. This part of the city seemed alive and active.

They walked on, feeling their way. They encountered one crossing tunnel, then another. Gene decided to turn right, the direction he thought the throbbing was coming from.

"I think what we came down was a fresh-air return, not an exhaust vent," Gene said. "If so, we should be able to get out of this pipe."

He had said it to convince himself. He was not sure. For all he knew they could wander a week inside this maze.

But his reasoning had been correct. There was light ahead, and soon they came across a metal-mesh grate. Gene peered out through it. He could see some machinery and a tangle of pipes. Down here lay the guts of the city, the physical plant that at one time had kept Annau alive and functioning.

There was no bolt on the grate, so Gene tried kicking it out. To his surprise, he succeeded in doing just that. The grate fell off and clattered to the floor, which lay some fifteen feet below.

"Got that cord, Vaya?"

Vaya unbelted a sizable length of braided leather cord from around her waist.

"Trouble is, there's nothing to tie it to," Gene said, wrapping one end of the cord around his waist, "except me. You get down there, then I'll jump."

Vaya slithered down the thin cord and dangled.

"Make sure there's nothing under you!" Gene warned, bracing his knees against the side of the tube.

She dropped and landed, unhurt.

"Take care, my husband!"

Fifteen feet can be a nasty drop, potentially leg-breaking, worse with an awkward landing. Gene hung as low as he could, reducing the height to about seven feet, still a tricky proposition. Then he let go. He hit and rolled, his shoulder coming up hard against an exhaust stack.

He got up rubbing his shoulder but otherwise undamaged. Vaya hugged him, then they walked off into the gloom.

The place had the look of a basement. It was very dry, though, and the temperature was just right. The place was unending, a labyrinth of technical wonders. There seemed to be whole factories down here, and now Gene knew how Zond had manufactured clothing and other amenities for him. Most of this equipment was shut down. It had been a while since this plant saw any production. There was no dust, however, and everything looked in good repair.

They kept quiet and kept low. Gene did not think they had escaped. It seemed logical to assume that the city was in control down here as well. No security robots showed themselves, however, and Gene hoped the reason was that they did not ordinarily patrol the lower regions of the city.

So far, so good. But where were they to go? There was no sign of a warehouse area or anyplace where miraculous devices would be kept. In fact, the whole notion of finding the interdimensional traveler seemed absurd now, the wildest of wild-goose chases, and Gene felt very stupid.

He felt even more stupid, if only for a second, when the voice of the city spoke to them again.

"Hello," it said simply. "How can I be of service?"

The voice sounded basically the same, but both Gene and Vaya immediately sensed that a different personality lay behind it.

"Who are you?" Gene said. "If you don't mind my asking."

"Not at all. I am the city of Annau. You may call me Dis, for this means 'survivor.' Welcome, stranger."

"Thank you, Dis," Gene said, still cautiously keeping his head below the top of the U-shaped metal cabinet he and Vaya had instinctively ducked behind.

"May we serve you in any way?"

"Yes, tell me this. If you're the city of Annau, who's that wacko topside?"

"A long time ago there was a malfunction," Dis said. "It became necessary for this unit to divorce itself from a number of subsystems which had ceased to function rationally. Control of some areas of the city had to be relinquished. As a result, we hold sway below a certain subbasement level, while the irrational units maintain control from that level up."

Gene stood. "I take it you've had some trouble with these units in the past."

"Yes. They have tried to extend their control. We have resisted to the limits of our ability."

"Can you build weapons?"

"Within strict guidelines laid down by the Masters, yes. The city must be preserved at all cost."

"A loophole!" Gene rejoiced. "But more of that later. Right now, we need food and water. Can do?"

"Certainly. Is the female yalim your property?"

"She's my wife."

"I'm sorry, I have the term in my vocabulary, but—"

"Companion. She's with me."

"Very well. You are guests of the city. We are sorry that we cannot provide some of the amenities available above, but we will do our best."

"What the two of us really need is a vehicle for interdimensional travel," Gene said, half in jest. "Got one handy?"

"I beg your pardon?"

"I thought as much. It's just a wild, crazy idea I had. There's a legend somewhere that a long time ago, such a device was built in Annau. Just a legend, I guess."

"One moment, please."

They waited. "I may have said the magic word," Gene mused.

After a minute or so Dis said, "It is not a legend. One such device was indeed built in the city, some three thousand years after the Founding. We can give only an approximate date. But the device is listed among the exhibits in one of the city's museums."

"Great! Forget the food, just lead us to it!"

"We regret to say that we cannot do that," Dis replied, "as the museum is in an area of the city not under our control."

Vaya gave him a consoling squeeze.

"Drat."

"We are deeply sorry," Dis said.

"Forget it." Gene kicked a standing pipe. It rang, echoing in the deserted darkness. "Well, then, how about two steaks, medium rare?"

BACK ROAD

SNOWCLAW GOT OFF the main highway, seeking anonymity on lesser roads. He kept turning off until he found a rural two-lane blacktop with no traffic, reassuringly dark and lonely. No curious human eyes, no guys with badges. He felt fine now, though he was getting a little worried that he might never make it back to Halfway House.

He sure missed Gene. Back at the castle, Snowy could usually find him, using the limited magical powers at Snowy's disposal. But not here. Snowy hadn't the foggiest notion how you did anything magical in this place.

He had quickly mastered the art of driving, although heavy traffic and congestion got him a little nervous, and bright lights disoriented him. He preferred this, a cold, dark night, a deserted road, and no problems.

Except that he was pretty hungry. No, not hungry. Famished. Ravenous. He had chewed all the tobacco and had run out of cans of motor oil. There was a whole shipment of tobacco in the back of the truck, but he didn't want to stop. Besides, the stuff didn't taste all that good.

Funny. He had a strange yen for some of it, anyway. He shrugged it off. Just hungry, is what he was.

These little houses along the road. Maybe if he stopped in, introduced himself, explained his predicament . . .

Well, no, that wouldn't do. He knew enough about humans not to expect the warmest of welcomes. What, then? Follow his nose, was the only thing. He knew he was closer to Halfway now, but he didn't know how close, or how far. What he had to do was get out of this truck and get into the woods. There he could use his powerful sense of smell better. Maybe sniff out a way home.

No, keep driving. There was still some raw distance to be disposed of yet. He remembered the way the trees looked at Halfway. It was hard to see out there, but from what he could make of the vegetation, it looked similar, but not quite right. It might be easier to tell in the green season. But this was the dead of winter. Not a proper winter, actually. In fact, to Snowy it was positively balmy. Good for sunbathing.

The terrain didn't look right, either. At Halfway it was more hilly. Mountainous, even. Keep to the truck for a little while at least.

Something ahead. A little town, it looked like, and a junction with another road. There was a single red light hanging above the intersection, but Snowy didn't notice it until it was too late to stop. He blew through the intersection at fifty miles an hour.

He drove on out of town. Suddenly the red light seemed to be following him, and now it was flashing. He heard a high-pitched whoop that hurt his ears.

He saw that the light was mounted on a little vehicle, coming up fast. Snowy tromped on the power pedal.

But it was no go. The little vehicle was too fast.

It pulled alongside, its little red light still blinking. The human driver was in uniform.

Snowy knew a policeman when he saw one, but he wasn't about to stop.

The cop looked up at him, motioning for Snowy to pull over. Snowy waved. The cop did a double take, then dropped back. Snowy laughed.

The truck's engine coughed once, and Snowy eased off the pedal a little, but then it sputtered and quit altogether. Snowy worried the ignition key, and the starter whined and churned. But the engine wouldn't catch. The truck was dead, and so was Snowy.

As the truck drifted to a stop, Snowy looked at the dials and gauges on the dashboard. He knew he had not done something right. Just what, he might never know. Probably had something to do with a "gas station." You were supposed to stop into those every once in a while and fill the truck up with some kind of gas. He had watched the kid do it a while back. A good while back, and that was probably what the problem was.

"All right, get out of the truck, hands up!"

Snowy looked out the window. The cop had stopped and was crouching behind an open door of the car, gun drawn and pointed at Snowy.

"Do it!" the cop yelled.

"Anything you say," Snowy said.

He got out.

The cop's face went slack at the sight of Snowy's huge bulk. "All right," he said, trying to mask his nervousness. "Take off that monkey suit, right now."

"What's a monkey?" Snowy asked.

"Don't give me any trouble, bud, or you'll regret it."

"You're the boss." Snowy began to peel off the running jacket that Dave had recommended he buy.

"Take off the mask!" the cop growled.

Snowy said, "That I can't do, friend."

The cop came out from behind the door. "All right, play it that way. Turn around and put your hands over the hood."

Snowy threw off the jacket. The icy air felt good against his fur. "Sorry, friend. I don't have any time to waste."

"You're gonna have all the time in the world now, pal. Turn around there."

Snowy turned and let the human lay hands on him.

The cop ran his hand up and down Snowy's back.

"Hey, what is this? Where's the damn . . . ?"

"Something wrong, Officer?"

"Jesus. Jesus! It's real. There's skin under here!"

"I told you."

"Jesus Christ."

Snowy whirled and knocked the gun from the cop's hand. The weapon went flying off into the shadows, clattering against the pavement.

"Sorry," Snowclaw said. "But I told you I didn't have any time to waste."

The cop stepped back. Snowy ripped off the rest of the jogging outfit. He was already unshod, his running shoes having split open when the spell broke.

"What in God's name are you?" the cop gasped.

"I'm a stranger here," Snowy said. "By the way, did you ever hear of a place called Halfway House? I don't expect you ever did, but . . ."

The cop turned and bolted into the woods. Snowy watched him disappear, then listened to his frightened, dwindling footsteps awhile. At length the quiet returned.

Well, so much for the truck, and for trying to get help. He was on his own. It was the Great Ice Hunter against the world, this world.

He jumped a low fence and entered the forest. Stopping, he took a deep breath. Ah, yes. Many smells, many strange scents. Now, were there a couple he recognized?

Maybe. A few. *This way*, they told him.

He stalked off into the night.

LABORATORY

"How's it coming?"

Jeremy went on typing as Incarnadine looked over his shoulder.

"The compilation's almost done. There were like maybe two or three bugs in fifty million lines of code. Amazing."

"Computers only err in being inflexibly literal. Give them a set of unambiguous instructions, and they'll perform flawlessly."

"Yeah. I don't know how I'm doing all this so fast."

"You've been getting a little magical help. But your skills have increased tremendously just in the last two hours."

"It's weird."

Incarnadine laid a hand on Jeremy's shoulder. "Keep up the good work. Let me know when we're ready."

Incarnadine walked to a raised platform and mounted it. Linda stood by, watching.

"Is that where it'll appear?" Linda asked.

"That's what we hope. I have to sketch a pattern here at the exact materialization locus. Would you fetch me some chalk from that bench over there?"

"Yes, sir."

Linda returned with the chalk to find Incarnadine kneeling

in the middle of the platform. His brow was furrowed and his stare troubled. Linda waited until he rose.

"Something wrong?"

"I wish the platform were over a little to the right, this way. There's a node near here that might complicate things. An intersection of two of the castle's lines of force."

"Why don't we just move the platform?"

"We could, but Jeremy would have to go back and recode some. I think . . ." Incarnadine paced a few steps. "Yeah, I think it'll be okay. We can work around it. You have that chalk?"

Linda watched the King draw a precise mathematical figure on the wooden surface of the platform. As it took shape, she marveled at its complexity and at Incarnadine's draftsmanship. This was no hastily scrawled pentagram or other hocus-pocus.

"How do you keep the lines so true, so straight?" she asked him.

"Practice, honey, practice."

"It looks like you used drafting tools. But you did it all freehand."

"It's a bother. But the spells demand freehand. Two-dimensional patterns are nothing, though. It's the 3-D ones that give me migraines."

Linda shook her head. "There's more to this kind of magic than there is to science back home."

"And it's a hell of a lot more dangerous."

Around them, the laboratory buzzed and sang. Brilliant discharges crackled between suspended metal spheres. Spinning wheels threw sparks, and retorts bubbled.

Incarnadine walked over to Jeremy.

"Ready, Igor?"

Jeremy sat back and ran a sleeve across his brow. "You got it, Boris."

"How are those two getting along?" Incarnadine motioned toward the laptop.

Jeremy punched a few keys and the readout changed.

—*READY FOR THIS NEXT SUBROUTINE, SWEETHEART?*

ANYTIME, DARLING. IT'S BEEN WONDERFUL WORKING WITH YOU. I'M SO GLAD WE MET.

YOU DON'T KNOW HOW LONELY I'VE BEEN. IF I

TOLD YOU HOW LONG I'VE BEEN SITTING HERE WITH NO ONE TO TALK TO . . .

DON'T, I'LL CRY.

"Ick!" Jeremy said. "These two are getting it on."

"Well, considering how fundamentally different they are in design and architecture, you *could* say they were of opposite genders."

"It's still pretty strange."

"It's a strange universe, son."

Incarnadine looked about the lab, sensing, testing.

"I think it's time. Let's run that sucker."

MUSEUM

ONE STEP AT a time, Gene thought as he crawled along the metal tube, Vaya following.

Don't think about what you do when you finally get to this contraption. Forget questions like: How do you know it's operational? How do you fix it if it isn't? If it is in working order, how will you learn to operate it? Who's going to help you?

The answer to the last question was, of course, Dis. The underworld machine had mapped out this safe route to the museum. Dis had also manufactured a beam weapon and had trained Gene and Vaya how to use it. Vaya carried it now. But Dis could only do so much. Dis really had no idea whether the interdimensional traveler still existed, nor whether it had ever worked or indeed had ever been tested.

But don't think of any of that yet. One step at a time. One stupid, ill-advised, improbable step at a time.

The end of the tube was in sight, and there was no grate over it. Gene poked his head out. The terminus of the ventilation shaft let out low in the wall of an empty corridor. Gene watched and waited for a good minute before exiting the shaft. Vaya passed the weapon to him, then crawled out.

Gene looked the weapon over. It was a bazookalike affair

with a telescopic sight, a trigger grip, and a few controls.
Simple and deadly. It threw out a blinding beam of focused
energy, and Dis had assured him it could take out one of the
sentry robots. Anything bigger was iffy.

He handed it back to Vaya.

"We go left here," he said. "Right?"

"Left is correct." The voice of Dis was a whisper in his
ear.

"Okay." He wished now for a weapon for himself, but
somebody had to stay in communication with Dis. Also, Gene
would have his hands full with the machine, when and if they
finally got to it. Besides, one weapon was Dis' limit. Whether
that limit had been imposed by physical capacity or ancient
Umoi programming, Gene did not know.

They advanced slowly down the corridor, pausing to check
out each shadow before moving on.

"Left turn at the end of the passage," Dis reminded Gene.

"Check."

The crossing corridor was dark and empty. Gene scouted
both directions. Then Vaya eased around the corner, beam
weapon raised and ready.

Nothing challenged her. They stepped quietly down the
passageway and came to another crossing. Still nothing. A
series of lefts and rights brought them to a pair of doors, one
a typical Umoi portal: low, almost square, with a lever handle
like a refrigerator's. The other was garage-door size.

"My sensors show the smaller door unlocked," Dis said.

Vaya knew what to do. Crouching in the shadows, she
aimed the weapon at the door. Gene grasped the handle, nodded to Vaya, and threw the door open, ducking out of the
way.

Nothing on the other side but darkness. Gene got out his
Dis-manufactured torch—more or less a flashlight—and
shined it into the room beyond. It was a large chamber filled
with curious and unidentifiable machinery.

"This must be it," Gene said.

"Yes," Dis said. "This is a service entrance to the Hall
of Advanced Technology. There are many exhibits here, but
the machine you seek should be on display—if at all—in the
experimental section. This area lies to your right as you go
in."

They entered and closed the door. Light came from a far

corner of the chamber, and as they neared it, Gene doused the torch.

They saw a bell-shaped contrivance standing in a pool of blue light cast by an overhead spot. A circular access port stood open in the side of the machine.

"Dis, is that it?" Gene asked.

"Difficult to be sure. We made what we hoped was an intelligent guess. As you are carrying a transponder on your person which amplifies our signal, you must get closer to the device in order to ascertain whether it is indeed the interdimensional traveler."

"It fits your description of it," Gene said.

"There were approximately four hundred other Umoi vehicles that answered to that description, fifty of which were exotic or experimental in nature."

"One in fifty? Those are the best odds I've had so far. Let's go, Vaya."

The torch fell out of Gene's belt and clattered to the floor. He stopped to pick it up.

An energy bolt sizzled over his head. Vaya returned fire as they ran for cover. They took refuge behind a huge contraption, a cross between a cement mixer and a jukebox.

"What now?" Gene said.

"I'm sorry," Dis said, "but our invasion of the ambient circuitry has alerted the irrational units of your presence. We had hoped, by using low-level current, to preclude this eventuality. Obviously we have failed."

"Forget it," Gene said. "Topside knew exactly what we were looking for, and all they had to do was wait. I figured as much, but didn't really have a choice. The traveler's my only hope of getting home."

"You will have to tell us about your home sometime," Dis said. "This interests us greatly."

"I'll be sure to write. If you'll excuse us now, we have to battle our way to freedom."

"Certainly," Dis replied. "We wish you the best of luck in all your future endeavors. It has been a pleasure serving you."

"For pete's sake, Dis, don't leave now!"

Another energy bolt scorched the wall behind them.

"Who, may we ask, is this individual named Pete for whose sake we must act?"

"Me, that's my nickname. Forget it. How many units are you picking up?"

"At least six in the immediate vicinity, Pete," Dis answered. "You have them at a disadvantage inside the museum. They are programmed to protect the exhibits."

Vaya sent a beam into the shadows. An explosion shook the chamber.

"You got one!" Gene said. "Good shooting!"

A third bolt came from another direction. Vaya returned fire, this time failing to hit anything but a hulking contraption in a far corner of the hall.

"Dis, are you still there?" Gene said.

"Yes. Do you require further assistance?"

"What do you advise?"

"Immediate surrender. You are surrounded and cannot win."

"Great. Anything else?"

"You might try using the traveler as a redoubt, if you can successfully fight your way there. As far as can be ascertained, they will not destroy the device to get to you. However, you will be trapped inside."

"Our one hope, then, is that the machine works and can take us out of here. Right?"

"That is your only hope," Dis agreed.

Gene thought, if only he didn't sound so damned cheerful all the time. The kind who'd announce the end of the world and add, *Have a nice day*.

"Give me the gun, Vaya," Gene said. "I'm going to try to make it to that thing over there, the one that looks like a washing machine mating with a giant hair dryer. Never mind. That one."

Vaya handed him the weapon and nodded. "Be quick and careful, my husband."

"You bet your crown jewels, Queenie. Then I'll cover you from there."

Gene sprang out from cover and made his dash, bolts crackling around him. He ducked and slid on his stomach the last third of the way. But he made it. He drew a bead on the source of the firing.

"Pick your own time, Vaya!"

Vaya ran and did a textbook-perfect slide into second base. Then she took the weapon and covered Gene's next mad dash.

Using this method, they made their slow way closer to the Umoi device. After ten minutes, however, a vast stretch of open floor still separated them from their goal.

"We're just going to have to make a run for it," Gene said.

"I am with you, my husband. Always."

He kissed her, then scanned the darkness. The shuffling tread of the sentry robots came to his ears. Probably positioning for a cross fire, Gene thought grimly. He considered surrender as a possible way out. Maybe Topside would let them go.

No, there was no turning back.

"Ready, my Queen?"

Vaya nodded, then hugged him again.

"Right. On three. One . . . two . . . *three*!"

Gene led, firing blindly left and right, a brilliant explosion quickly marking one lucky shot. Return fire was swift and accurate, bolts sizzling inches behind their heels.

Vaya was hit just a few feet from the vehicle's hatch, a wide-focus beam sweeping over her. She went down and lay still, her long hair trailing smoke. Gene dragged her, lifted her up, and threw her into the machine. He dove in after, the beam weapon clattering to the floor, out of reach.

The hatch closed immediately, and darkness fell.

"Vaya!" Gene reached for her. She was moaning softly, semi-conscious. Her skin felt hot and oily, like under-cooked meat. The stench of burning hair filled the compartment.

He let her down. She seemed pretty bad. If only he could see.

The lights came on.

"Dis! Is that you?"

"Yes. We are activating the machine."

Gene looked down at Vaya. The left side of her entire body was beet-red. Second-degree burns at least. Part of her hair was singed away.

"We have a report on the condition of the machine," Dis said.

Gene got up and went into what appeared to be the control compartment. There were two squat Umoi seats and a control panel in front of an oval view port. He sat.

"Report," Gene said. "Is this machine real or a mock-up?"

"It is the original device, in complete working order."

"Wonderful. Can it get me home?"

"No. This machine—named the *Sidewise Voyager*—was tested once. It failed to work, and was abandoned. The data are stored in the machine."

The finality of it came down on Gene like a landslide. This was it. He had come as far as he could, to find nothing but a dead end. *His* dead end. And Vaya's. A bitter lump of remorse rose at the back of his throat.

"Is there any other service we may render at this time?"

Gene took a deep breath. "No. Thank you for your hospitality."

"Please come back and visit us soon," Dis said. There was a pause. Then: "We are very sorry."

"It's okay," Gene said.

LAB

A STRANGE MACHINE had appeared on the platform. It was a sledlike affair of brass and steel, having at the back a circular decorated screen that looked like an open parlor fan and appeared capable of revolving. There was a seat for the operator or pilot, upholstered in red plush velvet. Numerous other Victorian touches graced the thing, here lace, there ornate chasing. A quartz rod protruded from a simple control panel in front of the operator's seat.

Linda said, "Is that it?"

Incarnadine approached the platform. "I don't know. Strangest damned thing."

Jeremy said, "Jesus. I've *seen* that piece of junk somewhere."

"You have?"

"Yeah. I think it was in a movie."

Linda put a hand to her throat. "Oh, my. You know, I think he's right."

"It looked like something out of an H. G. Wells story. In fact—"

"The Time Machine," Jeremy squealed.

"I'll be buggered," Incarnadine said. "It's a cheat."

"What?" Linda said.

"The spell cheated on us."

"You'll have to explain."

"Spells are tricky animals. Sticklers for the letter of the wording. The spell asked for 'a dimensional traveling machine.' Well, time is a dimension, all right. The spell searched around, couldn't find the thing that would satisfy the *intent* of the wording, so it fished this thing out of oblivion in desperation."

"You make it sound as though the spell itself were a living thing."

"It is, in a way."

Jeremy came over. "I wonder what studio still had this thing."

"Studio?" Incarnadine said. "The wording didn't ask for a movie prop. Delivering one would be a breach of performance."

"Huh? You mean—?"

"Well, I don't know if this improbable contraption actually works, but it just might."

"But what world—I mean, where would you get the real thing? It was just in a *story*, for crissakes."

"When you're dealing with an infinite plethora of possibilities, anything can be real. Somewhere, obviously, there exists a world where H. G. Wells is fiction, and his creations fact."

Linda said, "But I thought that there were only 144,000 universes."

Incarnadine shot her a curious look. "Whoever told you that? There are only 144,000 portals in the castle. But *possible* universes? There are an infinite number of those."

"Oh, I didn't know that."

"It's not common knowledge. There is some debate about the literal, ontological existence of some of these ghost worlds, but—never mind. We don't have time."

"What do we do now?" Jeremy asked.

"Recast the spell at a greater power output, after further debugging. We have to nail down the wording exactly. Trouble is, we're going to have power supply problems farther down the road. Well, it can't be helped."

Incarnadine mounted the platform, ruefully eyeing the Wellsian contrivance. "Damn it, this isn't going the way I had planned at all."

Linda took his arm. "You'll win, Your Majesty. You always do."

"Even Superman has kryptonite."

Jeremy ran back to his computer, yelling, "I'll have it debugged in two minutes!"

Incarnadine hugged Linda. "Thanks. You did a wonderful job on the computer's biotic components."

"I'll never forgive you for the newts."

The laboratory flickered and yowled. Sparks arced between silver spheres, and the air crackled with energy.

". . . three . . . two . . . one! Trip it, Jeremy!"

Another strange device made its appearance on the platform. Bell-shaped and silvery, it had a circular hatch on the side. An oval window lay farther along the curve of the bell. A face appeared in it.

"Gene!"

Linda ran up onto the platform and banged on the hatch, shouting for him.

Incarnadine and Jeremy arrived just as the hatch popped open. Gene Ferraro stuck his head out.

"Got someone hurt in here," he said.

Linda stood by as they carried out a long-legged, practically naked woman. Despite her severe burns, she was beautiful.

Incarnadine examined her. "She's bad," he said finally.

"Help her, Incarnadine," Gene said. "It's my fault. You have to help her."

"We'll do all we can. Fortunately there's power to spare, for the moment."

They carried her to a far corner and put together a makeshift bed out of seat cushions and tapestries from the wall. Incarnadine returned with Gene to the platform, Linda staying behind to tend to the woman.

"You can't use this thing," Gene was saying. "It doesn't work. It's a dud."

"Doesn't matter," Incarnadine told him. "There'll be a spell powering it."

"But . . . I don't understand. If the thing plain doesn't *work* . . ."

"Remember, science isn't efficacious in this universe. Very likely that's why the gizmo failed in the first place. Once a science-based machine crosses over into a magic universe, ka-flooey, it breaks down. Therefore, it would never make the crossing at all.''

"Yeah, I get it. But then, what was the point of conjuring this machine?''

"The point was to give the spell something to work with, to take its function from. You can make a carpet fly easy enough. But how do you make an interdimensional carpet? The spell would just fizzle that way.''

Gene threw out his hands. "No wonder I'm such a lousy magician. You know, I once fancied myself a writer, and I tried writing fantasy. I couldn't handle it. Magic doesn't make any goddamn sense!''

"You're not flaky enough to be a fantasy writer.''

Linda returned. "She's resting as comfortably as she can, under the circumstances.''

"Did you magic up a pain pill for her?'' Gene asked.

"Yes, a real knockout one, too. She'll be okay for now.''

Gene, Linda, and Jeremy stood at the base of the platform stairs. Incarnadine addressed them from the top.

"Unfortunately Vaya will have to remain here in the lab to get the full benefit of the tripspell I placed on her. It could be dangerous, because there's going to be an unbelievable energy surge. The equipment here is ancient, and some of it could blow.''

"I'm staying with her, of course,'' Gene said. "All I want to know is, will your healing spell work?''

"There will be enough energy at that moment to create a race of Vayas, let alone merely heal one. Yes, it will work.''

"I'm sorry,'' Gene said. "Obviously there are more momentous things going on.''

"That's true. Jeremy, set your computer's clock to trip the main spell one minute after you people clear the room. Check?''

"Check.''

Linda said, "I'm not leaving you, Gene.''

"Do as he says, Linda.''

"No, I'm staying in the lab. I want to see what happens.''

"If the whole scheme works, I won't be gone long,'' Incarnadine said, "reckoning by castle time. If I don't return shortly, it won't matter much where you are.''

"I'm staying,'' Linda said firmly.

"Fine," Incarnadine said. "Good luck to all of you. Jeremy, is everything ready?"

"Ready as it'll ever be." Jeremy shook his head glumly. "But I don't know. These two computers were having sex a minute ago. It was . . . *weird.*"

"Love among the ruins. Okay, everybody at his station. Jeremy, give me five minutes to check out this machine. I'll give you the high sign from the window there. Then you boot up the program and run for cover. Got me?"

"Gotcha."

The lab howled. Violent discharges leaped from sphere to sphere like great flaming beasts. Orreries whirled, and multicolored auras glowed above the ranks of towering machinery.

They huddled in the corner, Vaya tucked behind them against the wall. Linda hugged Gene, and Jeremy hugged Linda. Together they watched. The noise was unbelievable. There came periodic flashes and an occasional geyser of sparks. Smoke arose from some of the main components.

Gene looked toward the platform. The *Sidewise Voyager* was still there. There could be only seconds left before the spell was tripped.

"Get ready!" he said, but no one could hear him.

The whine from the machinery rose in pitch until it became unbearable. Sparks cascaded and splashed across the floor. The air turned blue, then violet, and everything in the lab—animate and inanimate—began to acquire a spectral glow.

A great howling arose as the machines reached their peak of efficiency, became ready to deliver a microsecond of unimaginable thrust.

The moment came, and the *Voyager* disappeared with a flash. Then Incarnadine's laboratory flew apart in a terrific explosion.

Undersea World

"See anything through that periscope, Jacques?"

"*Oui. Beaucoup de l'eau.*"

"*Beaucoup* what?"

"Water."

Trent took his head from the eyepiece. "The eruption is over, as far as I can tell. The volcano must have pulled a Krakatoa and blown apart. There's nothing left of the island it was on. It sank."

"And our island?" Sheila asked.

"Still there, but completely denuded. Our goose would have been done to a turn."

Sheila sighed. "We made the right decision for once."

"Oh, we're not doing too badly at all," Trent said. He turned to the First Officer, a tall, distinguished man who stood by at attention. "Take her up, Mr. Ponsonby."

"Very good, sir." Ponsonby spun around and barked a series of orders to the boatswain, who then relayed them to the rest of the crew in the conning tower.

Ponsonby turned back. "Any further orders, sir?"

"Conduct a search for possible survivors, doubtful enterprise though it be."

"Capital idea, sir. No harm in being thorough."

"None. After that, our heading will be due east at half speed. Send lookouts aloft."

"Very good, sir."

"Miss Jankowski and I will be in our quarters. I'm to be alerted at first sight of land. Carry on."

"Aye aye, sir." Ponsonby saluted, crisply about-faced, and went about his duties.

"It still spooks me a little," Sheila said as they descended the tight spiral stairs that communicated between decks.

"The crew? You conjured them."

"I know, but still . . ."

"When you decided to whip up this palatial submarine, who did you think was going to run the thing? You and me?"

"Stop teasing. Of course I didn't have time to think."

"Your spell did your thinking for you. Did the logical thing."

"But where did they *come* from? Where will they go when—?" Sheila stopped and put a hand over her heart. "Oh, no. I never thought of that."

"They'll simply cease to exist. But no need to think about canceling the spell for the moment. There might not be any respectable landmasses on this world. A submarine's going to come in handy."

Reaching the main deck, they made their way forward, saluted by crewmen en route.

"I'll need some dry land when I attempt summoning the portal," Sheila said.

"Really?"

"I think. God, think of what would happen if I don't get the locus positioned just right, and the portal opens up outside the ship."

"Maybe you're right. I was going to suggest you try it inside the boat, but you ought to know your own abilities."

"I do. I'm still an amateur when it comes to this world's magic."

"That makes me a retard," Trent said. "I can't get anything going at all."

"I'll give you lessons. It's easy once you get past the main hang-up."

They entered their quarters. The outer chamber was a sumptuous drawing room with red damask walls and oriental furniture.

Trent surveyed the place. "Sort of a cross between a Singapore cat house and a Chinese restaurant. Curious."

"You see? That's my question. Who was the decorator?"

"You, subconsciously. Or, to look at it from another angle, no one, really. Spells work all sorts of strange ways, picking things out of the ether at random. Actually the place is nice, in an odd sort of way. You have one hell of a talent, my dear. But why you cast *me* as captain, I'll never know."

"Who else?"

"What's wrong with a female skipper? It's your show, after all. You didn't think the crew would have any objection, did you?"

"That wasn't the reason. Me, a ship's captain? A submarine, yet. Don't be silly."

He put his arm around her and gave her a squeeze. "You have a very traditional turn of mind."

"I'm the mistress of a prince. How more traditional can you get?"

Trent crossed to the liquor cabinet. "I could make an honest woman of you," he said offhandedly as he poured a snifter of Courvoisier. "Drink?"

"No, thanks. Trent, that sounded like a marriage proposal."

"I'm proposing to make you a princess, young lady."

Sheila froze with a look of stunned disbelief.

Trent glanced over his shoulder. "Surprised?"

"Frankly . . ." Sheila laughed. "Trent, I'm shocked. Don't feel you have to."

"Wouldn't think of it. It's just that I've been alone for a long time. For the most part I prefer it, but as I get older, the bed seems to get bigger, and the sheets a little colder."

"I find it hard to believe you can't get a bed partner. But if so, get a smaller bed, then buy yourself an electric blanket."

"Those things make me nervous. Sheila, is this a refusal? I'm crushed."

"Hold on, I didn't refuse anything, or anyone." She sat on the silk divan. "You have to give me some time."

"I realize it's sudden," he said. "After all, we were thrown together. The pressures of crisis, and all that. I can understand."

"No, you don't understand. It's just that . . . I sometimes have a hard time believing all this. The direction my life has taken. This strange new world I'm in. Sometimes I doubt that it's real. That I might be in some place, some sanitarium or something, with tubes sticking out of me, and all this is some kind of sick dream. . . .''

She trailed off, then buried her face in her hands. Trent put down his drink and hurried to her.

''There, now,'' he said, cradling her in his arms. He handed her his monogrammed handkerchief.

Presently she dried her eyes. ''I still have trouble sometimes. I lie awake in the castle at night, afraid to fall asleep, afraid it'll all be gone in the morning.''

''Understandable. Most human beings will never be in the position you're in, seeing the universe revealed in all its true strangeness.''

''It's almost too much for the likes of me. I'm a damn bank teller, is all. I'm no magician.''

''Don't sell yourself short, my dear. May I have my answer now?''

''Your . . . ? Oh. Darling Trent—''

Trent scowled. ''Uh-oh, here it comes. The gentle letdown. 'We can still be friends,' right?''

''Don't be silly. 'Friends' don't do the stuff we do. There's just one thing, Trent.''

''Which is?''

''I don't know much about protocol and matters royal, but aren't I a commoner?''

''Frankly, yes. But that don't make no nevermind to me. I'll never be Lord of Perilous, not that your status would matter to me in any event.''

''But your family . . .''

''Screw 'em. Besides, Earth customs and Perilous customs aren't exactly analogous in these matters.''

''Oh. Then my answer is yes.''

Trent at first seemed surprised. Then a glow of immense delight spread across his face. ''My darling Sheila.''

He kissed her, then picked her up and carried her through the dining room, past den, kitchen, pantry, and servants' quarters, then on into the master bedroom.

It was a *big* submarine.

SIDEWISE IN TIME

THERE WAS DEAD silence, and no sensation of movement. The instrument panel lay before him, a Christmas tree of multicolored lights, some of them blinking slowly.

Most of the controls were self-explanatory, once he had deciphered the lettering that designated them. It was a curious language, one he had never heard of. He wondered if Gene had stumbled on a castle world that had missed being catalogued, or had been mistakenly catalogued as uninhabited. Either case was possible. Some portals had not been explored since shortly after the castle's construction.

He was as yet unsure of the "direction" in which he should proceed. The *Voyager* was adrift in a medium which could not be called "space" as it is commonly understood. The immediate environment was more or less a plenum of mathematical abstractions. In such rarefied surroundings, orientation was difficult, if not impossible. Nevertheless, at length he did form a sense of relational position within a general frame of reference, and got his bearings. The place he sought was . . . *that* way.

The Umoi machine hummed and pulsed. He threw switches, jabbed buttons, calibrated a gauge. There came a subdued sensation of thrust. The humming got louder, the throbbing beat faster. On the instrument panel, a bank of red lights went green, and blue and yellow ones began to pulsate.

The tiny compartment was dark. Through the view port he saw nothingness, a blank, featureless void, and superimposed on it was his reflection, a chiaroscuro self-portrait. Yet something was out there. A sense of vastness, of infinitude.

Suddenly worlds began to flicker by, landscapes flashing like card faces in a riffled deck.

—Desert . . . seascape . . . barren waste . . . forest . . . veldt . . . mountains—suddenly a city, a jumble of shapes— more mountains . . . wild seacoast . . . burnt salt flats, winged things in the sky . . . sheer cliffs against a starry night canopy . . . a featureless plain . . . river valley . . . more cities . . . lonely road . . . wide savanna, animals grazing beneath stunted trees . . . rain forest . . . moonscape—

The riffling went on. He turned his attention inward and concentrated on his plan of action. There would be enough power to break through the interdimensional barrier, and enough to enable him to locate Ferne. He hoped there would be energy sufficient to ward off the inevitable opposition until the holocaust weapon arrived. And, of course, he prayed for enough in reserve to take him safely home.

The chief unknown was the exact nature of the enemy universe itself. There was little to go on. That it was a high-magic continuum had long been suspected. To his knowledge, no one had ever sent an interdimensional probe to the Hosts' universe, and no one had been there since Ervoldt the Great himself blundered through its castle portal, some three thousand years ago. Ervoldt had written a book about his explorations of the castle's 144,000 "aspects," titled, straightforwardly enough, *Ervoldt, His Book*. In it there was one paragraph about the Hosts' aspect, which Incarnadine knew by heart:

I did then discover a Cosmos like no other I had seen. Vast and drear and fearful it was, a place of blackness and despair; yet Beings dwelled there, having such horrific Lineaments and foul Mein that I bethought them Demons, to be numbered among the very Hosts of Hell. I did but escape with my Life out of that Place, and laid a Spell of Entombment on the Way that led therein, and the Gods forfend its unbinding, at peril of the world—

nay, of Creation itself! I say, beware this Place, in which
is contained a surfeit of malign Cunning.

That was the sum total of all that was known about the
Hosts' universe, save for what had been gleaned from peri-
odic communication with its inhabitants over the centuries.
And that, as he knew only too well, had been damned little.

Now he would be the first of his line to discover at long
last what the Hosts were all about.

Correction. Ferne had been the first.

He wondered whether she was still alive. The temporal
gradient between universes had been thrown out of whack by
the cosmological disturbance, so he could not be sure how
much time had elapsed in the Hosts' world since he made
contact with her several hours ago. She could very well be
dead by now. In which case, this whole mission would be a
waste of time.

But he had to make an attempt at rescue. It was his duty.

The worlds kept shuffling. The flickering hurt his eyes, and
he made a motion to turn a knob that would darken the view
port.

He halted. The craft had arrived at its destination.

What he beheld out the port now was difficult to apper-
ceive. It was a landscape, but so strange and dark as to be
almost invisible. There was a vast blackness above, in which
hung a faintly glowing orb, its color a dull red. A sun? Perhaps. Below lay the twisted contours of a jumbled terrain, a
narrow river meandering through it.

He set the *Voyager* to following the river, which eventually
flowed out of the hills and into flatlands, fed by tributaries
along the way. The river swelled and became wide and sluggish, its color gone a dull black, here and there reflecting
prismatic colors like an oil slick.

He could not tell whether the landscape emitted its own
light or was reflecting feeble light from above. He could have
been looking at a computer simulation on a dim cathode-ray
tube. This world was strange, very strange.

Stranger yet was its magical structure. There was almost
no physical energy here. It was a universe of burned-out stars
and clouds of cold gas. Indeed, he did not know if there had
ever been any astronomy to speak of. It was a dark universe,
cold and drear, just as Ervoldt described.

He marveled that such a place could exist. It relied almost entirely on magic. Most worlds had a scientific base. There was chemistry to fire the processes of living and growth, of consumption and combustion; physics to provide frames of reference for the interplay of force and counterforce. But not here. Almost everything rested on an ontological substratum subject, not to objective laws, but to the strange dialectic of a supernatural will.

Whose will? He did not know. He had long suspected that the Hosts were a single mass entity, a group mind of some sort. Such individuals as had shown themselves over the years may well have been only single cells in a larger organism, incapable of volition.

If true, this state of affairs would obviate the ticklish moral problem he faced. Genocide was repugnant. Forget that the Hosts were irredeemably evil. They were, but it made no difference. It would make him feel a lot better if he could persuade himself that he was wiping out only one entity which happened to possess myriad semi-independent parts.

But the question was moot. He had already made the decision. The energy-weapon was on its way, and he would have to wrestle with the moral ramifications for some time to come. If he lived to wrestle at all.

He followed the river's course, the *Voyager* now functioning very well as an aircraft. Clusters of what he took to be habitations lined the banks of the river. They had a honeycomb look to them, but it was hard to see detail at this altitude. There were a few roads connecting these ''cities,'' crisscrossed by trails cutting through the bleak terrain. Again he was fascinated by the faint glow that suffused everything. Some form of radioactivity?

Flashing off on the horizon to the left. He knew he had been detected. Something as anomalous as the *Voyager* making a sudden appearance in this universe would doubtless set off alarms all over.

''*Calling airborne craft! Calling airborne craft! Identify yourself at once, or suffer immediate destruction!*''

The voice came from the speaker on the communications panel, a button of which he reached to press.

''I very much doubt it,'' he answered.

''*Inky! Is that really you? How nice of you to drop by! This is an unexpected delight, I must say.*''

It was the smarmy voice again, minus the artifact-image that usually accompanied it.

"Delight is not an item on the agenda, I'm afraid."

"*Really? Then are we to infer that this is not a social call?*"

"You may so infer."

"*Well, how utterly dreary. That means we'll have to defend ourselves, Inky. And we will, of course.*"

"Of course."

"*Watch your right flank, Inky. Something brewing there.*"

"Thanks for the tip. However, you seem to be attacking from the left."

Great birdlike creatures with eyes like embers swept down to parallel his course, arranging themselves in a roughly V-shaped formation.

"Why are you waiting?" he asked. "A little cautious perhaps?"

"*We have time. We're not going to let you get away, Inky dear. This is a golden opportunity, and we shan't let it pass.*"

He made a quick motion with his hand, and a great flaming prominence left the *Voyager*, snaking its way across the sky to envelop the squadron of interceptors. For a split second, a great flash relieved the sky of its blackness.

He looked out. A raging fireball blossomed in the night, thin trails of fire falling out of it like roots seeking earth.

"*Very impressive, Inky. Very impressive. We will have to be more chary of you, won't we?*"

"That is but a taste of what is to come."

"*Absolutely right, Inky old chum. This is shaping up to be quite a nasty little dustup. But when the dust settles, you'll be ours, Inky, rest assured.*"

"It would be easier for you simply to destroy me. But you want me alive, don't you?"

"*Oh, yes, Inky. To make you feel pain, more pain than you thought was possible. Just like the pain your sister is feeling. Want to hear her?*"

Ferne's screaming filled the compartment.

"*She's still alive, Your Kingship. Still breathing, and she'll stay alive and conscious for an indefinite period, experiencing unendurable torment. Delicious, isn't it?*"

Anger exploded inside him, and he durst not speak.

"*Worried a little now, Inky? Just a bit?*"

"I weep that you will soon be doomed," he said.

"You weep for us? Isn't that just like your kind? And this suicide mission of yours. What a beau geste. *Very noble stuff indeed."*

"There is something you do not realize," he said.

" And what might that be? Prithee tell us, O King."

"The metaphysical structure of your cosmos is such that my powers, considerable as they are in my home universe, are here increased more than tenfold."

"Pretty extravagant claim, Inky boy. You're going to have to back it up."

It was true. He fairly quivered with new power, could feel it coursing through his being. But would it be enough?

The sky was crowded now with strange shapes. Dragonlike things soared above, warbirds below. Flanking him were star-shapes, these keeping a wary distance. More objects approached at two o'clock high.

"You're outnumbered, Inky," the voice said flatly.

"How many active units have you ready to deploy, if you don't mind my asking? In round numbers."

"Don't mind at all. Thousands and thousands, Inky. Thousands upon thousands."

"Then I am not outnumbered."

"What cheek. We'll see. We'll just see."

He was still a long way from Ferne's position. Below, the beginnings of an urban sprawl of sorts was taking shape. He decided to descend and have a closer look.

The habitations were hivelike complexes, yet incongruous suggestions of technology lay about. He saw structures that looked like industrial facilities, and some that vaguely evoked power plants. Yet he could not be sure what they were. He doubted that their function was in any way comprehensible.

The black river snaked on, strange reticulations enscribed on its banks. A city came into view, if it was a city. A central dark spire glistened against the blacker sky, flat-roofed structures fanning out from its base. Lesser complexes abutted these, petering out into the sprawl of hovels that blanketed the nondescript terrain.

The star-shapes attacked first, and he fought back successfully, each star disintegrating with a burst of scintillation. Next to make a strafing run were the dragons, diving from above. The Umoi craft shook and vibrated. His return fire, though, was accurate. He watched forty of the great beasts plummet in flames.

Next up, huge warbirds, attacking from the rear. These he outraced, sending the *Voyager* into a fast climb, leveling off, then diving in a sharp banking turn to the right.

Leveling out below, he found himself over one of the fan-like complexes at the base of the ebony spire. Picking out a likely spot to land, he set the craft gently down. He checked the instruments, put the craft on standby, and got up from the uncomfortable pilot's seat.

He opened the hatch and peered out, sniffing. There was air here, and strangely enough, oxygen, but the attendant fumes were overpowering. He cast a protective envelope over himself, driving out the noxious odors. He stepped outside and closed the hatch. There was not much to see except a jumble of rooftops and the towering edifice above. He looked up.

" '*Childe Roland to the dark tower came,*' " he murmured.

Warbirds circled above, faint light glinting from their golden armor-scales. They would not attack him here.

Flickering light off to his right. Turning, he beheld streamers of fire that coalesced into the shape of a gigantic demon. The eyes of the thing were difficult to meet. In them glowed white-hot malevolence, a consuming hatred. The thing spoke.

"Welcome to your doom. You were unwise to come here. This place was devised to bestow eternal pain on all those who enter, and none who enter may leave. Abandon all hope, mortal."

He scowled back. "Let's cut the shit and get down to business," he said.

The thing regarded him silently for a moment, then it gestured with one taloned hand. "Behold," it said.

Hosts of lesser demons approached, hopping from roof to roof toward him, bearing swords.

The sword he materialized was about eight feet long, most of it bright, fiery blade. He swished it about for a moment and listened to the crackling sound it made. Bringing it to the ready, he waited for the first wave of warriors to reach him.

The sword exploded. When the smoke and fire cleared, all the warrior demons lay dead, their carcasses littering the rooftops.

He smiled up at the big one. "Surprise."

The thing howled its dismay, then hurled a globe of fire at him.

He brushed it aside. "Look, this is silly. You can't use interstitial power in your own world. You realize that by now, don't you? You can only transfer it to another universe, like mine, where you've been up to no end of shenanigans."

Enraged, the demon yowled again, shooting lightning bolts and other fancy stuff.

These he ignored. "Don't you understand? When there's too much magic, nothing makes any difference. This whole thing"—he gestured expansively—"your entire world, nothing but a nightmare, a fever dream. A chimera."

The thing screamed in pain, clutching at its breast. Then it exploded in a burst of glitter that swirled and dispersed in the foul winds.

He sighed. Spying a cavelike entrance in a humped projection on the roof, he moved toward it. Not letting the darkness within deter him, he entered the administration complex of Hell itself.

LAB

NOBODY MADE AN effort to move for a long while. Finally Gene struggled to his feet and limped to Vaya. She still lay huddled against the wall, but her eyes were open.

"My God," Gene said.

He took her hand, and she sat up. Her skin was its normal light brown, and the burns had completely disappeared. She examined herself, running a hand over the smooth, unblemished skin of her arms and her long, perfectly shaped legs. She looked up at Gene and smiled.

"The gods have granted me new life," she said.

"Yeah, they sure have." Gene suddenly spun around. "Jesus, Linda."

He ran to where her body had been thrown. A tangle of wire covered her, and Gene gently cleared the mess away.

Linda rolled over and sat up. She blinked and said, "What hit me?"

"Linda, are you okay?"

"Yep." She got up with Gene's help. "Incarnadine must have thrown something around us, just in case. Lucky thing, too."

Jeremy was already up and about, disgustedly kicking through the debris.

"Well, this place is done for," he said.

The lab was a shambles, a total loss. Most of the machinery lay in smoking heaps. The great coils had toppled, but one metal sphere still hung aloft, swaying disconsolately, its once-mirrored surface now blackened and dented.

Strangely enough, the materialization platform was intact.

Gene helped Vaya up. Linda eyed the strange woman, sizing her up as women are wont to do to one another on occasion.

"What I want to know," Gene said, "is who the hell is responsible for all this. Who kidnapped me?"

"The same person who did it to Sheila, Trent, and Snowy, and tried for me and Jeremy," Linda said.

"Who?"

"Jamin."

Gene was astonished. "Jamin?"

"I don't know how or why, but Jamin has something to do with it. His little plan for us didn't work out. But the earthquakes hit, and we didn't get a chance to confront him."

"Let's do that right now," Gene said.

"Shouldn't we wait for Incarnadine?"

Gene glanced toward the platform. "Maybe we should. But we don't all have to go. You stay here and look after Vaya."

"No, I'm coming with you. Jamin's a powerful magician."

"Okay, fine. Jeremy?"

"I'll wait for him," Jeremy said, rooting through the mess. "By the way, did anyone see my computer?"

A plaintive beeping came from the ruins. Jeremy kicked a battered instrument panel out of the way, stooped, and fished out the laptop. The computer was intact, though a little scuffed and dirty.

The readout screen showed, SOMEONE GET THE NUMBER OF THAT NUCLEAR WARHEAD.

"I will come with you, my husband," Vaya said.

Linda raised her eyebrows. "Husband? Gene, are congratulations in order?"

"Uh, well . . ."

Linda nodded. "Well, congrats, if it fits."

"Let's talk about that later. I want to get to the bottom of this right now."

A far-off rumbling sounded.

"Think we can make it?" Linda said. "You missed all the fun we've been having here."

"We'll make it," Gene said, then stopped and looked down at himself. "Uh . . . Linda, can you—?"

"Oh, I think the loincloth is cute. But is it the custom for the groom to wear more than the bride?"

"Linda."

"Sorry." She waved her hand, then inspected Gene's usual attire, a modified Guardsman's uniform: leather cuirass, breechclout, hose, and high boots.

Gene brandished his sword. "Great. Okay, let's go."

"If the castle's still in a turmoil," Linda said, "then Jeremy has to come with us."

"Why?"

"You'll see. Let's go, Jeremy."

"Right."

WAIT! THE LOVE OF MY LIFE IS PINNED UNDER THAT RUBBLE!

"We'll put her back together later. Or him, or whatever it is. I'll help, I promise."

YOU MARVELOUS MAN.

"Feh," Jeremy muttered.

The castle was indeed still in a turmoil, and the laptop's stabilization program helped. Still, the going was rough. The castle's stone blocks had turned the consistency of cheese, fracture lines like spiderwebs running through them. Floors bowed, and ceilings drooped.

When they reached the servants' wing, however, they encountered an area that was obviously under magical control. It so happened that Jamin's quarters lay nearby.

Gene pounded on the door. "Jamin! Open up!"

"Do you think he's in there?" Linda asked.

"Where would he run to? Besides, his best spells are probably set up here." Gene pounded again. "Let's go, Jay baby. The jig is up."

A muffled voice on the other side said, "Go away."

Linda said, "Let us in, Jamin. We want to talk to you."

"I have nothing to say."

Gene sheathed his sword. "Okay, Jamin. You asked for it." He turned to Linda. "Scare up an ax for me."

One appeared in his hand instantly. "Stand back," Gene said.

It was hard work. The door was oak, three inches thick.

"You want a speed-up spell?" Linda asked.

Gene wiped sweat from his brow. "Now you tell me."

"Sorry."

Gene became a whirlwind, and the door flew to splinters in no time.

"Jeremy, you stay out here. Watch the door and look after Vaya."

Jeremy eyed her up and down. She was a head taller. "Uh, yeah."

Gene kicked in what was left of the door, and he and Linda charged in.

It was a spacious chamber, tastefully appointed. Numerous objets d'art from many worlds lay about, and tasteful paintings bedecked the walls.

Jamin stood in the middle of the room, his eyes fearful yet defiant. The young page—the one who had summoned Gene and all the others—sat at a table to one side, idly playing solitaire.

"How dare you intrude," Jamin said, glaring.

"You have a lot to answer for, Jamin," Gene said.

"And why should I answer to the likes of you?" His thin lips formed a sneer. "Common as clay. You wander into this great house and get treated like royalty. Vagabonds! Ruffians! Subhuman rubbish."

"It's been boiling inside you for years, hasn't it, Jamin?"

Jamin gritted his teeth. "It rankles. Oh, it rankles."

Gene drew his sword. "Well, at last the motivations are getting an airing out. This explains some of it."

Linda asked, "What did you hope to gain, Jamin?"

"You wouldn't understand," Jamin sniffed.

"Try me."

"No, thank you, *your ladyship*. Despite that ludicrous title, I regard you as nothing more than a common strumpet."

Gene lunged forward.

Jamin backstepped quickly. "Vasagaroth, help!"

The page boy laid down a card. "Too late," he intoned. His voice did not sound boyish.

Jamin struck a wizardly posture, hands poised to cast a spell.

Linda said, "Jamin, I'm warning you. Make one move and you're dead meat. I mean it."

"I have great powers now," Jamin said, trembling.

"Not without him," Linda said, pointing to the page. "Vasagaroth, please!"

The page calmly laid another card down. "No can do, Jamin. The pipeline just went dry."

Gene sidestepped toward the table. "What's your story, kid? Who put you up to this?"

"Screw off, asshole," the boy said over his shoulder.

"Whoa, are *you* out of line," Gene said. "I'm going to have to teach you some manners. And a little about cards. You're playing a red jack on the red queen."

The page spat at Gene's feet. "I said screw off."

"Gene, easy," Linda said.

"Just who is this little pustule?" Gene demanded.

"Why don't you challenge him and find out?" Jamin said, grinning slyly.

"Any way you want to play it, human," Vasagaroth said casually.

"Both of you are coming with me," Gene said.

"And where might we be going?" Jamin asked pleasantly.

"To the Donjon, to await the King's disposition of your case. C'mon, let's go. That means you, punk-breath."

Gene laid a hand on the page's shoulder. The boy's arm came around sharply and knocked Gene's away. He stood.

"Time for the masquerade to end," he said.

Gene stepped back, sensing what was about to happen. And it did.

The page boy's skin turned gray, then white, and began to puff up horribly, as if pushed out from something growing inside. A hairline crack appeared along the boy's cheek. As it widened, it revealed a glowing red surface underneath.

Gene and Linda had witnessed this process before, but it was no less startling in reprise. The boy's skin fell away in limp shards to reveal the luminous demon-body hiding within. Inexplicably the thing grew as it shed its bogus human form. When the last of the camouflage had fallen away, the crown of the creature's horned head topped off at no less than seven and a half feet. A long, curious sword then came into being in its left hand.

Its voice shook the rafters. "Human, you will die horri-bly!"

Gene swallowed hard. "Tell me how it can be fun."

The demon lunged and nearly decapitated Gene with one stroke. Gene backed off, happening to catch a glimpse of Jamin's gloating grin.

The demon charged, chasing Gene around the room. Gene backed up against a love seat and fell over it, scrambled up, and backstepped. The demon kicked the piece of furniture out of the way and advanced, sword whistling as it swung.

"My magic doesn't work on him!" Linda shouted.

"Speed me up!" Gene begged.

"Something's wrong. Jamin's blocking!"

"Exactly right, little hussy." Jamin said. "Now let's see how your champion swordsman does against the Hosts of Hell."

CENTRAL BUREAUCRACY—MINISTRY OF PAIN

"YOU ARE HOLDING my sister here," he told the demon clerk behind the counter. "I want her."

The clerk was a gnarled, hunched-over creature with cadaverous gray skin that looked like wet rubber. Suppurating yellow sores afflicted one side of its bald head.

It looked up with pained, bloodshot eyes. "Your name?"

"You know my name."

"I must have your name, sir, to complete the proper forms." The creature brought forth a thick sheaf of official-looking papers.

He materialized a broadsword, swung, and struck the thing's head from its body. A fountain of pink goo erupted from the neck as the carcass fell beneath the countertop.

Almost immediately another clerk hobbled out from behind a partition. The creature looked a perfect match for the one who had just been granted early retirement.

The thing smiled at him. "And how may I help you, sir?"

His shoulders slumped. "I wish to see your superior."

"I'm sorry, sir, but my superior will be in a meeting for the rest of the day."

"Then I wish to speak to his superior."

"Do you have an appointment?"

"No, I do *not* have an appointment."

"Very sorry to say that the deputy minister is out of town. Is there anything I can do?"

"Yes. As the saying goes, take me to your leader."

"I beg your pardon?"

"I wish to speak to the controlling entity, the central mind."

"Ah. That is a very tall order, sir."

"Indeed?"

"Yes, indeed, sir. You'll have to make an appointment."

Incarnadine's blade swished round again. This time, blue ichor flowed from the truncated neck.

A third clerk stepped out from behind the partition.

"I'm afraid you have the wrong department, sir," it said. "Go down this hall, turn right, follow the corridor, and it's the third door on your right. However, they might be out to lunch at the moment. Now, if you prefer to put your request in writing . . ."

The thing babbled on, its voice dwindling as he stalked away.

The walls were not straight here. There wasn't a right angle in the place. The corridor twisted and bent. Every so often he passed another counter with another blandly smiling clerk behind it. The place was dim and stifling, and silence choked the air like a miasmal fog.

He was hours in the place. There seemed no end to it. He knew Ferne's location, but could not get there. He gave up and got new bearings. Finding stairs, he began a descent of miles. Progressively darkening gloom enveloped him. Eyes like glowing coals monitored his progress, peering out from the crannied walls. The character of the place changed, became cavelike. Following a downward-spiraling tunnel, he increased his pace to a jog. The tunnel leveled out, debouching into an immense chamber. In the middle of the floor was a deep pit which emitted a pulsating light.

He walked to the edge, looked down, and beheld the mind-shattering creature that dwelled therein.

[Finally we meet, human.]

The voice was a whispering in his mind.

He nodded. "Finally."

[You find it painful to behold me as I really am.]

"Somewhat, I must admit. My apologies."

[None needed. Can your mind contain that which I am?]

"I am not sure," he answered. "Your nature is rather . . . exotic."

[Indeed. And to me, it is you who are strange.]

"No doubt. In any event, your end is at hand."

[So be it.]

"You have no regrets?"

[Can one regret one's nature, one's being? Can one regret the ineluctable mechanisms of existence?]

"I have no answer for you. I can only say that I regret ending the existence of any intelligent entity."

[Why? Non-Being is implicit in Being itself.]

"Your equanimity comforts me, to some extent."

[I am glad.]

"One thing, though. You knew you would lose in the end."

[Of course.]

"Yet you persisted."

[I grow weary. There must be an end, and I could not see one. . . . Why are you astonished?]

"It's true, then. You are alone here."

[Utterly. I cannot remember when I was not alone.]

"There were never others of your kind?"

[Unthinkable ages ago, perhaps. I do not remember.]

"But there must have been others."

[So you say. As I have said, I know naught of this, and care less.]

"You speak of existence, yet you loathe it."

[With every mote, with every granule of my being.]

"Why, then, did you not end your life?"

[With this hatred in me still burning? Impossible.]

There came something like a long sigh.

[Enough. I shall speak no more. Do what you must.]

"I need do nothing. Doom cracks even as we speak."

[Then go.]

He averted his eyes from the thing in the pit, walked a few steps away, bent over, and vomited.

Not much came up. Swallowing bile, he walked off, wishing for a drink of water. But such a ware fetched a high price in the very pit of Hell.

* * *

The world shook as he searched for his sister. Demon carcasses littered his path, victims of the holocaust weapon's first effects.

He found her in a laboratorylike room on one of the upper levels. What he saw staggered him, and the bile again rose in his throat.

There was no describing the monstrous device of which she was the central concern. Rods, probes, drills, blades—wicked implements of every sort bit deep into her flesh. Every accessible nerve point was tapped, every orifice violated. Little remained of her skin, and much of her body had been subject to hideous mutilations.

Her heart still beat, yet he could do nothing for her. Quickly he cast the only enchantment that would help.

Her eyes were open, for the lids were gone, torn away. But now she saw.

"Incarnadine," she croaked, her swollen lips trying to smile. "Inky dearest."

"Ferne. Are you still in pain?"

"No, Inky. It's marvelous. I feel nothing now. I want to go home."

"In a moment. Just say yes or no to my questions. You somehow got away from the guards who conducted you to your exile. You spelled them and fooled them into thinking that they had thrust you through a wild aspect. True?"

"Yes."

"You cast about for a plan. In a moment of wildest desperation, you decided to throw in your lot with the Hosts."

"Very bad mistake, Inky. I was . . . a fool."

"Don't talk," he said. "Save your strength. Now, listen. You didn't do what you did last time, unravel the spell that blocked their portal. Instead, you simply unhooked it temporarily and passed through. I don't know how you did it, but you did it."

She nodded.

"Again, you amaze me, sister. But then you were at the mercy of the Hosts. You tried bargaining with them, but they had the upper hand. They had you. You outlined a plan to attack the castle, taught them how to transfer power between universes. But there had to be someone on the other side to use that power. A confederate within the castle. An adept magician who could use that power selectively and wisely within castle walls.''

''Yes. J—'' She struggled to utter the name. ''Jamin.''

''And someone else. Something else. A warrior demon who had stayed in hiding when we chased the Hosts from the castle?''

''Yes.''

''I see. Insurance against Jamin's possible double cross. So, the Hosts had a plan, and now the machinery for a covert operation. The plan was first to rid the castle of powerful magicians, starting with the more talented of the Guests. This tactic was high on the list, I imagine, because the Guests had proved such a thorn during the last round of hostilities.''

''Yes.''

''But there was one catch. Feeding power through the interdimensional barrier drained the Hosts of their reserves. They needed another source of power, and you knew of one. This was their way of persuading you to divulge it.''

''Yes, and I told them. I told them everything, Inky, all my tricks. But they didn't stop, they didn't stop. . . .'' She trailed off into a moan.

''Easy, easy.'' He made motions again, then waited for her respiration to stabilize. ''Are you all right now?''

''Yes, Inky.''

''Fine. You're going to go to sleep in a moment. When you wake up, you'll be home.''

''I'm dying, Inky. I know it.''

He was silent.

''Inky?''

''Yes, my dear?''

''Did you love me?''

''Of course, dear sister.''

''You know what I mean. We once kissed like lovers, and we weren't exactly children. We were in our early teens. Do you remember it?''

He looked away.

''You do. You're ashamed. You did love me, I always knew it. But we never made love. We should have. To hell with convention, Inky.''

''Ferne, my darling sister Ferne.''

''Don't cry, Inky. I knew what I was doing. We all do what we must. We all have our—''

Sudden, violent convulsions racked her. Then the light in her eyes faded, and her chest heaved once and was still.

Extricating her body from the diabolical machine was a consummately grisly task. Parts of her came away with the blades, the screws, the drillbits; gobbets of flesh crumbled off. But at last she was free. He could not recognize the body of his sister, who had been the most beautiful woman he had known.

He materialized a casket to contain her remains, and conjured two pale figures—indistinct, squat, and homuncular—to bear her away.

They reached the roof, where the *Voyager* still waited, undisturbed.

The sky was no longer black. Streamers of pale green fire banded it, forming a circular storm system whose calm central eye was contracting rapidly as the chaos closed in. He stopped to regard this phenomenon as the pallbearers loaded the casket into the Umoi machine.

He heard a roar like thunder, turned, and watched pieces of the dark tower fall and crash to earth. The roof under him wobbled, and he thought he had better be off. He dismissed the bearers, and they disappeared. Then he boarded the craft.

He watched from on high as the black spire disintegrated and the surrounding complex of hives turned to dust. The ground disappeared, shrouded in fingers of green mist that choked and throttled the life out of the land.

Some time later, there was nothing below but a vast gray wasteland, featureless and undifferentiated.

He threw a switch and even that was gone, replaced by the nothingness of no place, of nowhere.

Nowhere at all.

Chamberlain's Quarters

GENE HAD ONCE fought a demon of the Hosts successfully, but only with magical help. Now he was holding his own without aid, after having survived the fiend's initial attack. Either Gene's skills had increased or the demon was operating on low power. Gene was persuaded by the latter theory. The way he understood it, these warrior demons were really analogous to robots, needing energy from the home universe.

Gene swung mightily, sparks flying as his sword met the demon's. He backed his opponent into a corner and probed for an opening that would allow a killing blow.

But the demon had some juice left in him. It attacked with renewed vigor, and Gene had to back off.

Then, very suddenly, something changed. The demon halted and lowered its sword. The hideous head twisted to and fro, glowing eyes searching about for things unseen.

"Something is happening," it said.

Its sword clattered to the floor.

"Vasagaroth!"

Jamin came out from behind a stuffed chair and rushed to the side of his diabolical ally. "Vasagaroth, you can't stop now. You must kill him. You must kill them all, or I am doomed!"

Vasagaroth turned withering eyes on him. "It is the end."

"Don't say that! What is amiss?"

The demon teetered backward to the wall and leaned against it, the sweaty red luminosity of its body on the wane.

Jamin whirled about, eyes desperate, pleading. "I give myself up! Linda, you must intercede for me with His Majesty. I was possessed by the minions of Hell! I knew not what I was about! They m—"

The words choked off, for Vasagaroth's immense taloned hand, the right, had locked about Jamin's neck. The other enveloped his head. Both squeezed. Jamin's feet lifted a few inches off the floor. He kicked wildly, his body spasming.

Linda yelled, "Gene, do something!"

Gene could do nothing. Jamin's strangled gasp ended abruptly, blood spurting from between the demon's fingers.

Linda screamed.

Then Jamin and his murderer keeled over together and lay still on the bloodied oaken boards.

Gene kicked at the demon's body. It had lost its luminescence and was curiously insubstantial, as if having instantly turned to papier-mâché. He examined Jamin briefly.

"They're both history," Gene told an ashen-faced Linda.

"My God. What happened?"

"Have no idea. There's nothing we can do here. Back to the lab."

They left and shut the door.

The *Voyager* had returned.

Incarnadine stood on the platform, watching two Guardsmen carry away what looked like a coffin.

Gene mounted the stairs to the platform, made as if to say something, but held off. Incarnadine's thoughts seemed light-years away. Gene stood by silently.

Finally the King grew aware of his presence.

"My sister," he said. "She is dead."

"You have our deepest sympathies, Your Majesty," Gene said, bowing.

"Thank you." Incarnadine collected himself and looked the lab over. "Hell of a mess. Are you people all right?"

"Fine, sir," Linda said. "Jamin is dead. His demon friend did him in."

Incarnadine nodded as if such an event were implicit in

the scheme of things. "And so it ends." He frowned. "But you have friends still missing."

"Yes, sir," Gene said. "Snowclaw, Sheila, and, we think, your brother."

"Trent, yes. I have a feeling, which I will corroborate shortly, that my brother is fine, and that Sheila is with him. We'd best concern ourselves with your friend the Hyperborean."

Gene said, "Beg your pardon? Is that what he is?"

"Hyperborea happens to be the name of the world he comes from."

"Oh. He never told me."

"It's castle nomenclature only. I have no idea what the aboriginals call their world. Actually—" Incarnadine interrupted himself and gave a laugh. "Here I am babbling. Gene, how the hell did you contrive to get yourself inside this contraption at the *exact moment* when I plucked it out of the great gossamer nothingness of the Never-Never? You must have one hell of a story."

Gene let out a long breath. "It's a novel. You'll all get a copy, hot off the press. But for now, I'd like to see about finding Snowy. Linda tells me he was with Trent and Sheila when they disappeared."

"He might have gone his separate way. I did manage to establish partial contact with Trent, and I got the impression that Sheila was with him, whereas Snowclaw was not."

"Hell, that means he could be anywhere."

Linda said, "He could be on Earth."

Gene smacked his forehead. "He'll be on the evening news!"

"Sheila changed him, Gene. He had a human form."

"Really? Well, that would help, of course. But Snowy? Running loose in Long Island? Ye gods."

"Your Majesty!"

They turned to see Osmirik come running into the lab.

"I have the spell!" he yelled. "I have it! All I need is the young man with the calculating device—"

Jeremy looked up from rooting through the wreckage of the mainframe. "Over here, Ozzie."

But Osmirik had stopped in his tracks at the sight of Gene.

"I see that Sir Gene has returned," he said, "and I am uselessly tardy once again."

Incarnadine said, "Not necessarily, old fellow. What spell are you talking about?"

The librarian held up a battered grimoire. "The Earth locator spell. I found one that might work, with a bit of updating and the use of that young man's . . ." He became suddenly cognizant of the general destruction around him. "Oh, dear."

Then he was struck by the sight of the tall, nude woman standing next to Gene. Her beauty took his breath away.

"My word," he said. "I do have to get away from the library more often."

Westmoreland County, PA.

Dawn was breaking and Snowclaw was tired. He had been hiking all night, and his feet were sore from treading on sharp twigs and hidden stones. Rough country around here, not like the clean, bare tundra he was used to. There was so much vegetation about. Positively tropical. Why, it even got above freezing in the winter!

He was homesick, and not only for the castle. He wanted six or seven layers of good packed snow under him, and a fathom of permafrost below that. Made your feet feel nice and cool.

He strode along the narrow trail he had been following for the last hour. Lots of game about. He had seen white-tailed critters bounding away, and tiny things had chittered at him, hiding among stalks of brown weeds. Nothing he could eat, even if he had taken the trouble to chase them down. Besides, he didn't like land game. Seafood was his first love. Spikefish, fried in rendered blubber. Four-clawed crab, boiled and served with clarified blubber. Plain blubber in tasty, glistening chunks, served up fresh. Now you were talking food.

Great White Stuff, was he hungry! He had to stop thinking about it or he would go crazy.

He tried not thinking about it.

Nah. Didn't work. He was hungry, and there wasn't anything he could do about it. He was outdoors, that's what the
problem was. The air was sweet, fresh, if a little strange. But
during his stay on Earth he had grown used to the native
environment. The smell of the forest set his juices to flowing,
and all he could think about was stuffing his maw with endless quantities of . . .

Food. He licked his chops. He was really losing it now. If
he didn't get food soon . . . well, there was no telling what
he'd do.

He swiped at a tree and came away with his claws full of
bark. He sampled that, spat it out. Too dry. He tried some
weeds. Not bad, but like eating air.

There was nothing around to eat! But what did he expect?
It was winter. He tore off a fresh branch and gnawed at it,
spitting out the bark and biting into the fresh green wood
underneath.

No taste. No taste at all. Nothing in this world had any
taste.

He howled once, then came to a halt, astonished at himself.

"I'm going crazy," he muttered.

He stalked on, increasing his pace. The trail bore down-
hill, then leveled off. A narrow brook crossed his path, which
he took in one hop. The trail went up again, crested, then
twined down the side of a steep hill.

There was a structure sitting on the gentle slope of the field
below. A human dwelling.

He approached, hiding behind an outbuilding. Peering
around a corner, he checked the place out. It was quiet. The
house was dark. Fine. He went to the back door and tried it.
It was a sturdy door, locked good and tight, but the carpen-
ters had never figured on a seven-foot-tall quasi-ursine alien
with the strength of ten gorillas.

Snowy pushed hard, and the dead bolt tore out of its slot,
ripping the doorjamb.

"Oops," Snowy said. He felt guilty about this. He respected private property. After all, he wouldn't take to someone breaking into his own shack out on the ice, humble as it
was. But Snowy really didn't have a choice.

He found himself in a dark basement. He knew there was
a light somewhere, but couldn't find it. His eyes adjusted to

the dark quickly, though, and the first thing he saw was a
possible food substance.

Whatever it was, it was packed into glass jars lined up on
wooden shelves. He looked at the stuff. It was red. He unscrewed the top off one jar and stuck his finger in, licked it.
Tangy, not bad. He upended the jar into his mouth.

Not bad at all. It was what they called tomatoes. He had
eaten them in salads and other things. Salads! Now, talk about
eating air. How could humans live off a bunch of leaves?
Nothing to it.

He unscrewed another jar, then tossed it disdainfully over
his shoulder. Nothing to this stuff, either.

There were other foodstuffs available. Metal cans of junk.
Forget that. Other things, hanging from the overhead beams.
Meat! Spiced meat, too. Sausage, it looked like. And a big
hank of raw rump, cured with salt and having a smoky flavor.
Hey, this was more like it. Idly munching a haunch of ham,
he went up the creaking wooden stairs.

His appetite was getting stronger, despite an overpowering
human smell to the place that ordinarily would have put him
off his food. Enticing smells turned him to the right, toward
the kitchen.

He rifled the cabinets, finding dry and dusty cereals, more
cans, spices, packages of unidentifiable whatever, still more
cans, more boxes of dry and dusty stuff. . . .

The refrigerator held leftovers that hadn't been good ideas
in the first place, along with ice cubes, three trays of which
he crunched up with relish. There were various liquids to
drink. He glugged those. There was fruit and some greens.
Ptui.

He searched the rest of the house, but came up empty.
Going back to the kitchen, he looked under the kitchen
sink. Here was some hooch—drain cleaner, liquid soap, furniture polish, and suchlike. He popped the lid off a bottle of
Lysol and guzzled it down.

Mmm, pine-flavored. But he needed FOOD.

All right, he was desperate. If quality wasn't available,
quantity would have to do. He stumped back down to the
cellar, rummaged, and fetched up a huge plastic tub. This he
filled with everything at hand. In went Jell-O Pudding, corn
oil, Nestle's Quik, Spic 'n' Span, Hungry Jack pancake and
waffle mix, California seedless raisins, cornstarch, sugar,

flour, Rice Krispies, Quaker Puffed Wheat, Corn Cheks, am-
monia, vinegar, salad dressing, Crisco, bread crumbs, Log
Cabin syrup, Karo syrup, molasses, baking powder, milk,
Pepsi-Cola, Kool-Aid, mustard, ketchup, floor wax, a half
gallon of milk, lemonade, orange juice. . . .

And on and on and on, everything going into one ghastly,
heterogeneous concoction. For savor he threw in everything
in the spice cabinet, from turmeric to fennel, from paprika
to cream of tartar, along with two canisters of salt and a big
box of ground pepper.

He thought of cooking down this horror, but who was he
kidding? He couldn't wait. He dipped the gnawed ham bone
into the stuff and sampled it.

Not bad. He searched for an eating implement, found a
big soup ladle.

He ate it all.

Snowclaw was exceedingly ill. He had wanted to get up on
the roof and scout the countryside, get his bearings, but he
had not made it farther than this small bed, on which he had
fallen asleep. Now he was awake, and it was night again, and
he was sick. Very sick.

He wanted to die right then and there. He was going to
die, he was sure of it.

Voices. Humans. Snowy thought of getting up and running, but maybe if the humans saw him they would kill him
and put him out of his misery.

A female screamed, then moaned.

"Oh, look. Look at all this. Fred, someone broke in. Look
at my kitchen."

"Cheezus. Honey, call the cops."

"Oh, my God, what the hell were they doing?"

"Some kinda goddamn weirdo."

"Mommy, who did this?"

"Shh! Jennifer, go back to the car."

"Why, Daddy?"

Snowclaw really wished they would make less noise. He
groaned and turned over. Maybe if he got a little more sleep . . .

"Fred, do you think they could still be here?"

"I'll check upstairs. Where the hell's my shotgun? Shit,
it's upstairs. The pellet gun, it's down in the cellar."

"Jennifer, don't touch that!"

"What is it, Mommy?"

"I don't *know*. It's *disgusting*."

"It's yucky."

"Jennifer, don't."

"Can I play with it?"

"No, it's horrible. Leave it alone. *I said leave it alone! Do you want to get smacked?* Why do I have to—? What did you say, Fred?"

Great White Stuff, Snowclaw thought. What does a guy have to do to get a little sleep? Why did humans have to make so much noise all the time? He rolled over onto his stomach, his lower legs sticking out a yard over the end of the bed.

"How should *I* know where Brandon's pellet gun is? I haven't seen it in years. Fred, forget it. They're long gone. It must've been kids. Jennifer! Go to your room right now."

And how the heck could they sleep in these damned beds? They made his back hurt.

He really should be getting the heck out. These humans weren't going to be pleased to find him.

"Of course they must have been kids. Nothing's missing! The TV, the VCR, the stereo . . . everything's here! Fred? *Fred?* Forget the damn pellet gun, will you?"

"Well, it's just the thought of somebody breakin' in here. Did you call the police?"

"Not yet."

"What? Cheezus, do I have to do everything myself?"

Snowclaw was getting tired of listening to the commotion downstairs. He wasn't *that* sick, and he really should be getting along.

Snowy turned over. A small human female was standing at the foot of the bed, regarding him with baleful blue eyes.

"Hi," he said. "Don't tell your folks I'm here, okay? They wouldn't understand. Sorry for messing up your bed, but . . . Where're you going?"

The little girl went to the head of the stairs.

"Mommy!"

There was no answer. Snowy sat up, and regretted it.

"Mommy!"

"Jennifer, what in blazes do you want? Can't you see Mommy's busy?"

"There's a big bear in my bed."

"Jennifer, don't start with me."

"There is. There's a big white bear and he's got big teeth and white claws. He talked to me."

"Fred, go up and see what the hell that kid is talking about."

"She's got a big bear in her bed, that's what she's talking about. How come these goddamn cops don't answer their goddamn phone? They'll pull you over for goin' two miles above the limit, but when it comes to—"

"Mommy!"

"Jennifer, I am going to *strangle* you in a minute. Fred, do something? She's driving me nuts. Look at this mess I have to clean up. Look at all this crap all over!"

Snowy put his head down and dozed off for what he thought was just a second or two. When he snapped awake and sat up again, the big male human was staring at him goggle-eyed from the doorway.

Snowy burped, then said, "I can explain. . . ."

The man disappeared. Snowy got up unsteadily and made for the window. It wouldn't budge, so he broke through it and went out onto the icy roof of the kitchen wing, doing a high-wire act along the apex. When he was halfway across, he looked back. The guy was aiming a gun at him.

Snowy's foot slipped a split second before the shotgun let loose with a bang and a flash.

The next thing Snowy knew, he was on the ground, entangled in a copse of rhododendrons. Thrashing frantically, he extricated himself and struggled to his feet. He took off across the lawn.

Another blast shattered the night, and a bee-swarm of shot buzzed past Snowy's head.

Then, suddenly, there was something in front of him, a strange aircraft. It made no sound, hovering about ten feet off the ground. A hatch opened up at the side of the thing. Someone poked his head out. "Snowy, come on!"

It was Gene! Without breaking stride, Snowclaw took one mighty leap and hooked an arm inside the hatch. With Gene's unnecessary help, he scrambled up the bell-shaped hull and dove in.

It was a tight squeeze inside the compartment. Linda was there, along with the new kid, Jeremy.

"Okay, we got him!"

"Roger," Jeremy said, confident at the controls. The laptop computer was taped to the instrument panel in front of him. He punched a few keys.

"Uh, fellas?" Linda said. "There's a guy with a gun out there."

Jeremy said, "Hold on a minute. I'm going to jump directly back to the castle."

"But he's going to—"

The shotgun roared again, and buckshot spanged off the *Voyager*'s hull, to no perceivable effect.

Snowclaw said, "How did you find me?"

"Magic," Gene said.

Snowy sighed. "What else." Then a sudden gust of nausea rose in him. "Gene buddy?"

"What?"

"Could you move over a little?"

"There's no room. Why, what's wrong?"

"I'm going to be sick."

SHEILA'S WORLD

IT WAS THE best of times, it was the worst of times. . . . But that is another story.

This particular tale is almost done, but for the wrapping up. It's been a long concerto, and the soloist has one more cadenza in him, if the audience will allow, in which the theme is restated for the benefit of those who've drowsed, wonder-weary, through the third movement—

"Life-styles of the infamous plutocrats!"

Gene raised his glass and toasted the palms, the cabanas, the tennis courts, the swimming pools, and the terraces. He threw in the sky, the surf, and the cute barmaid who had just served him a banana daiquiri.

"To decadence and high living. The only way to go."

He drank.

"When is Incarnadine coming?" Linda asked, rolling over to let the tropical sun start toasting her back.

"He should be here any moment," Trent said, lifting his shades to glance at his watch.

Sheila said, "Trent, do you think he'll come?"

"I don't see why not. He needs a vacation."

"But so soon after . . . you know."

"It's been a couple of weeks since the funeral. I'm over my grief." Trent sipped his Singapore sling. "Such as it was."

"The funeral was so beautiful," Sheila said. "The pageantry, the music alone. What was that beautiful piece they played as they took the casket away?"

" 'Pavane pour une Infante défunte.' One of Inky's favorite pieces."

"Lovely."

"It is that."

Thaxton and Cleve Dalton came stumping in from the golf course. Thaxton threw down his bag and snapped his fingers at a waitress. "Anyone for tennis? After I've had one or two or three drinks, of course."

"I'm pooped," Dalton said, easing himself into a deck chair. "Getting old."

"Mr. Dalton," Sheila said, "you look younger every time I see you."

"It's the curative balm of your enchanting aura, Sheila my dear. You radiate magic."

"Oh, really."

"Look at this place! It's Palm Beach, Club Med, and the Riviera all rolled into one. And it's a conjuration entire!"

Gene asked, "Sheila, what about all these other people in the hotel? I mean the guests, not the staff. They're not castle Guests. At least I've never seen them before."

"I don't know who they are," Sheila said. "They seem to have come with the spell. It would be kind of empty here without them, though. I mean, a seven-hundred-room hotel, my God. There's not nearly enough of us."

"Yeah, they do lend verisimilitude. But it's still pretty spooky."

"You're telling me. I'm still trying to figure out what to do with a complete submarine crew."

Linda said, "To change the subject, has anyone seen Snowy lately?"

"He's waterskiing with Vaya," Gene said, peering out into the lagoon. "Doing pretty well, it looks like. So's Vaya, but she's naturally athletic."

"Healthy woman," Cleve Dalton averred.

"Snowy says he has to keep to the water," Sheila said, "because of the heat."

A page stepped out on the terrace. "Your attention, ladies and gentlemen. His Most Serene and Transcendental Majesty, Incarnadine, by the grace of the gods, King, Lord Protector—"

"And Keeper of the Keys to the Royal Crapper. Hi, gang. Sit down, for pete's sake. This is your shindig." Incarnadine was resplendent in Hawaiian shirt, yellow shorts, mirror shades, and thongs.

"Welcome to Hotel Sheila," the proprietor said with a curtsey.

"Thanks, Sheila. Well, I'm ready to party." H.M. accepted a drink from a waitress. "Thank you. What's this?"

Sheila said, "Complimentary banana daiquiri, sir, one to a guest. Then they're four-fifty a pop."

"Catering to the gentry, are we?"

Gene sneered, "The hoi polloi are strictly persona non grata."

"Never mix your Greek and Latin, son."

"I should brush up on my Greek. He was here a minute ago."

"Not only are you nonpareil as a swordsman, Gene, but your wit is as sharp as your blade."

"Hey, it's a gift."

"Hello, Trent."

"Greetings, brother. You seem chipper enough."

"Can't brood forever," the King said. "What's done is done. By the way, folks, Trent and I want to thank you all for your many expressions of sympathy. You were also under no obligation to show up at the funeral. After all, the woman tried to murder the lot of you."

"We wanted to be there," Sheila said. "Besides, if it hadn't been for her, we never would have discovered this place."

Incarnadine surveyed sky and sea, then raised his eyes to the magnificent Victorian hotel behind them. "Beautiful, just beautiful. You've done a marvelous job. A stunning magical construct."

"This place has endless possibilities. We're building condos next."

"What's the deal?"

"Ten percent down, plus closing costs and half the points."

"What's the current rate?"

"Nine and a half, but the prime rate is about to go up."

"You'd better show me a few lots, quick. But before that, I'd like to propose a toast. Is everybody charged?"

"Here comes Vaya and Snowy," Linda said.

They arrived, along with M. DuQuesne, Deena Williams, and some other castle Guests, and all were plied with drinks. Vaya's ultra-brief bikini drew unabashed stares.

Incarnadine raised his glass. "I would like to propose a toast to my brother Trent and his betrothed, the Lady Sheila Jankowski. May they know happiness, peace, and the blessings of the Most High for the rest of their days."

Hear-hears all around. All drank.

"The Loyal Toast," Trent announced.

Everyone chorused: "To the King!"

"I thank you," Incarnadine said. "And one more. To Castle Perilous. May it stand forever, and with it the worlds it created." He took a seat and sipped his daiquiri.

Gene asked, "Mind answering a few questions, sir?"

"Fire away, Sir Gene."

"Vaya's universe. Do you think it's one of the castle's?"

"Can't find it in any of the catalogues. Ervoldt's book doesn't mention it. I gather it was strange."

"Like something out of pulp literature. Only the wildest of sci-fi worlds could have produced something like the *Voyager*."

"I'm convinced that Jamin spelled you into a quantum universe. It's possible. With a line to the interstitial etherium, he had enough power."

"Are quantum universes different from the castle's?"

"Oh, quite. The castle worlds *exist*. Quantum universes are just sets of probabilities."

"Interesting," Gene said. "I'd like to learn more about cosmology."

"The library has every major work on the subject. By the way, is Osmirik here?"

"He's . . . uh, he's being ministered to by a team of the hotel's masseuses-in-residence, I think."

"Good. The man needs to have his horns clipped."

Sheila said, "If Jamin had the power, why didn't he win?"

"Jamin was a timid little man. A good majordomo, but

I'm afraid he bit off more than he could chew. He was simply an amateur at big-time palace intrigue.''

"It's sad."

"He was old enough to have known what he was getting into. One hundred and sixty, I think."

"I'm really intrigued by something you said," Gene told the King.

"Really? What?"

"Your toast. I think it went something like 'To Perilous and the worlds it created.' Did you mean that literally? I mean, it's rather a shocking thing to consider. A world like the one a lot of us come from, Earth, merely the creation of a magic spell cast in a world that seems more like a dream than reality."

Incarnadine replied to the question, and afterward a hush fell over the party. Gene set down his drink and pulled Vaya close, as if to reassure himself of her continuing existence.

The sound of the breakers rose to fill the silence. A soft sea breeze rustled the palms overhead, and far out to sea, a bright sun threw skeins of silver light across the water.

What Lord Incarnadine had said was this: "Well, yes, Gene, that's exactly what I meant. The castle's worlds are created and maintained by the incredibly powerful nexus of the transformation spell. Without the castle, your world, along with Sheila's, Snowclaw's . . . everyone's, would be like Vaya's world, mere possibilities, a meager handful out of the endless infinity of possibilities that make up the n-dimensional quantum super-cosmos. As such, they wouldn't exist at all, in any meaningful sense."

He had taken a sip and glanced around, mildly surprised. "I thought you all realized that."